REVEALED

BJ tipped her head back, needing to see Brodie's expression, needing to know he didn't judge her as some kind of freak.

She caught a glimpse of something wild and fiery before the gray eyes shuttered. "And now?" he prompted.

"Now it's happening all over again. I feel like I'm that scared little girl."

Brodie folded his calloused palm around her chin, capturing her in a grip somewhere between reprimand and comfort. "You're not that little girl anymore. You're a grown woman. And this time there's somebody on your side."

He touched his lips to hers, blotting out the power behind his guttural promise. His kiss was hard, hot, and over before BJ could respond.

JULIE MILLER

Immortal Heart

LOVE SPELL   ◆   NEW YORK CITY

For Gran.
Thanks to Mom and Dad for making me believe, and giving me the will to do it.
Thanks to Scott and Ryne for their support, and doing the male bonding thing so I could get this done.
And to the real Duke—you'll always be my sweetheart.

LOVE SPELL®

February 1997

Published by

Dorchester Publishing Co., Inc.
276 Fifth Avenue
New York, NY 10001

If you purchased this book without a cover you should be aware that this book is stolen property. It was reported as "unsold and destroyed" to the publisher and neither the author nor the publisher has received any payment for this "stripped book."

Copyright © 1997 by Julie Miller

All rights reserved. No part of this book may be reproduced or transmitted in any form or by any electronic or mechanical means, including photocopying, recording or by any information storage and retrieval system, without the written permission of the Publisher, except where permitted by law.

The name "Love Spell" and its logo are trademarks of Dorchester Publishing Co., Inc.

Printed in the United States of America.

Immortal Heart

Prologue

A remote corner of England, c. 1216

Flames ripped through the night as another timber fell from the ceiling to the dungeon floor, casting an eerie phantasm of light over the clanging swords and thrusting, twisting bodies of men in combat.

The rebels surged forward, sheer number giving them their only strength against their oppressors. The soldiers should have been easily taken, their cruel devices easily destroyed, but darker forces aided them. And the rebels had no such powers for themselves.

Simple peasants, the rebels knew nothing of war. Nothing of magic spells. Nothing of combating tyranny and oppression. They fought against the minions of a former counselor to the crown, a high priest of mysterious power bent on securing the loyalty and tribute of the remote villagers.

They faced an enemy, not of flesh and blood, but of shadows and evil. Soldiers could be gutted with a dagger or run through with a sword. But a sorcerer . . .

It seemed no weapon could defeat him.

Still, the peasants had a champion, an aging knight who had long stood against King John. He thought he had retired that day at Runnymede when he and other barons forced the king to sign the Magna Carta, putting into law the ideals of justice and honor he believed in.

But when he had passed through the peasant villages and seen how their spirits were abused, how their backs were broken, and how their hopes were shattered, the mighty warrior took up his sword once more. Weary of battle, but never of the cause of justice, he rallied the peasants and urged them onward through the sorcerer's dungeon.

He swung his heavy sword in a mighty arc, striking a guard in the neck and shoulder, felling him with the blow. Another uniformed opponent stepped out of the smoke. The warrior spun around, splitting the man in two with his knife.

He surged forward, his pale eyes cutting through the haze of smoke to spot the sorcerer. The evil man's silvery-white robe, with an odd arrangement of stars and half-moons embroidered with iridescent gold threads, glowed like a beacon in the dimness of the burning castle above them.

"Sorcerer!" he bellowed. The graying visage turned toward the challenge and the warrior strode onward. "These people are not yours to command and defile. Be gone from this place. Take your evil and suffering with you!"

He tucked his dagger beneath his tunic and clasped the sword in both hands. All the while, the sorcerer fixed his eyes on him. Those eyes burned into the warrior's memory. He would never forget them. Dark and mocking. Devoid of humanity.

"You threaten me?" The sorcerer laughed, not once flinching from the advancing warrior with his sword raised to kill. "Even now, your cowardly comrades flee. They run from what they cannot understand. They leave you to fight alone."

"I would die before I'd run from an evil being like you."

"If you wish." The sorcerer flicked his hand into the air and the warrior's sword crashed to the stones at his feet. "Your puny rebellion does not amuse me. You shall pay the price."

"I swear I'll kill you with my bare hands." He reached out but felt himself pushing against an invisible wall. Rage swelled within him. "Damn you!"

"Father!" A third voice severed their duel. "Please, no more!"

The warrior stumbled forward as the unseen wall crumbled with the sorcerer's distraction. A torch flared to life, illuminating the aura of dust and smoke engulfing him. Instead of closing his hands about the sorcerer's throat, he, too, turned.

The maiden stood between two peasants, a captured prisoner. Her tearstained face trembled as one man clutched her tightly and held the point of his sword to her throat. A second spoke.

"Release our village and farms from your spells. Take away your soldiers and return to the place from whence you came. Or else we'll slit your daughter's throat."

"No, she is an innocent!" The warrior's protest surprised them all.

"Do you not stand with us?" the peasant demanded. "Do you not see this is the only power we have over him? Look how his spells are broken when he fears for her safety."

A shadow passed across the sorcerer's black eyes. "If you harm her, I will bring a wrath of destruction upon you that your descendants shall never forget."

"Father, no. Please. No more."

The girl's plea touched a chord in the warrior's heart. He'd seen too much killing in his time to stand by and watch the slaughter of an

Immortal Heart

innocent, no matter where her allegiance lay. "Release her."

"You would betray our cause?" The peasant drew his knife and pointed it at the girl's stomach. In a brashness born of years of despair, he plunged the knife into the folds of her cloak.

But the warrior knew more of fighting than did the peasant. He lunged forward and twisted the peasant's arm, sending the knife skittering into the darkness. He shoved the peasant with the sword aside, and positioned himself beside the girl.

"Betrayer!" The first peasant rushed at the warrior. "He'll kill us all!"

The warrior pushed the girl toward her father and braced to face the angry peasant. In that same instant, the sorcerer flattened his palm and shoved it skyward, muttering a foreign incantation that sent the attacker flying through the air. The man landed in a heap, dead as though struck with a blow to the head.

The peasant with the sword ran, but the sorcerer touched his ring. The man stumbled and fell, his neck broken.

"No!" screamed the warrior. "She lives! Stop the killing!"

Enraged by the senseless deaths, and knowing there would be countless others if the madman wasn't stopped, the warrior picked up the sword of the fallen peasant. He raised it above his head.

The sorcerer didn't sense the attack until it

was too late. He reached for his ring. But before he could utter one word, his daughter jumped into the path.

"Not father!"

The mighty blade sailed through the air. The warrior cried out, powerless to stop its flight as it sliced through the only shield the sorcerer possessed.

His daughter.

The girl toppled to the floor, instantly dead. The sorcerer wailed unintelligibly and dropped beside her, cradling her spiritless body in his arms.

Horrified by his deed, the warrior fell to his knees. He bowed his head and prayed for a forgiveness he could not give himself. "I didn't mean . . . Forgive me. . . ."

He lifted his gaze to the sorcerer. There were no words he could say. He had slaughtered the very innocent he meant to protect.

The sorcerer rose, removed his cloak, and draped the silver and gold shroud over the girl's body. "For this, they will all die."

"No!" The warrior shot his head up. "Take me instead! Punish me!"

"I intend to." The sorcerer's voice echoed with a hollowness that extended to another time. He turned, extending his hand toward the warrior. But it was not a gesture of conciliation. His eyes blazed with an eerie force before he spoke again. "You have taken the one thing that mattered to me in this world. My child. My future.

Immortal Heart

You shall know the same anguish I know."

A chilling numbness crept into the warrior's limbs. He grew weaker, powerless to fight off the dizzying sensation.

"My wife is long dead, and my daughter was all that remained of her. You, too, shall never know a woman's love. Nor shall you ever sire a child."

The warrior collapsed to the floor beside the dead girl. The smoke thickened. His lungs struggled to fill with air. The sorcerer was killing him. Through some evil power of the mind, he was killing him. Slowly, by degrees.

The warrior's mouth went dry. "Spare the villagers. Punish me alone, I beg you."

"Punish you, I shall. I swear eternal vengeance upon your soul."

Smoke clouded the warrior's vision. He lay paralyzed on the cold stone floor.

"Not until the one you love is willingly sacrificed in exchange for your life will you ever know peace."

Mist filled the warrior's head. The sorcerer's incantations made no sense. The sorcerer touched the warrior's chest, scorching his skin. "I mark you now. You are a visible tribute to this day's battle. You will bear witness to every battle you fight.

"You wish to fight for a noble cause. You wish to give your life defending those weaker than you." The sorcerer looked down on the warrior, laughing with a sound that haunted the warrior's soul. "I promise you will spend eternity doing just that."

The warrior's eyes shut and the last mortal gasp left his body.

Chapter One

The Present

"A monster of a man."

Brodie read the teenage boy's opinion of him as easily as he might read a road sign. He ignored the curious gawking. Other heads turned but quickly looked away. He knew what they were thinking. He banished mirrors in his house so he, himself, couldn't see the monster.

He stood a shade over six-feet six and weighed in at 250 pounds, with impossibly broad shoulders, brawny arms, and legs like tree trunks. But the brutish appellation didn't stop with his size and dimension. Strands of silver sliced through his coffee-colored hair, which he wore cropped to a short length that emphasized the harsh angles of his face.

That face, an unforgiving landscape, reflected the horrors of his existence. His once-aquiline nose bent at two separate spots, reminders of a couple of lucky punches. Mottled ridges of a grayish-white scar filled the hollow beneath his left cheekbone and zigzagged into the corner of his mouth. The inflexible tissue pulled his face into a grotesque grimace whenever he smiled.

Long ago he had learned not to smile. Not even with his eyes. His steel gray gaze scanned his surroundings at the LadyTech headquarters building in Kansas City. He routinely memorized the number of people, their positions, the accessible exits. The icy eyes missed nothing of the chaotic, cluttered environment around him, just as they revealed nothing about the man inside.

Another old habit.

No one had ever called him handsome. His driver's license said he was forty, but life-experience beyond his years had taken his ugliness and shaped it into something more than physical. It shrouded him like a tangible thing, a shield he wore to keep all but the bravest and most foolish at a distance.

Brodie Maxwell liked it that way.

Once familiar with the layout of the first floor, Brodie strode from the entryway. Judging by the bustle of activity and torn-up work stations, some major redecorating was going on. He crossed to a makeshift table with a sign marked

Immortal Heart

"receptionist." But the chair behind it sat vacant.

The high school-aged boy, carrying a stack of boxes, stopped several feet away. Brodie felt his stare, curious, fascinated, repelled. Brodie turned his head and nailed the boy with a piercing look. Startled and ashamed of being caught, the boy lowered his gaze to a point about equal with Brodie's collar. He cleared his throat awkwardly, "We're getting ready for our open house, sir. The receptionist is . . . I'll see if I can find someone to help you."

The boy tucked in his chin and scooted past Brodie. Most people did that to him. Too lazy to strain their neck muscles, or too afraid of what they might see, strangers rarely made eye contact with him. Brodie didn't mind their rudeness. That way he didn't have to see their shock and revulsion when they got a good look at his face.

"Hey, you, punch up the con panel and see if the screen lights up."

Brodie's gaze shot around the foyer again, scanning for the source of the disembodied female voice. It made him edgy to think he had missed accounting for everyone in the area. It wasn't like him to make that kind of mistake.

"Hit any button on the keyboard." The voice drizzled into his eardrums a second time. From the vicinity of his feet.

A woman's hand popped out from under the

table and groped at the toe of Brodie's snakeskin boot.

"Yoo-hoo, out there, can you help me?"

Brodie stared at the hand, an ordinary left hand, without a fancy manicure or jewels to adorn it.

"Yes," he finally replied when the hand refused to let go of his foot. The woman couldn't see the whole package, he thought, or else she wouldn't be so relentless in asking for his help. Her voice sounded warm like honey and laughter. Not at all the sort of tone one used with a stranger.

Or a monster.

"It's okay if you don't understand computers. Just hand me one of the remotes. I can get it on-line from down here."

Brodie bit back the cutting remark that would have straightened out the woman's misconception. He was a creature of duty and chivalry. If a woman requested a favor, he felt honor bound to help. That was the only reason he'd agreed to this meeting in the first place. Because the widow of an old friend had asked for his help in finding out who was pirating creative designs from the LadyTech Software Communications Corporation.

Dutifully, Brodie searched the tabletop and picked up a small black box with a series of buttons on one side. He bent over and placed the remote in the palm of her outstretched hand. He lowered the bulk of his body, casting his

Immortal Heart

shadow across the hand and darkening the opening beneath the table.

"Hey, who turned out the lights?"

Once, he would have bristled at the remark. Now he accepted it without comment.

Seconds later, a company logo flashed to life on the computer screen. "It's on," he rumbled, reporting reluctantly.

"Piece of cake."

A body materialized at Brodie's feet.

BJ Kincaid scooted out on her backside, the remote clutched in one hand, a tray of tools in the other. She paused a moment, leaning back on her elbows to look up at her unwilling assistant.

"Whoa." *Land of the Giants*, she thought to herself.

BJ's gaze started at the booted ankles and travelled up a pair of jeans that fitted over the longest, sturdiest legs she had ever seen, past a black suede bomber's jacket, beyond an outdated necktie, over a vicious network of scars, all the way up to the stark gray eyes of the man who towered above her. It was a long trip. From her perspective, his spiky, military-short hair seemed to brush the ceiling.

A living mountain. A dark, battered, unsmiling mountain.

An image from a Frankenstein movie leapt to mind. Immediately, she shook off the comparison, ashamed of even thinking it. BJ knew bet-

Julie Miller

ter than most what it was like to be different from mainstream society. She should be the last person to judge someone else by a first impression.

Hoping she hadn't revealed her uncharitable thoughts, she scrambled to her feet. She dropped her tools on the table and brushed at the untucked hem of her Kansas City Royals baseball jersey. Standing eliminated only part of the distance between them. He still stood chest, shoulders, and head above her five-feet-five-inch frame.

She stuck out her hand and looked him squarely in the eye. "Thanks for your help. I'm BJ Kincaid."

Ironically, he seemed the one unwilling to touch her. A silent moment passed before his hand, nearly double the size of hers and scored with a dozen scars around tanned knuckles, wrapped around her fingers and swallowed them in his handshake.

"One of the partners." BJ could see him sizing her up, checking his internal data on her. "Along with Emma Ramsey and Jasmine Sinclair. You're the creative one. You design LadyTech's programs."

"Most of them," she amended, pulling her hand away. This man knew more about her than a regular customer would. The observation put her on guard. "Can I help you?"

"I'm here to see Emma. I'm Brodie Maxwell." He flipped out an ID that labeled him a security

Immortal Heart

consultant. Before BJ could question exactly what that meant, he returned his billfold to his back pocket. "She hired me to investigate a security leak. I worked with her husband in the Corps."

Emma's dead husband had led a team of crack Marine intelligence operatives. That meant this man possessed certain skills at which she could only guess. All of Jonathan Ramsey's men had been specialists. BJ wondered what this guy's specialty was. Stopping tanks with his fists, perhaps?

BJ shivered. Emma had mentioned bringing in outside help. She knew Emma had only the best interests of the company at heart. But Brodie Maxwell's presence confirmed that she was a traitor to both LadyTech and the partners who were her two best friends.

BJ had developed the missing designs. They had been her responsibility. Hell, the only way an industrial spy could get past her self-designed fail-safe systems would be for her to give out the access codes. Which she hadn't. She would never betray her partners. She would never betray herself. LadyTech was her baby, after all. Most of its concepts and products originated inside her head.

Therein lay the problem.

BJ had mapped out preliminary designs for languages, games, and programs that could mean millions of dollars to the company. Yet no trace of them existed. Not on printouts, not on disks, not on any hard drive at LadyTech or her home office. Her own shadowy memories provided the only evidence that those ideas had ever existed.

But could her memory be trusted? Where was the proof? Brodie Maxwell looked like a man who wouldn't quit until he found answers. BJ dreaded what those answers might be.

She averted her eyes and busied her hands with rearranging her tools. "I guess you're really here to investigate me, then."

"Excuse me?"

She swiveled her face up to his, unable to retrieve a welcoming smile. "You want to solve the mystery, right? I'm giving you your most likely suspect. Me. I'll show you to Emma's office. She'll be expecting you."

BJ cleared the screen of the computer she had just installed before pivoting and crossing to the grand staircase leading to the executive offices on the second floor. Brodie's long shadow overtook her, chilling her with the impression of a beast closing in on his prey.

Brodie ascended the staircase three steps at a time. He debated the woman's sudden mood swing. She had been smiling, unguarded, almost accepting of him when she first crawled from beneath the table. But when he mentioned the purpose of his visit, she closed up. Grew defensive. A fire lit in her eyes, indicating anger

Immortal Heart

and distrust. And something else. Fear perhaps?

But of him? Or his mission?

Her rear swayed on the steps ahead of him. The loose shirt and baggy jeans camouflaged her figure, but they couldn't mask the rigid set of her spine. What was she hiding?

Brodie knew the first step in drawing information out of a suspect was to engage her in innocent, neutral conversation.

"BJ stands for Bridget Jacoba, doesn't it?"

"You've done the research; you should know." The sharp bite of her words bounced off Brodie's tough exterior, but the visible sagging of BJ's shoulders told him she regretted saying them.

She softened her voice and flashed an apologetic smile over her shoulder. "My mom was Bridget. My dad was Jake." She topped the stairs and pointed down an empty corridor. "Emma's office is at the end. You'll probably . . ."

BJ froze mid stride. Her voice faded. "No. Not now."

Brodie collided with her back, and would have sent her flying if he hadn't snatched her shoulders, steadying her. "Miss Kincaid?"

"Get out of my head!"

"BJ?"

Her hands flew to her temples, her fingers dug into the short curls there. "Get out!"

Alarmed, Brodie turned her, keeping the shelter of one arm around her shoulders. He gripped her chin and tilted it upward. Her eyes squeezed shut. Was she having some kind of seizure? He couldn't recall any mention of a physical disorder in her profile. He searched her twisted features for an answer.

"Stop it!" Her voice sounded like cracked, brittle pottery smashing to bits on concrete. Thinking his touch frightened her, Brodie immediately released her.

Wildly, she clutched at his arm, clenching it with both hands until her knuckles turned white. Then she began to shake all over.

Her fingernails bit through leather and cotton into his forearm, but he ignored the bruising pain. If she needed something to cling to, he presented the most solid object at hand. He hardly qualified as an adequate nursemaid, but at that moment, he appeared to be the only one available. "What's happening? Do I need to call someone?"

"Not this time. I won't let you."

Brodie realized she wasn't answering him. He wasn't sure she even knew he was there with her.

"BJ!" He shook her, roughly. "Bridget!"

The demon that possessed her disappeared as swiftly as it had come. Her body went limp. Her knees buckled and he scooped her up in his arms. Her head lolled against his chest, the crown snuggling just beneath his chin.

Damn. The woman was a cuddler. Even sem-

Immortal Heart

iconscious, she turned and pressed her soft cheek into his neck. Every protective instinct that had ever gotten him into trouble surfaced, unbidden. Briefly, Brodie tried to remember the last time a woman had nestled against him so needfully without hesitation or fear or an ulterior motive.

Nothing came to mind. He muttered an angry epithet and refocused on the situation at hand.

He carried her to the first door on his right and kicked it open. He allowed himself a moment of stunned surprise when he entered the room. Other than the antique oak desk with its two computers in the center, it looked like a child's playroom. A truckload of toys lay scattered about the floor and on the furniture. Dolls, models, a train set, games. Floor to ceiling bookshelves, filled with collections of several kinds, lined one wall. Baseball cards. Heart-shaped pillows. Videotapes.

Without a conscious thought as to why, he knew this was her office. BJ Kincaid, former child prodigy with a Mensa-level IQ, multimillionaire partner in one of the hottest companies on the market, worked in an office overflowing with toys.

He determinedly thrust away a flood of unwanted emotions, and moved to a sofa behind the desk. Brushing aside a slough of quilted teddy bears, Brodie laid BJ on the cushions, propping her head on a stuffed plaid heart.

"Monster in my head . . ." she murmured,

stirring as he elevated her feet.

Brodie knew all about the monsters that haunted a person's dreams. He got a reminder of his own tortured demons each time he caught his reflection in a storefront window or rearview mirror. For him, it was natural, as much a part of him as breathing. But for BJ, this couldn't be right.

He squatted on the floor beside her. With one hand, he took both of hers and began rubbing them, kneading warmth into her limp fingers. He smoothed her bangs from her forehead. Her skin was cool to the touch.

She had short, soft curly hair, in a nondescript brownish-blond color. He saw nothing striking about her even features. She wasn't pretty. She wasn't plain. She was just—average.

Brodie thought it odd that he noticed her looks. And even more odd that he wasn't disappointed. Maybe it had something to do with the friendly, open smile with which she had first greeted him. Or the way her eyes boldly met and held his gaze, despite the way she had to crane her neck to do so.

Or maybe it just had to do with the fact he was a male animal who had been too long without a mate, and the sensation of holding a living, breathing female in his arms was all it took to send his hormones into overdrive. It wasn't a comforting thought.

"Wake up, BJ," he whispered, his voice dark and bass deep. "C'mon. Wake up."

Immortal Heart

Footsteps on the carpet alerted him to company. "BJ!" Emma knelt beside him, frowning with fear. "Is she hurt?"

"Don't know. She hit the top of the stairs and had an attack of some kind. When it stopped, she collapsed."

"This isn't the first time. Sometimes she loses track of hours. I have no idea how to help her. That's why I went through Jonathan's journal to track you down." Emma went to a built-in bar and brought back some wet paper towels to dab on BJ's face. "I wasn't sure you'd come."

"We all made a pact to look out for whomever was left behind."

Emma flashed him an apologetic look. "I led you to believe that I needed help, that the company was in trouble. But it's really BJ I'm concerned about."

He shrugged off the misinformation that had gotten him here and jerked his chin toward BJ. "Looks like she needs a physician or a psychiatrist more than she needs my services."

"There's a slight problem with that. BJ has some real hang-ups about men in lab coats, especially shrinks. I can't get her near one. Jas and I have both tried."

Brodie wondered what someone as smart mouthed yet ingenuous as BJ had to fear from a psychiatrist.

Emma continued, "Besides, tomorrow at the stockholders' party, we're announcing the opening of our new Tokyo office. BJ doesn't want any bad publicity concerning her mental condition to scare off potential backers."

BJ moaned, shifted on the pillow, then groaned again. "Tell him all of it, Emma. If he's the savior you say he is, you'd better tell him everything."

Her eyes fluttered open. For the first time, Brodie noticed their unusual color. Not just green, but dark and blue-flecked, like a shadowy spruce forest. Earlier they had sparkled with humor, gleamed with intelligence. Now, a haze of uncertainty and fatigue clouded her eyes.

Her gaze wavered over Emma, then settled on Brodie. "It's not just my ideas that are being stolen. They're taking my sanity. Somebody's playing with my head. It's as if they're tapped into my brain, pulling out ideas before I can even get them on paper."

"Enough." Emma chastised BJ with a worried frown. "Nobody believes you're going insane."

"So what just happened was normal behavior?" BJ's caustic remark echoed in the quiet.

"What did just happen?" Brodie asked. He rose and walked around the room, looking for hidden surveillance devices, getting a feel for BJ Kincaid.

Emma helped BJ sit up. BJ waved aside any further help and focused on Brodie. "You won't find any bugs—audio, visual, or tapped into the computer lines—I've checked."

Brodie admired her astuteness. Nonetheless,

he remained quiet. A long silence passed before BJ continued.

"These episodes happen two, three times a week. For about three months now. It's like . . ."

He heard her breath catch. The recollection obviously pained her. But he said nothing to ease her discomfort. It wasn't his place to do so. He agreed to help Emma because he owed her husband a favor. But when the job was finished, he intended to get back to his own life, solitary hell that it was. He didn't need to worry about anybody else's pain.

"It's like a shadow creeping into my brain. I feel it coming, pushing out everything else. Suffocating my ability to reason. Sometimes I beat it back, like today. Other times . . . I don't know when I lose it. Next thing I know I wake up. I have a memory of the time passing, but nothing tangible to show for it. I'd write them off as dreams except they're too real. And afterward, I have the most awful headache you can imagine."

Brodie paused at the videotape collection on the shelves. The movies consisted mostly of science fiction, including a vast assortment of old monster movies. Frankenstein. The Thing. Godzilla. She must think him a real-life extension of those video monstrosities.

"See anyone you know? You're not even listening to me."

Decades of training in steely self-control kept

him from starting at the sound of BJ's voice near his elbow.

"I heard every word." He angled his face toward hers. She had incredibly expressive eyes. And the deadly message she broadcast to him now was unmistakable. He had to admire her courage. People rarely stood up to him. A savage look or sharp word usually deterred any challengers.

He'd enjoy going a few verbal rounds with BJ. She didn't intimidate easily. She spoke her mind and teased him more than most people ever dared try. But while the idea sounded provocative, he was in no position to indulge himself. Personal involvement meant risk. It meant the possibility of caring. And caring meant death.

He would never take that risk again.

Brodie hooked his thumbs into the front pockets of his jeans, hunched his shoulders and scowled at BJ. "You talk about monsters in your head. Ghosts taking over your thoughts." He nodded toward the videotapes. "You're sure you're not imagining this?"

Color flooded her cheeks. Her fists rode to her hips. Then she caught him completely off guard and shoved at his chest, knocking him back a step. "You . . . You . . . Get the hell out of here!"

After the emotional release of the first blow, BJ attacked him in earnest. Brodie shifted his weight to balance himself, and stood immovable while BJ punctuated each word with a furious, desperate shove.

"I'm . . . not . . . crazy . . . !"

"BJ, stop." Emma gently reprimanded her friend and hurried over to help. But Brodie shook his head and warned her off.

BJ couldn't damage him, so Brodie took the brunt of her outburst, lifting some of the burden of coping from the two women. That much he could do for them.

"I am not crazy," BJ repeated through sobbing breaths, clasping his hands and clinging to him like a lifeline. "Somebody's doing this to me. I'm not crazy."

He absorbed the last of her fury and frustration into his calloused palms. When she was spent, she leaned forward and rested her forehead against him, seeking comfort.

From him?

The trusting gesture surprised him even more than the first blow of her attack.

She must have finally realized he had nothing to offer her, because she pulled away. She took a step back and hugged herself tightly, giving herself the solace he could not. She lifted her face to his.

BJ's eyes were dark, desperate, hopeful.

"I'm sorry. I shouldn't have done that. I promise to keep it all together if you stay and help me. Please."

This wasn't right. Expecting him to be anybody's rescuer. Missing data he could handle.

But asking him to help a damsel in distress? In the cobwebby recesses of his mind, he tried to remember what laughter sounded like. He should be laughing at their ludicrous expectations of him.

Emma stepped behind BJ, squeezing her shoulders in support.

"Jonathan said you handled unusual cases for him." Emma's concerned focus was on BJ, while BJ still concentrated her pleading eyes on him. "But more than that, he said you never quit until everyone was safe. Until everyone was accounted for. You weren't on his last mission, were you?"

Brodie shook his head. Jonathan Ramsey never returned from that last mission. The team had searched for over a year but found no body. Brodie still followed up any remote lead that presented itself. But his friend seemed to have vanished from the face of the earth.

Emma blinked moisture from her smoky blue eyes. "I believe if you had been on that mission, Jonathan would have come home to me. He believed in you that much. Because of that, so do I."

"Emma, I don't deserve that kind of trust."

"Beowulf."

Brodie's attention quickly attuned to BJ's husky, honeyed whisper. "Beowulf?"

"That's you."

He thought he had left fear far behind, but

the innocent hope in her deep green eyes frightened him.

"You're comparing me to one of the monsters in the story?"

"No." She reached for one of his hands and gently spread it open, palm up. With her thumb she traced the expanse of his long, blunt-tipped fingers, touching each scar and callus as if his hand were a rare, precious thing. "You're the slayer of monsters."

Even more than her words, BJ's guileless, gentle touches rocked him to the core. She didn't even know him. The damn fool didn't have sense enough to understand that he could break her neck with that hand. Yet she held on to him, fearful only of the monster inside her head, not of the one standing before her.

Brodie swore violently to himself. This job was going to get personal, he could tell. Yet, despite his misgivings, he accepted that he had already signed on for the duration.

Delaying the inevitable, he thrust BJ and her soulful eyes away from him and stalked across the room. He swiped a hand over his stubbly hair before turning to speak.

"I don't think you're crazy." He wasted no time in getting down to work. "I suspect you're under the influence of mind control."

"Mind control?" BJ and Emma echoed together.

"Posthypnotic suggestion. Brainwashing. I can't be certain, but that's my guess. The attacks come on suddenly, then vanish, leaving a vague memory, but no tangible proof." He saw the wheels turning in BJ's head. First evaluating, then accepting his hypothesis.

"You think someone has programmed me? How? Who?"

He shrugged his shoulders. "Figuring out how it's being done, and who's responsible, won't be easy to do. It will be pretty damn difficult, in fact."

"But not impossible."

"No." He paced the room, needing an outlet for the sudden wellspring of energy coursing through him. He always experienced this rush when he geared up for battle. And this affair could only be described as a battle, a battle with an unseen enemy haunting an innocent woman's mind, and an ongoing battle within himself. He couldn't afford to lose either one.

"I'll become your shadow at home and at work." he explained. "I'll learn your habits, meet your friends. I'll need to observe these episodes firsthand, plus see who has a motive and the opportunity to trigger them. You'll feel like a lab rat with the scrutiny I'll put you through."

He paused when he saw that his words made her look uncomfortable.

"Lab rat? Just what does that mean, exactly?" she asked.

"It means I'm going to move in with you. I'm going to drive you wherever you need to go. I'm going to be at every meeting you attend. I need

Immortal Heart

to know everything in order to figure this out. I'll be closer to you than your own shadow."

"Is that really necessary?"

He could see some backbone returning, and he felt encouraged rather than put off by her accusing look. "It is if you want me to find out the truth," he said.

"Can't you just ask me some questions?"

"Do you have the answers?"

Defiance sparkled in her eyes. Then she looked over at Emma, and sighed with quiet resignation. "Okay."

He wondered what concession she had just made. "Everywhere, BJ. I mean it."

After a tense moment, she smiled, like the sun breaking through the clouds. Bright and beautiful. The kind of smile you couldn't resist returning. Unless you never had any reason to smile. Like Brodie.

"I'll get used to it. I'm warning you, though. Folks will talk. I don't usually keep company with tall, dark strangers."

She was teasing again. Where the hell did she get her misplaced faith in him? Slayer of monsters? Ha! Couldn't she see the truth right before her eyes?

Still, her innocent trust touched something in him. His intrinsic code of honor, no doubt.

"I'll help you," he heard himself promise. "I'll find out who's playing with your head, and how it's being done. I'll put a stop to it."

Or else he'd always be haunted by BJ's frank

green eyes, wide-open and trusting. Looking to the big, ugly monster of a man for answers. And asking for—of all things to expect from a man who held none for himself—hope.

Chapter Two

BJ pushed a series of buttons on a keypad to unlock the front door and push it open with her hip. Inside, she sidestepped stacks of reading material, gadgets, and toys littering the floor and furniture of her clean, but cluttered home. She dumped her purse on a chair en route to the kitchen.

BJ had enough money to build several mansions if she wanted, but she had insisted on a traditional ranch-style house. The landscaper had left most of the natural trees and groundcover plants intact, giving her place the feel of the country. It was located on the outskirts of Lee's Summit, a suburb south of Kansas City, about a thirty-minute drive from LadyTech headquarters.

It was a drive that, thanks to Brodie, had taken her over an hour this evening. As promised, he had been a menacing shadow following her through evening rush-hour traffic. Each time she stopped, once to buy gas and once to pick up a pizza for dinner, his Explorer pulled up right behind her. Then Brodie was at her side, almost before she could open her truck door.

His proximity didn't faze her too much. After all, he had promised to shadow her. But his endless barrage of questions stretched her nerves to the limit: *Why do you broadcast your truck with license plates that say WIZ-KID? Do you always travel the same route? Are these the same people who always wait on you?*

If she could just come up with the right answers, maybe he'd stop hounding her. He hadn't once offered any bit of information about himself, yet BJ began to feel as if he knew every detail about her. He was studying her, taking her apart, finding out what made her tick.

The inquisition left her head throbbing, but she had to let him do it. He offered BJ her best shot at finding out the culprit sabotaging her mind. And LadyTech.

But Brodie's scrutiny and analysis, done without revealing his opinions, what he thought of her, or even whether she was helping any, tugged at a memory she had purposefully buried. His use of the term "lab rat" struck a little too close to home. Some demons from the past

Immortal Heart

deserved to stay there. BJ knew she'd have to tell him everything, sooner or later.

She preferred later.

She swallowed her retort and answered another question about her home security system.

Brodie seemed to think the place was a tactical nightmare. He wanted to know why there wasn't any human backup to her fully automated system at the gates. He advised her that the trees gave excellent cover to anyone who climbed over the perimeter wall.

He listened to her explanation about the workings of the motion-detector system she had installed, but he kept coming back to the concern that automated systems could fail. She needed physical and mechanical backup as well.

"You don't have a lot of faith in modern technology, do you?" she said without looking back.

He followed her into the kitchen. "If someone wants to get to you, they'll find a way."

She put two fingers to her mouth and whistled through her teeth. A high-pitched bark answered her immediately. "If it makes you feel any better, I do have a guard dog. Duke! It's me, sweetie. Here, boy!"

A heartbeat later, a miniature black missile shot through a flap in the back door and hurtled itself at BJ. With familiar devotion, she dropped to her knees to scratch in the pits of Duke's bouncing legs and lowered her face to accept his wet, welcoming kisses.

Julie Miller

"Your guard dog is a poodle?"

The voice rumbled from above like thunder, shifting the dog's attention to Brodie. The lionhearted fluff ball growled in his throat, planting himself squarely between Brodie and his mistress, barking and growling, lunging toward Brodie's boot, then pulling back. The tiny thing bared his teeth and stood ready to defend BJ against the strange giant.

"Duke! Bad dog." She scooped the dog up in her arms and stood, surprised by his reaction to Brodie. Duke stretched his neck and nearly jumped out of her hands. Brodie retreated a step and Duke quieted his yapping to a low vibration BJ could feel shaking his ribs. She shook her head, perplexed. "I'm sorry. I've never seen him act this way before. He's usually putting on a show to get attention or a treat, not attacking my guests."

Brodie looked first at the growling dog and then at her. "You rely on that for protection? Dammit, BJ, it's hardly as big as my foot."

BJ's chin jutted out defiantly at the insult. " 'It' is a he, and he sounds an alarm better than anything I could invent. Duke's big where it counts the most, in his loyalty and in his heart."

Brodie pointed a finger at the dog. "He's just a little noisemaker."

On cue to illustrate the point, Duke's growl increased its intensity. He shocked BJ by snapping at Brodie's outstretched hand. Brodie dodged the sharp little teeth.

Immortal Heart

"You need more backup than that. He could be taken out just as easily as your computer systems. Technology and puppy dogs can be dismantled."

His callous observations spurred her to escape. Snitching a bite of hamburger from the pizza, she fed it to Duke and carried him to the back-porch door where she set him down. "Duke, room."

She watched proudly as the well-trained dog reluctantly obeyed his mistress by crawling through the door flap onto the porch. Then she turned on Brodie. "Do you have something against pets? Or is Duke just one more thing about me that you want to pick apart and criticize?"

Brodie didn't apologize. "The dog's heart is in the right place. But he's hardly a deterrent to the mastermind we're up against."

"We don't know what we're up against."

"Precisely." He leaned forward slightly, casting an ominous shadow over her. "Don't be lured into a false sense of security, BJ. You have to question everything. Everybody. I'd bet good money that your mind-stalker has already compromised your security systems. Anyone smart enough to do that would hardly be intimidated by a little dog."

Brodie's icy eyes melted a little, as though he regretted driving home his point so succinctly. But the apology she wanted to hear wasn't forthcoming. "Can you think of anybody with your same technical know-how? I'm not asking if you suspect anyone, just who would be capable of dismantling your security designs."

More questions. BJ released a vexed sigh. Brodie seemed determined that she know nothing of peace until the security leak was resolved. She wanted to pig out on junk food and play with her dog.

He wanted to expose every painful detail of her life.

"I guess it's pretty arrogant to think I'm the only hacker on the planet. I can think of one or two people who might be able to break into my security program."

"Who?"

She spoke without really thinking about her answer. That was one of the downsides to higher brain-function activity. You could give an intelligent answer while thinking about something totally different, like the formidable man who was at once her protector and inquisitor.

"There's a guy who works for us, Rick Chambers. I'm not his favorite person, but he's an ace at debugging programs, so we keep him around. Also, I did a couple of internships at the Morrisey Research Institute. The director, Damon Morrisey, is brilliant. He could probably decipher how my mind works."

Brodie paced the length of the kitchen while he jotted something on the notepad he pulled from his jacket pocket. "This Chambers guy,

Immortal Heart

why aren't you his favorite person?"

BJ wasn't fooled by Brodie's apparent nonchalance. His icy, nearly colorless, gray eyes scanned the room, memorizing each knickknack, each piece of furniture, each nuance of her reactions to his probing questions.

"Rick thrives on creative competition. He keeps a mental tally sheet where he tracks every patent and profit we bring to LadyTech. I have a few more victories than he does. I don't think my success sits too well with his ego."

"Do you have any enemies at the Morrisey Institute?"

Brodie worked like a machine. Emotionless and tireless. BJ didn't know how much longer she could last with that intense scrutiny directed solely at her. Every question Brodie asked, every notation he made, drove her deeper into a pit of uncertainty and self-doubt. Could she have betrayed LadyTech? Would she do it again? Was she losing her mind?

"I left Morrisey on good terms. I go back as a consultant sometimes. Damon has given me rock-solid support through all this. I still visit him a couple times a week, just to shoot the bull and get my mind off things."

"And you're positive no one else knows your security codes?"

"Not even Jas and Emma know the sequences for my home office. We set it up that way for safekeeping."

"The missing designs were transmitted from here as well?"

BJ nodded. She weathered the subsequent onslaught of questions by distancing herself from the situation. Her keen imagination turned the tables and studied Brodie Maxwell instead.

Unusual didn't begin to describe this man of paradoxical contrasts. Despite his imposing size, he moved with a natural grace that she would attribute to someone who practiced the martial arts. Poised and precise on his feet, he looked solid enough to either deliver or survive a deadly punch.

His dark hair was short and studded with just enough gray to hint that he had endured some real stress in his forty or so years. But he was obviously physically fit. His jeans hugged narrow hips and a firm set of buns. BJ definitely counted herself a tush fan, and if she concentrated on Brodie's body instead of his face, she saw some good material for her errant fantasies.

But she couldn't ignore his face. He bore so many scars, his skin looked like a crazy quilt that had been pieced together. His left cheek and jaw were a distorted washboard of hardened tissue, pulling his mouth into a taut, straight line. Imagining a couple of bolts sticking out of his neck completed the picture forming in her mind.

"BJ." The brittle ice in his voice snapped her

Immortal Heart

back to the present. She had been staring at him. No matter that some of her impressions had been rather flattering, she had been rudely gawking. Obviously, Brodie didn't appreciate the scrutiny.

"Sorry." She smiled contritely. "I didn't hear your question."

"It can wait." He closed his notebook and put it away. "You don't like to answer questions, do you?"

He leaned his hip against the counter and hunkered his shoulders down a bit. BJ thought he did that to appear smaller, less threatening. Though he still towered over her, BJ found his effort oddly touching. She suspected Brodie Maxwell rarely made such a concession to anyone.

That concession gave her the courage to delve into the past.

"You want to know why I freaked out when you called me a lab rat this morning?"

BJ kicked off her shoes and padded past him into the living room, needing some time to choose her words. She sat on the sofa and pulled her legs up beneath her, pretzel style.

Brodie moved the beginnings of a space-shuttle model out of the chair across from her and sat. He leaned forward, resting his elbows on his knees, again making his bulk appear smaller. "I'm listening."

BJ breathed deeply and expelled the air

slowly. "I'll give you a brief history of my childhood."

She found the steadiness of Brodie's gaze reassuring, and she concentrated on his steely eyes as she launched into her story. "My mother died when I was born, leaving Jake—my dad—to take care of me. He was a good man, and I loved him dearly. He was a digger for Jasmine's father, Austin Sinclair."

"A digger?"

"Austin's hobby is archaeology. After an accident on one of his early expeditions, Austin promoted Jake to foreman. Gave him steady work. So he travelled a lot, all over the world. Jake used to take me sometimes. Those were the best adventures. I have memories from a very early age." Her heart warmed as she recalled those brief, special times with her father.

"But he was never in one place for very long, so he let Austin enroll me in a boarding school when I was four. Almost from the start, I was in trouble all the time. Missing curfews and meals because my nose was stuck in a book. Asking the wrong questions in class. Challenging teachers. At first they diagnosed me as hyperactive and put me on medication."

A sour taste coated her mouth as she recalled the school nurse prying open her mouth and jamming the pills she didn't want to take down her throat.

"It didn't seem to have much effect other than to make me depressed and combative. The ad-

Immortal Heart

ministrators sent me to several doctors who tried different medicines and treatments. I was dismissed from two schools before I was six. Jake pulled me out of a third school when they labeled me mentally retarded—"

Brodie's crude expletive interrupted her. "That's about what Jake said."

"I think I would have liked your father."

BJ saw understanding shining in Brodie's eyes. The kindness and compassion there softened his harsh looks. BJ rubbed her hands together, feeling an eerie chill of remembrance. For an instant, she was a terrified five-year-old, praying that some kindhearted hero would rescue her from her captors.

"Can you go on?"

Brodie's gentle prodding and secure presence made the painful memories recede a little. "Jake never believed there was anything wrong with me, but he didn't know what to do with me, either. We lived in California at the time, so he checked me into a research school in Berkeley. The professors and grad students ran all kinds of tests on me. They poked and prodded and quizzed me eight hours a day for several months."

"You were so young. You must have been terrified."

She had been. Through a child's viewpoint, the machines were alien creatures that gave her nightmares. The adults in white lab coats were witches and warlocks who trapped her in sterile-walled torture chambers from which she couldn't escape. Needles pricked her. Electrodes stung her. Questions hounded her.

"One doctor finally thought to give me an IQ test. I was off the scale for a six-year-old. Then the testing really began. They wanted to find out just how smart I really was." BJ slipped back to those terrifying months, reliving the fear and loneliness.

"Once, they locked me in a room and gave me math problems to solve. They tied my hands together so I couldn't use them to count. They wanted to get an accurate measure of how complex a problem I could do in my head."

She shuddered as the memory became real to her. No longer a twenty-seven-year-old woman, she regressed into a confused child who felt imprisoned and abandoned and frightened for her life. "I got every answer right. But they said I cheated. They strapped me down every morning until I finally figured out that if I gave a couple of wrong answers, they'd let me go."

The brush of something soft and solid against her cheek pulled BJ back to the present. The smell of worn leather tickled her nose. Warmth surrounded her. She didn't know how much she had actually said out loud, but she shook with tears that burned her eyes and paralyzed her throat.

She hadn't cried like this since she was a girl. Not since she buried Jake. She'd shared her sorrows with Jas and Emma, and confessed trou-

Immortal Heart

bling problems to her mentor, Damon Morrisey. But she'd never wept like this. She'd never bared her soul. She never thought anyone could understand.

No one had until Brodie cradled her in his lap, and wound his sheltering, titanic arms around her. His long fingers smoothed the fringe of curls at her nape while he murmured deep voiced nothings against her hair.

BJ burrowed into his ample chest, finding solace and security in his immeasurable strength. Finding comfort and peace in his gruff, rumbling voice. She discovered a kinship in his strong arms. He was an ally who truly understood her darkest fears.

She didn't want to leave the haven she found unexpectedly in Brodie's arms. He made her feel safe. His size and warmth and awkward gentleness formed a barrier against both the dangers of the present and the demons of the past.

"That was back before schools had programs for the gifted," she finally continued. "The doctors recommended to Jake that I stay with them. I started with tutors for a couple of years, but when they found out how quickly I assimilated information, they enrolled me in college courses.

"Talk about a freak. My classmates thought I was some kind of joke, an eight-year-old in a freshman algebra class. They stopped laughing

Julie Miller

when they found out how high I raised the grading curve."

Brodie's arms tightened around her. "Didn't Jake know what you were going through?"

"Yes. But what could he do? He was a single parent who had no understanding of little girls and no idea what to do with a genius child. When he visited, he took me to ball games and showed me how to build model airplanes."

Her story indirectly explained the mess in her house, the tomboyish clothes she wore. She'd never had a childhood. So she had created one for herself as an adult. She had been a lonely little girl surrounded by people who treated her as an object, a phenomenon, not as a person.

She knew Brodie understood.

Her fingers tightened their grip on his jacket. He'd push her away soon, but for now she clung to him, seeking the strength to finish. "Jake was the only person who treated me like a child. To everyone else, I was a case study. A scientific experiment."

"A lab rat," Brodie concluded.

"When I was older, I went through some counseling. You can imagine how I handled their probing into my life. Damon was a huge help. When he took me on as his protégée, he gave me a purpose. He helped me discover ways to use my talents. I thought I had put all of those old fears to rest. Until now."

She tipped her head back, needing to see Brodie's expression, needing to know he didn't

Immortal Heart

judge her as some kind of freak.

She caught a glimpse of something wild and fiery before the gray eyes shuttered. "Now?" he prompted.

BJ didn't question his reaction. Anger and mystery seemed to be a big part of who he was. "They're playing with my head again. All those years as a child I thought someone wanted to take over who I was, wanted to control me. I felt as if they wanted to cut open my head and take my brain for themselves. Now it's happening all over again. I feel like I'm that scared little girl."

Brodie folded his calloused palm around her chin, capturing her in a grip somewhere between reprimand and comfort. "You're not that little girl anymore. You're a grown woman. And this time there's somebody on your side."

He touched his lips to hers, blotting out the power behind his guttural promise. His kiss was hard, hot, and over before BJ could respond.

With abrupt force, he lifted her off his lap and plopped her on the cushion beside him.

"Brodie?" Her lips burned from the incendiary contact. His brief caress kindled the spirit within her, bringing her to her feet a second behind him. "I just wanted to explain . . ."

"I need to check the grounds outside." He strode to the door, forcing her into double time to catch up to him. When she touched his arm, he pulled away from her and looked down at her with such fury that she wondered if she had dreamed his tenderness and concern.

The hinges hung on for dear life when he swung the door open. "What's the security code?"

"No way."

"What?"

She recoiled to a safer distance. "N-O-W-A-Y. The numerical equivalent."

He didn't comment on how clever or ridiculous her password sounded, he was beyond civil conversation. "Lock it behind me. If you need me, yell. I'll be here."

The door slammed shut on his promise, leaving BJ in the fallout of Hurricane Brodie. She hugged herself protectively and licked her lips, tasting salty tears and something more. Something he had stamped there. She wasn't the only one surprised by that kiss. Brodie's abrupt departure confirmed it.

BJ rubbed her arms and headed to her office. The male of the species was one subject she hadn't aced. She didn't presume to comprehend this one.

She sat down and turned on the monitor. Computers she understood. They never called her eccentric or judged that she was too successful.

Today she had sought security and acceptance from Brodie, a man who very clearly liked to keep his distance, a professional who didn't like to get personally involved. With the episode at the office and the confessions here at home,

Immortal Heart

she had probably invaded every bit of personal space that Brodie guarded.

No wonder he'd left so suddenly. By choice a recluse, Brodie had reluctantly come out of hiding only to repay a debt he felt he owed a friend. She didn't doubt he had gone outside in order to escape her company, to be alone again to recover his icy composure.

She should honor his need for privacy. She should keep her distance for her own sake as well as his. But a part of her couldn't help wishing that the fire would return to his eyes. And that for a few moments out of time, he would drive away the demons that haunted her mind, and make her feel the way no man except her father had—normal.

The stars rode high above a churning bank of clouds. The still heat hit him like a wall. Thunder rolled in the distance. Static lightning charged the sky, like torches blinking on and being snuffed out. The scent of rain told him the downpour would reach here any minute.

The violence matched his mood.

Brodie ran into the darkness, pushing his body to its top speed. He ran until he felt alone and swallowed up by the swirling night.

Then he braced his feet, tipped his head back and howled his endless rage at the coming storm. Somewhere in the distance, Duke barked. In that moment, Brodie hated the little dog. He hated him for seeing what BJ could not.

That Brodie Maxwell was a freak. That he was a monster inside and out.

Brodie dropped to his knees, conceding a begrudging bit of respect for the dog. Duke did everything in his power to protect his mistress. But the fiercest dragon in the world couldn't protect anyone from Brodie. Once the cycle had started, their doom would be inevitable.

And the cycle had started. Damn it all, he had kissed her!

He hurt for her. He went to her and gathered her in his arms when her memories grew too difficult for her to bear. Could there be anything more dangerous than caring for a woman? The injustices of her childhood churned the anger inside him. It was his nature to protect, and she had been so vulnerable.

Thunder cracked and the moon vanished behind the clouds. He tilted his face to the heavens that had forgotten him, and he waited for the cold rain to pelt his skin.

BJ looked at him as if he were a man, not an object. She expected decent, normal behavior from him. She stood up to the monster, yet turned to the man for comfort.

The rain hit his forehead and ran into the crevices of his cheek. Lightning forked to the ground in the distance. He should seek the heart of the storm and let the next bolt strike him. But that wouldn't help BJ. Nothing could help her now.

For what seemed a lifetime, he had managed

to keep the danger at bay. But somehow, on this day, he had slipped. Irrevocably and unforgivably. He sealed BJ's fate just as surely as the criminal who stole her thoughts and ideas.

Because Brodie had started to care.

Thunder echoed in the distance by the time Brodie finished circling the grounds surrounding the house. Wet jeans plastered his legs, and his shirt collar clung like a clammy second skin beneath his water-stained jacket. He had walked the duration of the storm, become one with the elements until he could push everything out of his head except his sense of duty.

As Brodie neared the house, the mantle of warrior awareness slipped over his shoulders. Forget today, he chided himself. Tomorrow's investigation would be more insightful. Sassy women with tell-all eyes would not affect his ability to ferret out the truth.

But when Brodie stepped onto the porch, his cool detachment evaporated. Something was wrong. His scalp tingled in anticipation, his radar sensing danger before he saw it. The interior lights were out and the door stood ajar. Could a power failure have tripped the security system? He thought BJ had mentioned a backup generator.

Slipping into the shadows against the house, Brodie reached behind him and pulled a knife from the sheath on his belt. He rolled the leather handle until it fit snugly in his hand and became a lethal extension of his own body.

He slid along the siding to the door frame, nudging the door with his boot. In one smooth motion, he swung the door open and dropped to the floor inside. He crouched low behind the furniture, keeping his eyes open for anything, straining his ears to hear some sign of BJ.

He heard crunching and scratching through the kitchen. The damn guard poodle was eating a midnight snack.

With an ugly sigh, he rolled to his feet. BJ probably was sound asleep in her room. The open door was probably just a fluke. Still, his instincts had carried him through many battles. He wasn't ready to discount their warning signal just yet.

His boots squeaked with dampness as he systematically checked the rooms. He found everything dark and silent until he reached the far wing of the house.

A pulsing light flickered through an open doorway at the end of the hall. He crept closer and looked inside.

BJ's office.

The only light in the room came from the computer monitor on the desk in one corner. Gray illumination flickered from rows and rows of data scrolling across the screen. A second desk with another computer setup lined the opposite wall. In between were scattered stacks of drawings and printouts, a battered recliner, and a trail of discarded clothing.

Immortal Heart

"I've been waiting for you."

Brodie whipped his head around as a shadowy figure emerged from the corner. The husky honey drawl belonged to a woman who looked like BJ, yet didn't.

"You should be asleep. Are you all right?" He sheathed his knife without taking his eyes off her.

"I am now."

The differences in her appearance became apparent as she sauntered toward him. She had removed her jeans, socks, and shoes. She still wore the baseball jersey, but looked nothing like an innocent kid in it now. The hem fell to a tantalizing line near the top of her thighs where the curve of her hips began. She had unbuttoned the top to a point halfway down her cleavage. One side fell open, revealing the swell of a breast.

Brodie's gut clenched inside him. She wasn't wearing a bra. In fact, he could pretty well guess that she wasn't wearing much of anything beneath that clingy, unexpectedly sexy jersey.

He didn't need this. "BJ, what's going on?"

Cotton rustled as her hips swayed beneath the fabric.

"Did something happen?" His eyes narrowed questioningly, then accusingly as she pressed herself against him.

"I got scared. But I feel safer with you here."

He was ready to wrap a comforting arm

around her when she stepped back. "You're soaked."

Her fingertip caught the top button of his shirt and unhooked it. "You'd better get out of these before you catch a cold."

She slipped to undo another button, and he grasped her wrist to stop her. "I'm fine. What scared you?"

She lifted her free hand and tugged open the zipper on his jacket.

"BJ."

She giggled secretively, seductively. "You're dripping on the rug."

When he looked to see the damage, she pushed his jacket off his shoulders and down his arms. She twisted behind him and pulled the sodden leather off, letting it fall to the floor.

"Oh yes."

He turned and questioned her downward focus. "What are you doing?"

"Fantasizing."

She sounded as if she were joking about his backside. He reached for the light switch near the door, but she pushed him back. She had two more buttons undone before he snatched her by the wrists. "Stop this. You don't know what you're doing."

"You said I was a grown woman."

"It wasn't an invitation."

"Of course it was. You try to be tough, but you're still a man. A man I want." BJ tipped her head back, exposing the long column of her

Immortal Heart

throat down to . . . damn. Her jersey had picked up the dampness from his clothes, clinging and revealing high, firm breasts whose pouty tips flirted with him.

Suspicious mistrust flamed inside him even as his jeans grew tight. His anger fluttered into focus again. Not at BJ, but at himself for reacting like a man instead of her protector.

She ignored his grip on her and rose on tiptoe, pressing her lips against an aroused male nipple. Her touch sent a shockwave straight through him. He had never imagined this forthright woman to be such a tease. Did she think toying with his baser needs was some kind of joke?

He might be a living, breathing freak of nature. But he still felt normal male desire.

He gave her wrists a slight shake, not wanting to hurt her, but wanting her to realize that she played with fire by taunting him. "BJ, you're exhausted. I don't think you know . . ."

She inched her body forward, rubbing herself against him. She knew exactly what she was doing. The tips of her breasts brushed against his stomach and he caught his breath.

If her honey sweet voice warmed him, her body set him on fire.

But her actions angered him. He had sworn an oath to protect her. Did she think she needed to pay for his help by sacrificing her self-respect? Was this the kind of comfort she craved?

He released her wrists and grabbed her shoulders. "Don't do this. You don't know anything about me."

Her response was to unfasten the top button of his jeans and pull out the tail of his shirt. "I know all I need to."

Brodie felt the vestiges of self-restraint slipping away. Nobility became hard to hold onto. Years of denied need slowly eradicated an age-old promise to never become involved with a woman again.

BJ was intelligent. She had the IQ to prove it. She had to know where this was leading.

"BJ. Stop."

It was a pathetic command. He wanted it. He wanted her. He had found no true release outside. His rage still simmered below the surface. Now, the embers of passion mingled with it.

This wasn't right. Yet she was so seductive, so sure of what she wanted. He hated that he had misread her so. He hated himself even more for losing control of his self-imposed distance.

Dear Lord, part of him was still human. Muttering an oath about eternal damnation, Brodie scooped her up by the buttocks and lifted her high off the floor. He crushed her mouth beneath his, locking her in a fiery conflagration that consumed them both.

Chapter Three

He wrapped her legs around his waist, swallowing her triumphant cry. Her hands clutched wildly at him, ripping his shirt open, digging her fingers into the hard muscles of his chest. Her nails teased his skin, eliciting shockwaves that made him dizzy. She fired his cool, damp skin everywhere she touched him.

Brodie collapsed in the chair and reclined it backward, stretching her out on top of him. Her lips left his to softly trace the trails marked by her fingernails. His hands roamed beneath her jersey, finding nothing but a pair of plain cotton panties to impede his progress.

Brodie loved the feel of her, solid and curved in all the right places. And not so fragile that he felt she was going to snap in two beneath his big hands.

With impatient clumsiness, he unfastened her jersey and tossed it to the floor. When his mouth found her breast, she arched her body backward, snatching at his hair and clasping his head to her.

BJ's guttural response fueled his need for her. Briefly, he thought of slowing things down for sanity's sake. But BJ had other things on her mind. She shifted and guided the other breast to his willing mouth. Her bold maneuvers enticed him into a trap from which he didn't want to escape. Brodie obliged her by rolling his tongue around the rosy peak, teasing and sucking until she cried out his name.

Lifetimes had passed since he had known loving to be this good. This free. This passionate. He was mindless with her uninhibited need. Somehow he had misjudged her. This irresistible seductress simply couldn't be as innocent as he had imagined. He felt bound to claim her. To take what she so eagerly offered.

"BJ," he gasped, seeking her mouth again, dragging the lower part of her body squarely over his. She rubbed her heat against his, temporarily robbing him of the ability to speak. He slid his hands over her hips and stilled her provocative moves. "This isn't the best time to explain why I don't carry any protection. But I promise I can't hurt you. I can't get you pregnant."

Immortal Heart

"Just shut up and kiss me again." BJ lifted her head and smiled wickedly at him, her lips swollen with his kisses, her eyes . . .

That was when he saw it. The blank look in her eyes. Like an invisible curtain shrouding the natural light and sparkle.

That look carried him back centuries in time. Back to a time when sorcerers cast spells and damned warriors with curses.

Her eyes could see, yet saw nothing. He clasped her head between his hands, squeezing a little roughly, forcing her to look at him when she wanted to return her attentions to his body.

"BJ, look at me." He shook her without hurting her, and tried to capture her hands to stop them from bewitching his body with their erotic play.

"Dammit, BJ! Do you see me? Do you know who I am?"

She wedged her peach-soft thigh between his legs, and he damned his body for its involuntary response.

"Bridget!"

Suddenly BJ froze, stock-still above him. Even by the dim light of the computer, he could see the color draining from her body. She blinked rapidly, like a sleeper startled into wakefulness.

Her tentative fingers traced the most hideous scar on his body, the abstract zigzag that covered his heart. He knew she was seeing it for the first time. Really seeing it. She started to shake.

"Brodie?"

A panicked whisper replaced her husky sexiness.

In a sudden, jerky movement, BJ rolled off the chair and stood, shaking, clutching her arms across her naked breasts.

Her gaze darted around the room and back to him. Brodie slowly straightened the chair and got up, moving cautiously, never taking his eyes off her. She cowered like a cornered animal, expecting to be attacked at any minute from any direction.

"BJ?" He ignored the protests of his body and kept his voice low and steady. "Do you know where you are?"

She glanced around her. Her nod was quick, rabbit-like. "Home."

"Do you know who I am?"

Her eyes bored into his before she nodded, very slowly. "It happened again, didn't it? I mean . . . I'm not sure . . ."

She shivered. Brodie removed his shirt and draped it over her body, overlapping the front to cover her. Then he stepped away from her and turned on the overhead light so she wouldn't be frightened by a monster in the shadows. When the light came on, she saw his unfastened jeans and her own clothes on the floor.

Immortal Heart

Red blotches dotted her cheeks. "Oh my God. Was I? Did I?"

She covered her mouth, clutched the shirt together, and dashed into the hallway. Brodie followed her to the bathroom where she slammed the door in his face. He heard the toilet flush and water running for several minutes. Finally, it grew quiet.

He retrieved his jacket from the office floor to cover himself, and rebuttoned his jeans before knocking on the door. "BJ, are you all right?"

Silence. He tested the knob. It was unlocked. "I'm coming in."

Brodie found her sitting on the edge of the tub, huddled inside his shirt. The thing hung past her knees, making her look like a little girl playing dress up. Curly wisps of hair clung to her skin where she had splashed water on her face. She looked deathly pale except for the pink rims around her eyes, evidence of more crying. Her eyes were dry now, but shadowed with trouble.

He closed the toilet lid and sat across from her. Brodie wanted to hold her hand or pull her into his arms, but thought it wiser to keep his distance. He didn't want to startle or alarm her in this disoriented state.

She glanced up at him, but quickly averted her eyes.

"I'm so embarrassed. I'm mortified. Brodie, I'm so sorry. You must think I'm an idiot. I kissed you, didn't I?" She bent her head with a strangled groan of frustration and self-reproach. "Hell, I was practically naked when I woke up. I'm so sorry."

"I should have realized sooner."

"I couldn't have been in my right mind to throw myself all over you like that."

"Quit apologizing!" He barked the order more harshly than he intended. The sight of BJ cringing away from him tore him in two. How could he have been so stupid to let BJ put herself in such an awkward position? He should have been looking out for her welfare from the outset. He should have seen her dazed expression. He should never have inflicted the kind of pain he saw etched in her eyes.

Brodie softened his voice and hunched his shoulders. "Do you remember anything?"

He held himself still, giving BJ the time she needed to summon herself once more. She leaned forward, lifting her fingers to his lips, tracing them with the delicate inquisitiveness of a blind person reading Braille. It required all his will not to jerk away from her tender, unwittingly arousing fingertips. A frown crinkled beside her eyes. She concentrated, trying to replay the episode in her head. He kept still because this was his mission, and BJ needed to find answers.

"I don't know." She leaned even closer, trying to see with her eyes something her memory could not. "You were wet and cold and we kissed. I think."

Immortal Heart

Brodie couldn't account for what possessed him then. He fleetingly excused it as research for the case when he pulled her hand away, closed the distance between them, and kissed her.

Slowly, reverently, less volatile than before. He kissed her until her lips shyly responded. Until her hand cupped the less damaged side of his jaw. Until her mouth opened to let him taste the honeyed softness inside. She had been fire before. Now she had changed into a soft rain, mesmerizing and life-affirming.

He pulled away even more slowly, hesitant to believe that he wasn't under some kind of spell. Her eyes fluttered open, close to his. They were clear and bright—and aware.

"I remember," she whispered. "Nothing else is clear. But I remember this. I remember you."

When she looked at him with those honest, trusting eyes, he could almost wish . . . he could almost believe . . . Hell, this was too much. Too soon. It would never be right to have feelings for BJ. It would never be safe.

Abruptly, Brodie cleared his throat and stood. He steeled himself against her visible withdrawal and the habitual way she had of crossing her arms and hugging herself. "That doesn't make any sense. You can't remember what you were doing in your office. But you can remember what I did?"

"Vaguely." BJ spoke quietly, almost apologetically. "I remember the sensation more than the actual embrace. I knew I wasn't alone. I knew it was you."

Nothing made any sense. "You don't recall anything else?"

She struggled to find an answer that remained just out of reach. "No. Not until I woke up, on top of you."

BJ winced at the last phrase, looking acutely embarrassed by the intimacy she had unconsciously shared with him. At that moment, Brodie felt the sting of every wound ever inflicted on him, every tragedy of which he had been a part. To have let his sordid, sorry existence touch this innocent woman felt unforgivable. Instinctively, he zipped his jacket to the neck and turned the more frightening side of his face away from BJ.

"Do you remember what you were doing before you went into the trance?"

BJ couldn't blame Brodie for his abrupt change in manner. Somewhere along the way she had crossed that indefinable barrier between employer and bodyguard and gotten very, very personal. Even if she didn't remember much of what happened in her office, she could tell that Brodie was extremely uncomfortable at being reminded of just how personal things had gotten between them.

She wanted him to protect her and comfort her as he had earlier. She wanted to know the true man inside of him. Was he the gentle giant of a moment ago or this cold, fierce warrior?

But just because she felt unfamiliar desires and curiosity didn't necessarily mean he wanted anything from her. In fact, Brodie had gone out of his way several times to show her how much he needed his privacy and distance. BJ felt rather selfish for violating those needs, regardless of whether she'd been sane at the time or not.

BJ did remember the tender kiss they had shared moments ago. His crooked mouth had been unbending, but infinitely gentle. Brodie's raw, sensual touch scattered the murky clouds of shame and confusion in her mind, and replaced them with the clarity of awareness. Of him and of herself. Man and woman. Not damsel and rescuer. Not monster and misfit. Brodie and BJ.

If he could deny the connection between them, then so could she.

She answered his question in as businesslike a manner as she could. "I couldn't sleep. The storm came and I knew you were outside. I went out on the porch and called, but I guess you couldn't hear me. I came back in to play on the computer until you got in."

Her recollection went fuzzy.

"I don't know." She shoved her fingers through her hair, frustrated with herself for being so confused. "What's wrong with me?" she demanded, to no one in particular. "My mind is so screwed up!"

Julie Miller

"When the other incidents occurred—when your designs were stolen—do you remember anything at all about them? What you were doing when they started? When you woke up?"

"I don't know."

"Think!" His clipped command forced her to concentrate.

She closed her eyes and tried to picture the episodes that had left her feeling violated. "Usually they happen late at night. When I've been working really hard. But tonight I wasn't doing anything. Just playing a game."

BJ's cheeks grew hot. That wasn't all she had been doing. She had been thinking about Brodie. In her mind, there were no scars. There was only strength and understanding, enough to make her feel feminine and desirable. In her imagination, his comfort became a caress. He smiled with her.

She snapped her eyes open. Brodie still wore his perpetual frown. BJ channeled her thoughts back to business. "I kept myself awake by rewriting the game program."

Suddenly her thinking skipped off on another tangent. *The computer. Something about the computer.* A flash of insight toyed with her consciousness.

"What is it?"

BJ shot to her feet, shoving her arms into the sleeves of Brodie's shirt. She darted back into her office. His question hung in the air, unanswered, while she focused everything on the computer in front of her. Brodie moved behind her chair while she typed in a command.

Nothing.

She banged her fist on the table and typed again. When she pushed the enter button, a myriad of geometric shapes floated across the screen.

"Damn!"

"What are you doing?"

She ignored Brodie's question. Clutching the oversized shirt together with one hand, she crawled under the computer table and checked the wires on a recording box she had installed.

Nothing.

The word became a mantra in her head.

BJ slid out from beneath that table and repeated the same manic process on the other computer. She stared at the figures moving randomly before her, pressing the heels of her hands against her temples, desperately trying to make sense out of the garbage on the screen.

Nothing.

She jumped to her feet, grabbed the computer monitor, and slung the machine into the corner of the room. Brodie grabbed her by the collar and jerked her away from the shower of sparks and glass that followed the impact of wall and hardware.

BJ turned willingly and buried her face in his jacket. She breathed in shallow, erratic gasps. She shuddered violently against him, dry-eyed and totally lost. But just when she felt his blessed arms close around her shoulders, she shoved herself away from him. She didn't need to escape into his comfort right now, she needed to think clearly. If only her brain would cooperate.

"It's playing games with me."

"What is?" Brodie remained cool and unruffled by her bizarre behavior.

"The computer!" She gestured wildly at the broken machine. "I know I input new information on that thing tonight. But there's nothing there. No file. No dumpsite. Nothing. I even gerry-rigged the damned thing to record any use or transmission that doesn't show up in the server log."

"Speak English, Beej."

She shook her head exasperatedly. "I know I worked on the computer tonight. I installed a device to record every time that machine goes on or sends or receives any message. But there's nothing. That machine says nothing happened."

"There were words on the screen when I first came in."

"Yeah?" His throaty reminder gave her a threadbare spark of hope.

"Yeah. On the surviving computer."

BJ clutched her arms tightly over her stomach, tucking the long ends of Brodie's sleeves underneath and binding her in a mock straitjacket. She almost laughed at the symbolism. Yet, something about the external control calmed her. It released her mind from its frenetic activity.

Immortal Heart

"At least that proves I'm not totally nuts. You actually saw the computer working. I didn't imagine that."

"You said you were playing a game."

"Yes, but it was more than that. I think." A dull ache rimmed her skull, constricting her ability to reason clearly. "I don't know. There's something more. But I can't remember."

She squeezed her thumb and forefinger together. "I'm that close, but I can't figure it out."

"BJ, you're exhausted. Give your brain a rest."

"Damon says my brain never shuts down." If only it would. Then she might know some peace.

"This ex-boss of yours doesn't know everything." She smelled the damp leather of Brodie's jacket and knew he had moved closer. She felt his hands beneath her elbows, guiding her to his side. She sagged against him, grateful for his strength, never questioning why she trusted him so completely.

He walked with her into the hallway, his arms supporting her more than her own legs. She went with him willingly, not sure of their destination, but happy to see him turn into her bedroom. He kept an arm around her waist while he turned back the quilt, flipping her menagerie of stuffed animals onto the floor.

He turned her and sat her on the bed. Then he lifted her feet and laid her down gently, tucking the top sheet and quilt snugly under her chin.

Julie Miller

"Do you want some aspirin?"

BJ felt too tired to sit up and swallow. "Could you let Duke in? He likes to sleep with me."

Brodie looked uneasily out the door. She remembered the dog's reaction to him. At least that was clear. She laid her hand over his, keeping him from leaving her side. "Never mind. I forgot how he growled at you. He'll be okay tonight."

Brodie surprised her by sitting on the edge of the bed. His long, blunt fingers tenderly smoothed the curls off her forehead. "I'll stay with you until you fall asleep."

BJ nestled into her pillow, the feeling reminiscent of her earliest memories with Jake. Brodie gave her the same secure, protected feeling. But with something more. Through the fog of encroaching sleep, she looked up at him.

Beyond the frown, beyond the scars, she saw a determinedly gentle man. He bore the marks of incredible torture and suffering, yet he never let the hell he must have endured hurt her. She suspected that he had killed before. Yet she didn't believe that he would ever harm her.

She tightened her hand around his, feeling small and delicate and inadequate next to him. "Brodie?"

"Hmm?"

"What did I do? When I was out to lunch earlier?"

"During the trance?" She nodded. Her eyelids grew heavy, but she concentrated her hearing on his deep, halting words.

Immortal Heart

"You were concerned about me catching cold after being out in the storm."

"There was more," she murmured sleepily.

"You, uh, offered me the shirt off your back."

"I did?"

"You're a sexy woman, BJ. Full of unexpected surprises that may drive me crazy."

"I didn't embarrass you, did I?" The muscles in her eyelids stopped working.

"No, darlin'."

The mattress creaked and something warm brushed across her cheek. A kiss? Or a dream?

"Go to sleep."

BJ nodded obediently, then turned on her side and curled into a ball. Brodie had given her a gentlemanly, watered-down version of tonight's episode, she was sure. She recalled something about bare skin and searing heat. And had he called her sexy? And darling?

Gray mist filled her head, muddying her disjointed thoughts. The image of a lightning bolt blipped into her dreams. Poor Brodie. That hideous brand on his chest. A twisting scar of puckered skin that cut a track through the soft, dark mat of hair.

Or was it silver and black? An image forged in metal.

BJ's foggy brain tried to latch on to the picture.

Nothing. It's nothing, Bridget.

"It's nothing." Drowsy lips repeated the words. The picture vanished. Sleep won.

Chapter Four

"I said you didn't need to wear a tie. We may call it a ball, but tonight is strictly casual."

Brodie adjusted his collar for the sixth time in nearly as many minutes. "I'm here as a security consultant, not a guest."

BJ smiled up at him and shook her head. "Even our regular security guards don't wear a tie with their uniforms."

"I'm not regular security."

She shrugged her shoulders, giving up the argument. Or so he thought. "You could lose the tie, but keep your shirt buttoned to the collar. You'd be in style and you could still hide the scars on your neck."

"The scars?" Brodie sighed raggedly, curbing the flare of his temper. The woman didn't miss

Immortal Heart

a trick. She possessed a sharp eye for detail, using keen insight to translate her observations into facts. No wonder she kept beating herself up trying to piece together clues to the piracy case. She could figure out almost anything else, from repairing the band's speaker, to rerouting computer lines for tonight's presentation. But her episodes still eluded her comprehension.

He kept out of the way, watching BJ, Emma, and Jasmine greet their guests. Did BJ really remember every guest's name? She made it seem that way by drawing them into conversation and subtly extracting the information on the four or five out of two hundred whom she didn't recall.

He could almost see the brain cells ticking behind her intelligent eyes, quickly processing and retaining information. On top of a busy day at LadyTech and the trauma of last night, which she refused to discuss, she still managed to notice how awkward he felt tonight.

He did wear high collared shirts and long sleeves to cover himself when he ventured out into public. His face and size alone were enough to make most people squeamish and uncomfortable. If they could see how bad the rest of him looked, they'd be running away in droves. It was his way of protecting them—and himself from unintentioned cruelty and rejection.

But BJ noticed. The notion didn't sit well. With everything going on in her head, she shouldn't be worrying about him. It was absolutely imperative to him that she didn't care about his problems. Yet a sheltered remnant of his soul warmed to the idea that maybe she did.

Today, she insisted on devoting her time and energy to LadyTech's annual open house for investors, clients, and friends. She felt obligated to prove her loyalty to LadyTech. Not that Emma or Jas doubted her for a minute, but BJ persisted in the idea that she had sold out her friends, whether consciously or not. She worked herself into a state of mental exhaustion trying to atone for the wrongs she swore she had committed.

He watched her shake hands with a portly Asian man. "Mr. Takahashi. You've recovered from your jet lag, I hope."

"Yes, Miss Kincaid." He returned her smile. "Jasmine's tour of your offices and adjoining warehouse and gardens was most intriguing. I look forward to the unveiling of your new program this evening."

"I look forward to showing it off, sir."

Jasmine, a striking, petite blonde, crooked her arm through Mr. Takahashi's. "Let me introduce you to some of our guests, Kiro."

After Jas escorted their newest prime investor away, Emma turned to BJ. "Why don't you sneak upstairs and grab a catnap. You've been at it all day, and quite frankly, you look tired."

"I'm okay, Em."

In reality, BJ's sleep had been fitful. She

Immortal Heart

thrashed under the covers, mumbling incoherent words. Brodie stayed with her until close to dawn, when utter fatigue finally pulled her into deeper, dreamless sleep.

"Emma's right," he heard himself add. "Take a break and relax."

BJ glared at him with obstinate eyes. "I have to double-check the program to make sure tonight's demonstration goes off without a hitch."

"You've checked it once already," argued Emma. "Besides, you'll be inundated with questions afterward. You won't get a chance to rest again until really late."

BJ bristled defensively, ready to take on Emma, Brodie, and anybody else who tried to tell her what to do. But a yawn betrayed her. "All right," she conceded. "But fifteen minutes, that's all. I'll be lying down in my office."

With a humph of resignation, she twirled around and went up the stairs. He watched her until the creamy shoulder exposed by the draped neckline of her peasant blouse winked out of sight.

Brodie felt a hand on his arm.

"What happened last night?" Emma challenged him, as though she thought him responsible for BJ's fatigue. Jonathan had often mentioned his wife's soft-spoken ways, which hid a backbone of steel and motherly preservation where her loved ones were concerned. Were all the LadyTech women this stubborn?

Brodie wondered how much of BJ's past

Julie Miller

Emma knew. Having a third party to bounce ideas off sounded like a good idea, but he didn't want to divulge any of BJ's confidences.

"She had another episode," he said simply.

Emma's smoky blue eyes flashed with anxiety. "Was she hurt? Did you find out anything?"

He found out she was built the way a woman ought to be, curved and healthy, not pencil slim. He found out she could melt him into putty when her honey, husky voice lowered in a bewitching tone of arousal. He found out that grilling her with questions triggered abusive childhood memories for BJ.

He found out that the darkest moment of his life held some connection to BJ, that a scar burned into him ages ago had meaning to her, even though her conscious mind denied the connection.

I couldn't have been in my right mind to throw myself all over you like that.

Not in her right mind. BJ meant the words as an apology, but Brodie knew they were true. He had foolishly wanted her to want him, to the extent that he had abandoned all reason and common sense and practically forced her.

Not until he had seen the glazed look in her eyes did he realize the scope of the evil force manipulating her. He had been out of his mind with need for her, and she had no clue to the passion ignited between them. Even afterward, she had responded to him with the tender shyness of a first kiss. She recalled the essence of

Immortal Heart

what happened, but concrete memories eluded her.

"No, I didn't find out anything useful," he said. "Only that she's in a lot of trouble. And that I'm not sure I can help her."

"You're not giving up, are you?"

How could he? In twenty-four little hours, BJ Kincaid had become an integral part of his life. How could he leave without knowing she'd be safe?

"No. But this case may be a little more complicated than I originally thought."

"You won't leave her until she's okay, right?" Emma prodded him again.

Ages ago, he had taken an oath to fight the injustices of the world, and to protect the innocents harmed by those injustices. Like BJ. Even if he could control his emotional response to her, he could never quit until he eradicated the evil thing attacking her mind. His conscience wouldn't let him.

"I won't leave."

With each promise to protect her, he came closer and closer to sealing BJ's fate. He might be able to save her.

But he could just as easily destroy her.

"Dammit, Rick, I'm not in charge of personnel. I can't make you any promises like that."

Rick Chambers had knocked on BJ's office door within seconds after her eyes closed. She found no respite from the ache digging in at the

Julie Miller

base of her skull. And Rick's argument was getting old.

"I deserve that promotion. Nobody has worked harder to get the Tokyo office up and running."

"I know. You put in a lot of hours on the project, and I made a recommendation. But Emma has to review all the candidates and bring her final choices to the board for a vote."

Rick's handsome, toothy smile held no charm for her. "Then I'm one of the finalists, right?"

"I don't know." BJ returned his smile with as much sincerity as she could muster before dropping down to her hands and knees to retrieve her sandals from beneath the desk. "Look, can we discuss this tomorrow? I want to do a final check before we run the program tonight. I'd hate for a glitch to show up with all those people watching."

"I set it up myself. It's running fine. If you kept regular office hours, we wouldn't be having this conversation now."

BJ rolled over on her rump and put on her shoes. "I recommended you, Rick. That's all I can tell you." Hell, she'd give him the job right now if he'd just leave her alone.

By the time she had the second shoe on and had adjusted her Aztec-print skirt, Rick stood over her, holding out his hand. BJ took it, expecting to be helped to her feet.

Instead, he pulled her right against his chest and pinned her there with his hand at the back of her waist. Strong cologne assaulted her nostrils, sharpening the sting of her headache.

"There are only three of you on that board. Isn't there anything I can do to persuade you? We've worked so well together for over two years now."

He brushed his fingers over her shoulder. It could be her headache that made BJ feel nauseated, she wasn't sure. The arm around her waist wouldn't budge, so she used sarcasm as a weapon.

"Two whole years and you're just now making a pass at me? I didn't think you were the shy type."

She felt his temper vibrate through him. Then he pushed her back against the desk, trapping her with his body. "You three are raking in big bucks. I deserve a piece of it."

"Stop it, Rick." His implied threat made BJ fighting mad. "I can't just give you the Tokyo job, but I can fire you."

She tried to twist free, but Rick grabbed a handful of her hair and jerked her head back at a sharp angle. Myriad tendrils of pain shot through her scalp. "I could be as big as you, Beeeej." The way he slurred her name made BJ's skin crawl. "My ideas are as good as yours."

His hot breath washed over her face, "I deserve—"

BJ felt a jerk, and then Rick went flying. He landed in a heap beside the door.

"Back off."

The low warning echoed in the room and the immovable presence of Brodie Maxwell positioned himself between her and Rick.

"Are you all right?" Though he uttered the question gently, BJ saw such fury in Brodie's eyes when he looked over his shoulder that she herself moved away from him a step.

"I'm fine."

"I'm not!" Rick's voice raised to a whining pitch. He scrambled to his feet and pointed an accusing finger at Brodie. "I'm going to sue you for assault."

"The lady is the one who can press charges."

Rick advanced on Brodie like a puppy dog challenging a grizzly bear. Brodie didn't move. Rick wisely halted. "I don't know why you hired this thug, Beej, but he's got no business interfering in our private conversation."

"Our conversation was over when you came in! You threatened me!" When she would have moved past Brodie, his hand on her elbow stopped her. He made sure she stayed out of Rick's reach.

"Did I?" Rick relaxed unexpectedly, smiling in a way that made BJ's stomach turn over. "I made a pass at you and you weren't interested. It's not against the law for a man to try."

He smoothed the wrinkles from his polo shirt and tucked in a few strands of his long hair while BJ replayed the conversation in her head. Rick was right. His only threat had been implied. Bad manners and raunchy cologne didn't

Immortal Heart

prove he intended her any harm.

"You're smarter than I gave you credit for, Rick."

"Remember that when you vote for the new chief." He backed toward the open door. "I'll see you tomorrow at work."

Brodie released her and took a single step toward Rick. Rick nearly fell over, trying to hurry his exit. "You touch her again before this investigation is finished, Chambers, and I'll throw you out of here by your ponytail."

"Brodie, that's not necessary."

"It's all right." Rick oozed conceit once again. "We all know Emma hired him to help with your . . ." he paused to squeeze sympathy into his voice, "memory lapses. I'm willing to help in whatever way I can. You can count on my full cooperation."

After Rick closed the door behind him, BJ muttered, "In a pig's eye."

"What was that all about?" Brodie asked.

"I'm not sure. Rick can be rude and hot tempered, but he's never behaved like that before. Of course, he's got a lot at stake with that promotion. There's no other position he can advance to here at headquarters."

"Then he's never threatened you like that before?"

"No."

The protective rage that filled the room softened a little. Brodie had just been doing his job. But BJ felt as cherished and championed as any lady whose knight had just ridden in on a white horse to save her. Rick's unsuspected violence angered her, but what made the whole scene truly frightening was how out of control she felt. She was once more the victim, not the director, of her own destiny.

All day long she put off Brodie's attempts to discuss the night before. She knew she must have done something awful to find herself bare breasted and panting on top of Brodie. But despite her humiliation, Brodie had done nothing but treat her with gentleness and respect. He kissed away her fear and confusion, and tucked her into bed. Her sixth sense told her that he had even stayed in the room with her until she found restful sleep.

Her first impression of Frankenstein's monster altered into another fairy tale. One where a man of true kindness and caring spirit had been enchanted with a hideous appearance to punish him for a crime. BJ couldn't imagine what crime her gentle giant could have committed.

Her giant? Where did that possessive, protective feeling come from? Brodie could definitely take care of himself, and he had made it very clear by his words and actions that he wasn't interested in belonging to anyone.

"You're not all right." Brodie pushed aside some books and sat on the edge of her desk, bringing his body several inches closer to her size. He pulled her hand into his and brushed his thumb lightly across her knuckles.

Immortal Heart

It was hard to push aside her new feelings when he made it so easy to give in to his strength and caring.

"You look a little peaked." The archaic expression rumbled in his deep, soothing voice added to the old-fashioned charm and chivalry that BJ found so endearing.

"I'm okay," she whispered, feeling his comfort and warmth slipping around her, chasing away the stress of the unpleasant encounter with Rick. "I just can't shake this headache."

"Do you want me to take you home?"

"I can't leave. There are too many people downstairs waiting to see my latest invention."

"You don't owe them anything."

BJ reached for the right side of his jaw. She cupped her fingers gently there when he didn't pull away. "I can't run and hide, either. Besides, you'll be there with me, right?"

His eyes darkened to a turbulent storm cloud color before a shade was drawn and they reverted back to icy, emotionless gray. "I'll be there."

Despite his promise, BJ could feel him withdrawing, shutting the doors to his inner self. Respectfully, she pulled her hands away, allowing him that distance.

Brodie was the one to press her hand reassuringly before they separated entirely. "Let's go."

BJ preceded Brodie into the hallway, bolstered by his encouragement. A third figure came around the corner and BJ immediately slowed down, expecting Rick had returned.

But when she recognized the tall, distinguished man walking toward her, her anxiety vanished and she ran, smiling, into the welcoming arms of Damon Morrisey.

"Damon!"

Damon's sixty years were evident only in the distinguished silver of his hair and the crow's feet crinkling beside his dark brown eyes. He was a vital, intelligent man, with a wicked sense of humor and an affinity for giving bear hugs, which BJ loved.

"Bridget," he smiled down at her, separating himself a little but keeping her in his arms, "I'm sorry to be so late. That last meeting ran on forever. I haven't missed the debut, have I?"

"Not at all. I'm on my way to start the demonstration now."

BJ didn't know how she could feel any more secure than she did at that moment. The man she loved like a father held her under the crook of one arm, and the man who was becoming her spiritual as well as physical protector stood beside her.

"I want to introduce you to Brodie Maxwell." BJ tilted her head up toward Brodie, who stood in the middle of the hallway with his feet braced out in a vee and his massive hands balled into fists. A vein pulsed beneath the scar on his left cheek while his eyes bored icy daggers at Damon. Brodie looked the very image of the beefy

Immortal Heart

guard defending the gates of the castle.

Where was the danger, BJ wondered. Then she realized Brodie would be suspicious of everyone, and that without finishing the introduction, he had no way of knowing that Damon presented no harm to her.

She touched his arm, willing the mistrust out of his expression. Brodie's gaze dropped briefly to where she touched him, then refocused, just as unflinchingly, on Damon.

"This is Damon Morrisey, my mentor and good friend. It's all right."

Getting no help from Brodie, BJ turned and smiled an apology at Damon. Damon didn't disappoint her. Releasing BJ, he stepped forward. "Mr. Maxwell."

For a moment, BJ didn't think Brodie would accept the proferred hand. But then he relaxed his stance a bit and returned the handshake. "Morrisey."

Damon folded his arms together and rubbed his hand thoughtfully across his jaw. "Do I know you?"

Brodie answered without inflection. "You'd remember me if we'd met."

"I'm sure I would." Unlike Rick, Damon seemed curious about, but not intimidated by Brodie. BJ hadn't considered the possibility of the two men not getting along. Without conscious thought, she had imagined the three of them forming a team to track down LadyTech's pirate and stop whoever was playing games with her. Brodie's reaction to Damon concerned her, but this was obviously not the place to discuss it.

"Let's get this show on the road." BJ forced the lightness into her voice, hoping to prod Brodie into a friendlier mood.

No such luck.

With a grim, self-contained look in his eyes, Brodie excused himself. "You go ahead. I need to check a few things."

BJ questioned him silently, but he offered no answers.

Damon proved to be a more willing escort. He bent his elbow and winked at her. "Shall we?"

BJ tucked her hand through his arm. "By all means."

It didn't feel right to leave Brodie standing alone in the hallway behind her. She wanted to ask him what was wrong, and maybe offer him some of the comfort he had in abundant supply for her. She suspected he hated tonight's party, but endured it for her sake. Brodie gave and gave to her, accepting very little in return. She wondered what a man like him did for fun. She wondered if fun was even part of his vocabulary. She had yet even to see him smile.

A round of applause when they entered the warehouse startled her out of her theorizing. Damon dropped a chaste kiss at her temple and whispered in her ear. "My young protégée is a hit."

"I'm not that young, Damon."

Immortal Heart

"Please. Twenty-seven years old and a multi-millionaire, with the respect and envy of her peers? Go. Take your place in the spotlight."

Damon gave her a gentle shove. The crowd of guests parted to give her a path to the stage where Jas and Emma stood. "And here is the third member of the triumverate that makes up LadyTech. I can see I don't need to introduce BJ to you."

Jas continued with her speech about the new office opening in Tokyo, and plans to open a third network in Europe. "Most of you are familiar with the internet language for computers that BJ designed. That will still be the main focus at LadyTech. But tonight, BJ has prepared something just for fun. A sample of the games line we hope to launch in the future. If I could direct your attention to the big screen behind me, I invite you to the premiere of 'Legends.' "

The lights dimmed and the audience quieted. A familiar song BJ had composed on the keyboard jingled out of the speakers as pictures of superheroic androids introduced themselves on-screen. Mentally, BJ reviewed each command and waited for the resulting action in the program.

Slowly, the game unfolded. The androids played a battle of wits and strength against a master computer bent on destroying their homeworld. But as the game entered its second level, a sick feeling chilled BJ. This wasn't her game. Familiar images appeared, but she noticed subtle changes in the design. The androids looked more like monsters. The factual questions were worded like riddles. Lights blinked, and a graphic of a thunderstorm washed the androids off the screen, racking up thousands of points for the computer.

She hugged her arms tightly around herself, turning her knuckles white. Did the others see the same program she did? Or had she fallen into some demented dream? This was definitely her program, but it wasn't the program.

Her stomach heaved and the room spun. This was the game she had rewritten last night, killing time while Brodie wandered outside in the storm.

This was the last thing she remembered before coming to in Brodie's arms.

Panic overwhelmed her. Desperately she turned away from the screen, searching the darkness for the man who stood head and shoulders above the other guests. Too many shadows kept her from seeing if he was there.

She saw Damon, smiling at her and giving a thumbs-up sign. Quickly, she turned her attention back to the screen.

Emma leaned over and whispered. "When did you beef up the program? I thought you wanted to keep things simple."

Jas whispered from the other side. "This is terrific. Certainly a little irreverent, but the audience is eating it up."

Immortal Heart

"You can see it then?" BJ's whisper held none of the same excitement.

"What?" Emma turned around and saw how badly BJ was shaking.

"This isn't right." A headache pounded behind her eyes. "It's a pirated program."

Jas wrapped a steadying arm around her shoulders. "Are you sure?"

Emma frowned with fear. "I'll find Brodie."

"I need some fresh air." BJ pulled away from Jas's support.

"I'll go with you."

"No. Cover for me. Please. I'm losing it."

BJ quickly descended from the platform. She barely acknowledged the congratulatory remarks from the guests as she pushed her way out of the room.

Someone had gotten inside her head again. Images from last night wound their way into the android program, its intricacies mocking her with the clever style that only she could devise.

She left the warehouse by the back exit and ran into the parking lot. She had to get out of there. She had to find Brodie.

What kind of sick jokester would take a woman's private daydream and put it onscreen for two hundred people to see? Or was the joke for her alone? What kind of demon tormented a woman with a silly game, making her doubt her own sanity?

She dug in her pockets for her truck keys,

then realized Brodie had driven them to the ball. She glanced back over her shoulder, anxious to escape, but not eager to return to the scene of her nightmare to look for Brodie.

Instead, BJ hurried over to his Explorer, praying he would look for her there.

She paced beside the Explorer for nearly a minute before noticing the folded paper tucked beneath the windshield wiper. Responding out of distraction more than curiosity, BJ pulled it out and unfolded it. On a sheet of LadyTech stationery, laser-printed in standard type, were these simple words: "Nothing can save you from your fate."

Nothing. The word tormented her. Deathly fear consumed her. She hadn't been threatened before. The only danger had been inside her head. Why would someone threaten her? BJ paused. Then she realized the message was on Brodie's car. It was intended for Brodie. Someone didn't want him investigating the security leak. Someone wanted him out of the way.

Permanently.

"BJ?"

The familiar deep voice boomed across the parking lot. She turned from the crumpled paper in her hand to see Brodie searching the shadowy parking lot for her. BJ sagged with relief. She ran to him, wanting to fling herself into his arms and beg that he protect her from the nightmare unfolding on the screen inside.

But she heard another sound that stopped her

Immortal Heart

in her tracks. She heard the revving of an engine hidden in the darkness. When the tires squealed on the pavement, BJ remembered the note in her hand, the threat to Brodie.

A dark car lurched onto the roadway, picking up speed. Brodie jumped off the curb, running toward her.

She screamed his name and dashed forward, wanting him to move out of the path of the car. His gaze snapped from the oncoming vehicle to BJ.

"No!" The gleam of a chrome bumper flashed before her eyes.

With a flying leap, she launched herself at Brodie to push him to safety.

"BJ! No!"

When she hit the wall of his chest, he twisted and wrapped his arms around her like a shield.

She felt the horrible impact that knocked them both to the ground and sent them sliding several feet across the pavement. Brodie landed on top of her, knocking the wind from her lungs. She heard a crunch and Brodie's muffled "oof" and felt a burning along the side of her left leg and shoulder.

They came to a stop when they hit the grass at the curb. BJ lay stunned, smothered in the vice of Brodie's arms and chest. When she could breathe again, she squirmed until she wedged a little space to free her arms. She snatched Brodie around the neck, hugging him close and burying her cheek against his collar.

"This is all my fault. I'm so sorry I got you involved in all this."

Brodie rolled onto his back, bringing BJ on top of him, holding her securely with one arm. His hand roamed up and down her arms and across her back. "Are you hurt?"

The car speeding from the scene wouldn't register until later. At the moment, BJ could only revel in the warmth and strength of the man who held her.

"C'mon, darlin', answer me." His hand pressed a little harder. Then, when his fingers touched the raw skin on BJ's shoulder, she gasped and stiffened. "BJ?"

She relaxed against him once more. "It's no worse than skinning my knee. I think I did a really good job of that, too. But nothing serious."

"Thank God." He squeezed her tightly. BJ clung to him, needing his solid security to anchor her in the midst of fear and chaos. He understood. He protected.

He pushed her away.

Abruptly, BJ found herself sitting on the ground beside Brodie's prone figure. With an awkward lack of grace, he pushed himself up to a sitting position facing her.

"What the hell did you think you were doing?" Fury raged darkly in his turbulent eyes.

"What the hell was I doing? I saved your life! Someone tried to kill you."

"Maybe he was trying to kill you!"

Immortal Heart

BJ scrambled to her feet, searching for the note. She plucked the torn paper from the spot where it landed and returned to Brodie. She knelt beside him, ignoring the stinging wound on her leg, shoving the paper at him. "I found it under your windshield, 'Mister Attack Me Now When I'm Already Scared To Death' Maxwell. Somebody doesn't want you to help me."

With one hand, he unballed it and quickly read the contents, muttering a string of expletives when he finished. Just as quickly, he stuffed the note into his pocket and reached for BJ's hand. Slower to cool than he, she resisted at first. Then she looked into his eyes and saw the dramatic change there. Dark like worn steel, she discovered. When he let something besides his anger show, he had the most beautiful, unusual eyes she had ever seen on a man.

She softened under that unique gaze and clutched his hand in return. "I didn't want you to get hurt."

"They can't hurt me."

"Of course, you can be hurt. Look at your . . . scars." She finished badly, hoping he wouldn't anger and pull away from her again.

He only shook his head. "Promise me you'll never do anything that foolish again. Don't ever jeopardize your safety for me."

He leaned forward, cutting off her protest with a kiss. His touch was strong and sure, filled with a mixed message of compassion, lust and warning. BJ clung to him, needing his mouth on hers, needing his secure presence to make her feel whole.

Brodie pulled back all too soon, leaving BJ shaken and wanting more. "Promise me," he rasped in his deep, spine-tingling voice.

"Are you two all right?"

The rest of the world invaded BJ's private moment with Brodie when Emma knelt beside them, followed by Jasmine just a step behind. Shutters of ice closed over Brodie's eyes again before he answered.

"Call 911. I want somebody out here to check BJ as soon as possible."

"You, too."

Emma nodded. "I'll get right on it."

When Emma left to make the phone call, Jasmine took her place. Her blue eyes shimmered with worry. "I'm so sorry about getting the programs mixed up. To see it publicly displayed must have been a shock."

"It's not your fault," BJ assured her.

Brodie intervened. "It's tangible proof your ideas have been pirated."

"Yeah." If she and Brodie hadn't just been run down by an oversized Buick, she might have smiled. But there were still too many problems to solve. "What's the purpose of showing the game? The thief can't make any money off it now."

Brodie squeezed her hand again. "It's a display of power. His over yours."

"His? You think it's a man?" Brodie's expression shifted a little, as if he wanted to say more. "What?"

A low hum of voices interrupted before Brodie could answer. BJ looked up and saw several party guests coming out the back door, curiously moving closer to find out what had happened.

Jas looked over her shoulder, then back at BJ and Brodie. "I'll get them out of the way. You two work this out, okay?" She gave BJ a quick hug. "I leave tomorrow for Tokyo, and I don't want to be worrying about you."

"I'll be fine."

Jas patted Brodie's right shoulder before leaving to dispel the crowd of onlookers. "Make sure you have that arm looked at."

"Your arm?" Fear stabbed BJ. "What's wrong with your arm?"

She moved closer, inspecting first his right, then his left arm. A gasp of sympathetic pain escaped. A pool of blood dripped into the grass beneath the shredded left sleeve of Brodie's jacket.

"Oh my God." She ripped the rest of his shirtsleeve to expose his wound. She clamped her teeth together to keep from retching at the sight of the ghastly injury. Brodie's arm lay contorted at an abnormal angle. A tattered sliver of bone protruded from a wide gash near the joint. "A compound fracture."

"It doesn't hurt much." He tried to push her hand away, but she continued to work at pick-

Julie Miller

ing loose threads from the ripped material out of the wound. "I'm all right."

"Don't be so brave about it. Let me help." BJ pushed against his shoulders to get him to lie down again.

"I said I'm all right!" The harshness of his tone shocked BJ into stillness.

"You need a doctor."

"Trust me. I'll be okay." BJ searched his face for some kind of explanation, but the harsh landscape revealed nothing. Brodie cradled the broken arm in his lap and studied the injury himself.

After a moment, he wrapped his powerful hand around the wound and began to compress the area. He only grunted once as the broken arm snapped back into place.

She cupped his face and rubbed his shoulders, touching him, comforting him wherever she could. Chivalry might include some rule about hiding your true feelings, but even a man of Brodie's stature and bearing had to feel excruciating pain. "What can I do to help?"

"Just forgive me. And try to understand."

Her forehead wrinkled at the odd request. "Understand what?"

When he looked down at his forearm, BJ did the same. She looked back up into apologetic eyes, then down at the awful wound.

She pulled her hands away from him, too stunned to speak coherently. "Wha . . . ?"

"BJ—"

"No!" She jerked away from his outstretched

Immortal Heart

hand, no longer comforted by his touch. She pinched herself, trying to wake from this horrible, ongoing nightmare.

"BJ, I can explain." He had been rough before, dangerous and mad as hell. Now he pleaded with her, a desperate note shading the deep rumble of his voice.

She refused to see the pain in his eyes, the loss registered there. She could only stare at his arm, dumbfounded and disbelieving.

In a span of seconds, right before her eyes, the blood ceased flowing from the open gash. The rip in his skin narrowed, then fully closed. A pink ridge formed where the gash had been. Then the puckered skin turned whitish gray and sunk into his forearm, leaving a new, perfectly healed scar.

Brodie flexed his fingers and made a fist, testing the once-damaged arm. Then he reached out, tentatively, lifting that same hand to her face.

"Don't touch me!" BJ scooted away from him on her backside, leaving his outstretched fingers suspended in midair.

"Don't be scared of this. I can explain."

BJ shook her head. Her brilliant mind couldn't comprehend the miracle she had just witnessed. A miracle as maddening and frightening as the thought of an unknown tormentor snatching thoughts right out of her head.

"Who are you?" she whispered, feeling betrayed and humiliated by the creature before her. "What are you?"

Chapter Five

BJ ran. Through sculpted hedgerows and thorny rose beds she ran. Into a stand of dogwood trees, denuded of its flowers by the summer's heat, she ran. If she could run fast enough and far enough, she could escape the nightmare.

But how did you escape a giant who thundered after you in the night?

The sounds of the building storm blended with the sounds of Brodie crashing through the trees behind her. The first raindrops hit her face mere moments before he grabbed her arm and yanked her to a halt.

He swung her up into his arms, absorbing every kick and scratch she doled out. She pummeled him and fought for escape. She couldn't

Immortal Heart

hurt him. Her foolish, futile struggle couldn't hurt him one bit.

Hot tears ran side by side with chilling rain down her cheeks. She had passed over the edge into insanity. There could be no other explanation for Brodie Maxwell. As she accepted that fact, a peaceful calm shivered through her, leaving her spent and silent by the time Brodie deposited her into the dry warmth of his Explorer.

"BJ, can you hear me?"

He climbed in the driver's side, dripping water onto the upholstery. Peripherally, she saw him reach for her, but draw his hand back.

"I am so sorry. I'm sorry I didn't prepare you for this."

BJ stared at the windshield, entranced by the waterfall streaming down the smooth glass. Brodie's heavy sigh brushed across her ears without a response. He reached around her and buckled her into her seat, careful not to touch her. He started the engine and turned on the wipers, clearing her path of vision so she could see into the lightning-shattered darkness.

"I'll take you home."

BJ climbed out of the vehicle herself when they reached her front door. Brodie hovered around her, but didn't touch her. He pushed the buttons and opened the door for her. She walked through the living room and kitchen to the back porch. Duke greeted her, full of love and acceptance and furry, tongue-licking reality.

Julie Miller

She cradled him in her arms, rocking and loving him as if he were a baby, for a long while before Brodie's gruff voice made her tense. "We need to doctor those cuts and scrapes. And get you dried off and into bed."

Like a drugged patient dutifully obeying her nurse, BJ walked through the house to the bathroom. She sat while Brodie dug through drawers and cabinets to find first-aid supplies. Duke nestled in her lap, situating himself so he could keep an eye on Brodie.

BJ flinched at the first sting of peroxide on her shoulder and the dog growled.

"Sorry, boy," said Brodie, "but I need to do this."

With amazing gentleness for someone with such big hands, Brodie tended her shoulder and the scrape along her leg that ran from above her knee to her ankle. He applied cooling ointment and covered the worst part of the wound with a gauze bandage.

"Too bad I don't heal as quickly as you."

At the sound of her flat voice, he looked up from where he knelt beside her, a light of hope flickering and dying in his eyes. "I guess that's not a joke."

"Guess not."

He stood, taking several seconds to straighten to his full height. BJ experienced no fear or intimidation at his towering presence. Crazy women didn't get scared.

She rose obediently when he touched her el-

Immortal Heart

bow, though he quickly released her when Duke nipped at him. "You need dry clothes."

They went into her bedroom. BJ waited and watched Brodie open the drawers of her dresser, searching through her things for pajamas. He returned with a pair of panties and a Cubs jersey.

"Here." She looked at him, unmoving. He dropped the clothes on the bed when she didn't take them. Hesitantly, as though unsure where to start, Brodie grasped the hem of her shirt and pulled it up past her waist. Duke barked and Brodie dropped the material, stepping back.

"A little help?"

She tossed Duke onto the bed. "Sit." The dog minded, then she lifted her gaze to Brodie. "Go ahead."

Her compliance surprised him, she could tell. Good. Let there be at least one small thing she could do to knock his world off the edge.

His eyes darkened to shadowy pools. Testing him gave her a small measure of control. She was making him pay for earning her trust and then shattering it, and he knew it. The impatient, fortifying breath through his stiff lips proved that.

Brodie pulled her blouse up over her head and dropped it beside her. The air on her damp skin raised goose bumps. But she didn't move to rub them away.

He turned her by her upper arms and reached for the fastening of her strapless bra. His calloused fingertips teased her spine, hovering about the clasp.

With a sharp intake of breath, he pulled away from her. "Don't make me do this."

"You're my protector. Take care of me."

"Dammit, BJ. You think I'm some kind of a monster, but I'm not. I'm a man. I know I hurt you, and believe me, I'll pay for that. But don't, please don't taunt me like this. Don't punish me because I'm different."

She turned and looked at him then, fully conscious and fully aware of the heat from his gaze sweeping over her and then fixing on her upturned face. She could hurt him, after all. He wasn't invincible. *She* had the power to hurt him.

Some of her fighting spirit struggled to the surface. It went against her nature to knowingly cause anyone pain. "I want to understand, Brodie. Please help me understand."

A little of the tension eased from his expression. Tentatively, he touched his fingers to her cheek. When she didn't recoil, he traced the mark of her dried tears down to her chin. He tipped her head back and lowered his mouth to hers. Firm lips touched hers with gentle reverence. Her lips softened beneath his, trading apologies.

When he finally pulled away, his eyes shone with silvery promise. "In the morning, when you're stronger, I'll try to explain. But not now. You've had one shock after another tonight.

Immortal Heart

"Shut up, dog."

That earned him a bark. "Listen, dog, you'll wake up BJ if you don't quit your yapping."

Brodie strode to the door, feeling grumpy and frustrated enough to do battle with the little mutt. His hand was on the doorknob when common sense finally whacked him over the head. *The mutt sleeps with her.*

He plunked his coffee mug on the counter and ran to BJ's bedroom. He didn't knock. He didn't announce himself. He threw open the door and looked inside.

Her bed was empty.

And it was neatly made with that mountain of stuffed animals piled on top. She must have gone while he was in the shower. She'd snuck away from him before he had a chance to tell her anything.

Brodie ran to his room and grabbed the dagger and sheath from the nightstand. He strapped it to his belt and charged out the door.

He didn't bother checking the garage for her truck. He knew where she had gone. He jumped in the Explorer and floored it as soon as the engine turned over. Once he hit the highway, he called Emma on the cellular phone to get directions.

Emma plied him with questions, but Brodie hung up without answering them. If everything BJ told him about herself was true, he knew exactly where she had gone. If the man he had met last night wasn't an hallucination, he knew where to find her.

That knowledge transformed into a tidal wave of fear that tightened his gut like a vise.

BJ hugged herself, looking out the window of Damon's plush office at the spectacular view of the Missouri River near downtown Kansas City. "I don't think he meant to hurt me. Maybe I overreacted because of all that's been going on."

Damon found the tight spot at the base of her neck and massaged the tension from her shoulders. "I agree with him that broadcasting a pirated program was a ploy to show power. But I can't help but think this Maxwell isn't the right person to help you. You said he did 'weird' things last night. What exactly do you mean?"

BJ didn't quite know how to explain what had happened.

His hands stopped the massage. "He didn't harm you, did he?"

BJ laid her hand over his and turned into his concerned gaze. "No. Nothing like that."

Damon studied her a moment before clicking his tongue and leaving to pour them both a glass of bottled water. BJ trailed behind him and sat on his high-backed brocade sofa. She kicked off her shoes and curled her feet beneath her. Damon twisted a slice of lime into her glass and handed it to her.

By the time he sat across from her, she had prepared for his fatherly reprimand. "Mr. Max-

Immortal Heart

well struck me as nothing more than a brute beast last night. I daresay he's the kind of professional you need helping you right now."

He plucked at the seam of his summer-weight wool trousers, trying to appear detached, but BJ knew he was anything but. Damon rarely said or did anything without a plan. "You know I have several contacts in the medical field. I'd be happy to arrange a meeting for you, without any publicity that could damage LadyTech's reputation."

She took a cool, tangy sip before responding. "We've already had this discussion. You know my answer."

"Then what about loaning you one of my technicians?"

"Damon," she stopped him, "what are they going to find that I can't?"

He laughed then. "Of course. Nobody can outsmart you where computers are concerned."

BJ joined him, finding the laughter a welcome respite. "You make me sound like some annoying know-it-all."

"You'd only be annoying if you had the ego to go along with your talents." Damon patted her hand on her knee, then grasped it in a brief display of emotion. "You are too caring and too amusing to annoy anyone."

She squeezed his hand in return. "Try telling that to Brodie. I seem to be making a lot of wrong turns with him."

Damon set their drinks on the coffee table,

then captured both her hands in his. "Fire him. If he does strange things you can't tell me about, and makes you so edgy that you come running to me first thing in the morning, then he can't possibly be helping you. I know how terrified you've been. If this man has problems, get rid of him."

BJ considered his advice. True, she didn't need the emotional upheaval Brodie had brought into her life right now. He scared her. He was too secretive and mysterious for her to trust completely. Yet she did trust him to a degree. He hadn't harmed her. If anything, he had gone out of his way to protect her.

He listened to her ramblings about her childhood. He witnessed two episodes and still hadn't called the funny farm to come pick her up. He tended her wounds and put up with her dog.

He kissed her with swift, uncontrolled passion that woke her to the mysteries of womanhood, and with tender, bittersweet reverence that made every bone and fiber within her pulse with feminine awareness.

He made critical gashes in his arm disappear with the touch of his hand.

"I can see even you have doubts about him."

BJ looked into Damon's beloved, loving eyes. She had trusted this man's advice since he came into her life thirteen years ago. Should she trust reason and history? Or should she listen to instinct and the new indefinable feelings Brodie

Immortal Heart

stirred to life in her? "Emma says he's the best. Jonathan depended on Brodie with his life."

"Emma's husband is dead." The stunningly simple statement hung in the air.

Damon pulled BJ into his arms and rocked her soothingly against his chest. "I don't mean to sound cruel. I know Emma's husband thought highly of him, but a man can change in three or four years. Mr. Maxwell might not be the same man Colonel Ramsey knew."

BJ didn't think her confusion would ever go away. She had come to Damon this morning to try and make sense of her world once more. Her world bordered on insanity. If the man who knew her better than anyone couldn't straighten things out, then where could she turn? With her history, psychiatric help was still too frightening a proposition to consider.

BJ pushed herself away and slipped on her shoes. She needed to seize these clearheaded moments and reason the mystery out for herself.

She started by evaluating the pros and cons of Brodie Maxwell. "He's a good bodyguard, actually. He pried Rick Chambers off me when Rick got a little too fresh."

Damon seemed willing to follow her train of thinking. "Chambers? That sleaze? I warned you about him."

BJ smiled indulgently. "You warn me about every man I meet."

"Isn't a father supposed to?"

She leaned over and planted a kiss on his tanned cheek. "You bet he is."

She never minded when he called himself her father. Jake was Jake, the treasured dad every little girl wanted. Damon was her father, a loving, guiding force in her adult life.

"I'd better get over to work and help clean up the mess from last night."

Damon stood with her. "Don't you have people to do that for you?"

"You know I like to get in the trenches with the staff. Besides, I want to take a look at that program again, see if I can figure out where the transmission came from."

He walked her to the door. "You never quit, do you?"

She elbowed him in the side. "Now who was it who taught me that giving up without an answer is not an option."

"Did I say that?"

"Once or twice." Sharing laughter with Damon revived her spirits, giving her strength to open the door and face another day.

"You can't go in there! Doctor Morrisey has another appointment with him."

"Lady, I'm not big on manners or patience . . ."

"Brodie?"

BJ stopped the confrontation between the stern, gray-haired administrative assistant and the scarred, unsmiling giant.

Immortal Heart

He spun around at her appearance. "Are you all right?"

Raw, blatant fear leaped from his eyes, stunning her. "I'm fine."

Damon's calm voice intervened, dismissing his assistant. "Abby, it's all right. Shall we go into my office?"

"How the hell could you leave without telling me or without even leaving a note?" Brodie spoke over Damon, ignoring the invitation.

BJ flushed indignantly. "Am I a prisoner now?"

"Mr. Maxwell—"

"What did you tell her?" Brodie looked as if he might do physical violence to Damon.

BJ wedged herself between the two men. "Tell me about what?"

Damon's cool, cultured voice answered. "I recommended she get rid of you."

Brodie's eyes blazed like fire behind the ice when Damon put his hands on BJ's shoulders. "Judging by your behavior today, I'm even more convinced it's a good idea."

"Stop it! Both of you!" BJ placed herself in the age-old position of breaking up a fight, turning sideways and pushing a palm against either man's chest.

She looked first to Damon, the more reasonable of the two. "I know you mean well, but I'll make my own decisions.

"And you." She tilted her face to Brodie. "You have no right to barge in here like that. I'm sure you scared Abby to death."

"You weren't at home when I got up. You know what we discussed."

"You're staying at her home?" asked Damon. "I didn't realize the relationship was so personal."

"It's not . . ."

BJ lost her breath when Brodie's hand nipped around her waist and pulled her to his side.

"It's not anybody's business but ours," Brodie finished.

BJ would have argued the point, but she was distracted by the sensation of Brodie's hard, muscular body imprinting itself so squarely against her. The change in him was subtle but tangible. His hand spanned the right side of her ribcage, his thumb resting beneath the weight of her breast.

It wasn't a protective gesture so much as it was possessive.

She grew aware of the raw virility in his changed appearance. The T-shirt and trim jeans masked little of his strength and few of his scars. What he had at first worked so hard to keep hidden, he now brandished like a challenge, the impact of which hit BJ in the chest like a freight train, stealing her breath away.

Damon evaluated Brodie's implied message and BJ's reaction to it. Then he backed off, his finely manicured hands raised in surrender. "You're right, it's none of my business. But Bridget," she forced her focus away from Bro-

Immortal Heart

die, "Consider what I said. And know you can always count on me to support you."

"I know." Reluctantly, she stepped away from Brodie and kissed Damon's cheek. "I love you."

Damon winked. "I know."

The heat of Brodie's hand at the small of her back finally turned her away from Damon. When they shut the outer door of the executive offices, Brodie let go and tipped his face upward, exhaling deeply.

BJ wondered at the immensity of his relief. "Do you know Damon? I mean, before I introduced you last night, had you two met? He doesn't like you, and you certainly don't like him."

"I know his type." They walked down the hall to the elevator.

Brodie never once looked at her while they waited for the car to return to the top floor. "I thought the worst when I couldn't find you this morning."

She still couldn't shake the impact of his anger, nor the way her body had responded so dramatically to his possessive touch. But she felt honor bound to defend Damon. "He's family to me, Brodie. He would never hurt me."

"I'm counting on it."

His statement struck her as odd, but she didn't comment on it. The elevator doors opened and they stepped inside. In the small confines of the car, BJ could almost taste the palpable vitality in Brodie. Moody. Violent. Untamed.

BJ felt woefully nondescript by comparison in her cut-offs and baggy Cardinals jersey. Every time he inhaled, his cotton shirt stretched tautly across his imposing chest. Every time he exhaled, his potent masculine scent filled the car.

Her skin prickled with acute awareness of Brodie. She needed space from him. She needed to trust him again before she allowed herself to respond to her desire.

When the button for the seventh floor lit up, BJ pushed it impulsively. "You want to see where I used to work?"

Brodie paused in the elevator, obviously questioning her sudden yen for nostalgia.

She scrambled for a face-saving reason to put space and neutral people between them without insulting him or admitting her reaction to him. "You said you wanted to meet everyone I have contact with. I work here at the Institute every couple of months or so."

"It couldn't hurt to check out every possibility, I suppose."

With resignation, he followed her into the Morrisey Institute's main laboratory. Carpeted cubicles divided the perimeter into individualized research stations. In the center of the room were two large, free-standing fixtures that resembled telephone booths, with stainless steel side frames and top to bottom glass doors. Each unit took up about twenty-five square feet and had nothing inside but an odd-looking chair. Hundreds of round and flat cables ran from the units to the surrounding research stations.

BJ hastened past the two structures, averting her head from the always disturbing sight. She smiled a greeting that encompassed all the white-coated technicians in the room. "Hi, everybody!"

"Beej!"

She traded hugs and welcomes with several of her former coworkers, constantly aware that Brodie hung back a few steps. Even after introducing him to a couple of technicians whom she occasionally socialized with, he still kept his distance. No one made a rude comment or quizzed her about Brodie, but she grew sensitive to the number of curious looks directed his way.

A pillar of isolated strength, used to standing alone. The image haunted BJ. Growing up, she herself stood alone on playgrounds, she sat alone to study at the library. She watched from the sidelines while other, normal, people interacted with each other in friendly, everyday ways.

In a surge of protective empathy, BJ linked her arm with Brodie's drawing him into her circle of acceptance. The curious looks lessened, then ultimately disappeared. After everyone met Brodie, she led him to an empty research station, and let the technicians get back to work.

BJ plopped down in the only available chair and Brodie sat on the corner of the desk. Hidden from view of the others, she sighed wearily and noticed that Brodie did the same. "Sorry. I didn't realize there would be such a crowd."

"No harm done. I wouldn't want to keep you from your friends."

BJ absentmindedly turned on the computer in front of her, giving him time to regroup before they ran the gauntlet of small talk again.

"What's your aversion to those boxes in the middle of the room? They remind me of something out of the Inquisition."

She glanced quickly up at Brodie, then across the floor to the steel monstrosities. She measured her answer. "They're Damon's death chambers."

"Death chambers?"

BJ tapped random keys on the computer, uncomfortable with the subject at hand. "They're the only thing Damon and I ever really disagreed on. They're why I left and started my own company."

He shifted around the corner so that he faced her. "Tell me about it."

BJ punched in an old command and discovered with sickening awareness that the old program hadn't been purged. She tinkered through the system and found the subroutines she had written were still in place, even the ones she had

Immortal Heart

tried to hide. She leaned back in her chair and crossed her arms, warding off the mental chill.

"Mastery over death," Damon had called it. Their finest work together. His ideas and her brainpower. She'd never developed his affinity for playing God.

"Damon runs the Morrisey Institute like a think tank. He gathers groups of researchers and presents each unit with a hypothesis to test. He encourages free thinking, challenging each unit to develop alternative solutions if the original hypothesis proves inaccurate."

"Basic scientific theory." He jerked his chin toward the center of the room. "How do those things fit in?"

"Four years ago, Damon scored a contract with the penal system to develop more humane ways to execute death row criminals."

"My God."

"He put me on the team despite the fact I'm not an advocate of capital punishment. He wanted the best, he said. I threatened to leave then, but he convinced me that I had the perfect attitude for the project. Who better to find a kind way to end another person's life?"

Brodie leaned forward and closed his hand over her shoulder. "I can't imagine you trying to hurt anybody."

BJ started to smile. Instead, her gaze lighted on the newest scar near his left elbow. She pushed her chair back and stood, still not trusting her instincts toward blind faith in Brodie.

"Damon came up with the original design. I refined it. Theoretically, it works by charging the ions in the chamber's atmosphere, overloading the brain with electrical impulses. Eventually it shuts down and you die quietly in your sleep. It's painless."

"But the victim still dies."

She nodded, hugging herself and staring at the painful memories erected in cold steel and glass. "I couldn't be a part of it. I never wanted my work to be used in that way. I had to leave."

"BJ."

Suddenly nothing mattered but the need to have Brodie make her feel safe once more. She turned and walked willingly into Brodie's waiting arms. She pressed her face against the warm pulse in his neck, burrowing in the iron strength that protected her.

BJ wrapped her arms around his waist and linked her fingers behind his back, drawing even closer. "I know it hurt Damon at the time, but he came around. After a while, he realized that our relationship had become personal, not just professional."

Brodie's lips whispered against her hair. "Shh, darlin'. He's not going to hurt you again."

The husky promise made BJ curious. "You do know him, don't you?"

Brodie loosened his hold and pulled away. His bent, twisted features hovered inches from her own face. "I meant that as a vow that no one would hurt you again."

Immortal Heart

She placed her tender, caring fingers on the scar beside his straight mouth, wondering what horrible event had left that mark on him, and if it had healed as quickly as his arm or if he had suffered in pain.

"You're old-fashioned and gallant, Brodie Maxwell, but I don't want any promises like that. No matter what you say to the contrary, you can be hurt. I hurt you last night, and I'm sorry. I don't want you to make any promise that could hurt you again."

With tender, brave boldness, she pressed her mouth to that scar. Brodie closed his eyes and accepted her caress, allowing BJ the freedom to explore his craggy facade. BJ knew a strange, feminine power as this huge mountain of a man sat docilely before her, letting her kiss and caress each harsh mark on his face and neck.

She touched the scar on his brow, teased the bumpy ridge of his nose. She tasted the clean spice of his skin, blemished by unknown horrors.

When she reached the tiny nick on his chin, a primitive, incoherent growl rumbled in his throat. Like an ancient mating call, the sound triggered BJ's triumphant, husky response.

By mutual consent, Brodie angled his neck and moved his mouth over hers, hungrily taking her eager offering. BJ parted her lips, greedily seeking more. His tongue darted and danced with hers, eliciting a joyous moan in her throat when they twisted and joined.

Brodie slid his hands down her ribs, cupping her bottom and pulling her flush against the vee of his legs. BJ spread her fingers along the nape of his neck, rubbing her palms against the prickly provocation of his hair.

A heaviness like molten lead pooled at the heart of her womanhood. Striving for release from the erotic pressure, she rubbed her breasts against him and rotated her hips.

But hands stronger than her feverish need cinched her by the waist and pushed her away from the rock wall of Brodie's body. Brodie tore his mouth away, resting his forehead against hers, panting with the same uneven breath as she.

"God, woman, you don't know your own strength."

"Me?"

"Don't sound so incredulous." He lifted his head, clasped her jaw in his hands, and planted a firm, hot, dismissive kiss on her lips. "But this is hardly the place to succumb to your spell."

BJ giggled with a lighthearted remnant of ignited passion. "I thought you were the one weaving the magic."

Could that really be her own voice sounding so vampish and flirty?

Brodie took her by the hand and led her quickly out of the research area, down the elevator, and out to his Explorer. "Ride with me. We'll pick up your truck later."

BJ still tingled with the power of their kiss,

Immortal Heart

but she couldn't ignore the strange events unfolding around them. "I'm willing to listen with an open mind today. You said you could explain about last night?"

Brodie carried her hand to his lips and brushed a kiss across her knuckles. "I can try."

Chapter Six

"Do you have the power to cure everybody?"

"No, it's not like that."

Brodie pushed the door open from behind BJ and followed her into the house. Like a child who repeatedly asks why, BJ rattled off question after question. Thus far, he had managed to put off giving her any concrete answers, choosing instead to wait until they returned to BJ's territory. What he had to tell her would sound incredible enough. He wanted her to have the security of her own space around her to soften the shock and encourage her to understand.

She had already given him the precious gift of her acceptance: pulling him to her side and acknowledging him as an equal when she

Immortal Heart

introduced him to that crowd of intellectual researchers, touching him with her mouth and hands in the most forgiving, mind-numbing act of healing he had ever experienced. Letting him touch her. And, if he weren't too far out of practice to interpret the signs correctly, liking his touch.

For years Brodie had avoided getting involved with a woman. The risk was simply too great. Clarinda had suffered because of him. Zora. Lynelle. Jane.

He was responsible for all their suffering.

So he removed himself from society and settled in a remote, part of the Ozark Mountains, living off a legacy from the past.

But removing himself from society meant removing himself from women. He denied himself their kindness, their caring, their generous passion. Their beautiful, soul-brightening smiles.

Until he walked in the front door of LadyTech headquarters, he had denied those needs. Until he met BJ.

After a few days in BJ's quirky, unsophisticated, brilliant, surprisingly sexy company, he admitted how much he craved a woman's touch in his life. How much he craved her touch.

All the more reason to proceed slowly, carefully. He understood clearly the meaning of the note that had frightened BJ last night. There was no changing his future. But maybe, if he stayed in control and moved cautiously, just maybe, he could cheat fate just a little bit.

"It's close to noon. We ought to have some lunch."

BJ turned her perceptive, expressive eyes up to him. "This is really hard for you to talk about, isn't it?"

He wished he could give her a reassuring smile. "Yeah."

She provided the smile instead. "I don't think a bologna sandwich will change what you have to say."

"No."

She patted his arm, a light, familiar, everyday pat that made his heart flip-flop. "I'll fix us something to eat. I should let Duke out anyway. Don't worry, I'll put the little beastie out back where he can't hurt you."

Brodie watched her walk into the kitchen. He wondered if she had any clue how enticing he found her tomboyish attire. The snug fit of her knee-length denims revealed just enough curves to force him to imagine the feminine charms hidden beneath her oversized shirt.

And more than a little male ego swelled with the possessive knowledge of just how seductive she could make a man-sized sports jersey look.

Brodie realized how quickly he was losing his resolve to move slowly, to talk first, to gain trust and understanding before he and BJ moved on to anything else. Needing physical activity to douse his growing need, he launched himself into the task of straightening BJ's front room.

Immortal Heart

The furniture looked dusted and the big area rug on the hardwood floor had been vacuumed. But BJ had accumulated an amazing amount of stuff. Surely it made sense to store the jigsaw puzzles in the antique armoire. And move the models to a display area on a bookshelf. Set the handsewn dolls on their chairs beside the doll-house.

"My, aren't you the brave soul."

He straightened from his work and accepted the plate of sandwiches, chips, and sliced cantaloupe from BJ. "You're not offended, I hope."

"Are you kidding? It's hard enough to find a housekeeper who's willing to clean around my collections. If you want to volunteer for the job, I won't stop you."

Brodie speculated on whether a subconscious part of him had influenced his domestic endeavor. He had cleared the sofa, but not the chairs, leaving only one alternative for a seating arrangement. Side by side on the sofa.

They spent several minutes in companionable silence, taking the edge off their hunger with the plain, but filling meal. Brodie was glad to see BJ's healthy appetite since he couldn't remember if she had eaten anything substantial since the pizza two nights ago.

She must have sensed him watching her, because she looked up. She didn't appear self-conscious, only curious. "So, when are you going to tell me all about these secret powers you possess?"

Julie Miller

Brodie was literally saved by the bell. The telephone rang. BJ frowned toward the kitchen where the nearest phone was located. She probably had some fancy answering machine she had designed to take care of it for her.

But she surprised him by setting her plate down. "I'd better get that. It's probably Emma wondering where I am. I told her I'd stop in the office today. She's such a worrywart, bless her heart. Excuse me."

"Sure."

He used the temporary reprieve to try and come up with the best way to explain everything. Finally, he decided there was no good way to do it. He'd just let the conversation begin and hope he didn't botch it too badly.

BJ rode an emotional high, enjoying the simple companionship Brodie shared with her this morning nearly as much as she had thrilled to his embrace. They had hurdled some barrier together in that tiny cubicle at the Morrisey Institute. She had touched the soul of a man and he had awakened the heart of a woman.

She felt good enough to take the day off and devote her time to Brodie. That would shock Em, she thought. Emma of the common sense and caring nature who only criticized BJ about one thing, working too much.

BJ smiled as she picked up the receiver and relaxed against the kitchen counter. "Hi. This is BJ."

Immortal Heart

A voice distinctly different from Emma's answered. "Bridget. Rick Chambers."

BJ's mood did a nosedive. She tensed, psyching herself for another confrontation. "What's up?"

"We had an appointment today. You didn't come in, so I thought I'd check on you. I heard about that accident last night. Good thing your bodyguard was there to save you."

"Thanks for your concern. But I don't think I'll be . . ."

BJ suddenly went blank, losing her train of thought. She shook her head, feeling foggy and light-headed. The sunlight streaming through the window over the sink stung her eyes. She bent forward, shading her eyes with the palm of her hand.

"Beej? You still there?"

Where did that voice come from? She straightened, looking around, blinking in the brightness.

The moment she knew, she also knew it was too late. Her breath caught in her throat, strangling her. *No! Not now!*

The words couldn't get past the constriction in her throat. An ominous shadow, cold and frightening, seeped into the corners of her consciousness. *Fight it, BJ! Fight!*

"Beej, is something wrong?"

Her fingers clenched the plastic stick in her hand, squeezing until either it or the bones in her hand might snap. *An episode. Think. Brodie.*

Julie Miller

The membrane beneath her skull throbbed with the effort to push the dark presence from her head. She panted out loud, trying to catch her breath. *No. Not Brodie. The phone. Rick. Remember. You have to . . .*

In a last desperate burst of conscious thought, BJ snatched at the notepad beside the phone, pulling the whole thing off the wall as she ripped a sheet and wadded it in her hand. *No. Fight.*

Clutching a pencil in her dysfunctional fist, she scratched on a corner of the paper, pressing down harder and harder.

The lead snapped the same instant her head cleared. BJ blinked rapidly, focusing on a wall of tiles behind a toaster, wondering why she was in the kitchen with the top half of her body sprawled on the counter.

"Beej! Answer me!" A frantic male voice shouted in her ear. She looked dumbly around for the man speaking to her, then realized the sound came from the receiver on her shoulder. She steadied herself with a cleansing breath before picking up the receiver and speaking.

"Rick?" The fairly normal tone of voice pleased her.

"Dammit, Beej, you scared me. Why didn't you answer?"

"A twinge of a headache all of a sudden, that's all. It was nothing; really. Nothing."

"Well what about our discussion?"

Brodie. She had to find Brodie.

Immortal Heart

The shouting person ceased to be relevant. "Rick, I've got company and can't really talk right now. I'll catch you later."

"Beej—"

She placed the receiver back in its cradle. In a self-conscious, ego-boosting gesture, she fluffed the curls on her forehead and moistened her lips with the tip of her tongue.

"Brodie?" She returned to the living room and found him working with her doll collection again, brushing some dust from a doll that sat atop her curio cabinet.

He kept the doll in his hands. "Was that Emma?"

He had a broad, tapering back, even more inviting than the opposite side of the man. She curled her fingers into fists, controlling the urge to touch him. They needed to talk first.

"Rick Chambers."

The wry inflection in her voice turned him around. "Did he threaten you again?"

"No." She put her hands up in a conciliatory gesture, wanting to curb his temper before it started. "I put him off until tomorrow. For now, it's just you and me."

His eyes narrowed quizzically, studying her. "You all right?"

BJ waved her hands and turned to get the last couple of chips off her plate. "It's nothing. Rick's call kind of spoiled my mood, that's all."

She heard the hesitation in his movements behind her. But whatever he was about to say changed when she turned around again. Brodie gave the handmade doll another look. "He must be one of your favorites since he has the place of honor up here."

The doll with a woolly lion's mane, felt fangs, painted face, and a tunic of mallard blue silk, was indeed her favorite. "The lady who made him copied the illustration out of a favorite childhood storybook of mine, *Beauty and the Beast*, are you familiar with the fairy tale?"

The look he gave her over his shoulder blended disbelief with wounded hurt at her question. BJ chomped on her potato chip to drown out her regretful thoughts. She hadn't meant anything by the remark, but obviously Brodie questioned her motives.

She matched his silence, watching him replace the doll on the top of the curio cabinet. *Change the topic.*

Her eyes dropped to the tan leather sheath hanging from his belt, pointing a suggestive line down to the tight arch of his buttocks. BJ swallowed hard. *Not that topic.*

"You must do some collecting yourself." She mentioned the first thing that came to mind. "That knife on your belt looks like an antique."

Brodie's hand seemed to automatically moved to the knife's handle, as though her words were some kind of attack. She got up and crossed the floor. He relaxed as she moved closer. "Do you mind if I take a look at it?"

"No." His chest muscles flexed invitingly

when he reached behind him to undo the knife. He held it at both ends, laying it horizontally across her outstretched hands.

"It looks positively medieval."

"Thirteenth century."

"Wow." BJ studied the long narrow blade and leather-wrapped handle.

Brodie pointed to the crosspiece. "I reinforced the handle and replaced the original blade with steel."

"You don't carry a gun?"

"I own one," he reassured her. "I keep it in the glove compartment unless I need it for a particular case, though. But I prefer the dagger. It's quiet. Takes up less space."

"And you won't accidentally shoot yourself in the foot." BJ laughed alone at her additional reasoning. Brodie never laughed. He never so much as smiled. Maybe the injuries that had scarred his face also caused nerve damage. Maybe he couldn't smile.

BJ carried the knife to the sofa, turning it over to look at the small carvings etched into the blade. The markings continued beneath the newly wrapped leather handle. She wondered what they might represent.

"Did you do these?"

His shoulders stiffened and straightened. He spoke to her, but his eyes looked to a faraway place, a place beyond her home and this time.

"Brodie?"

"Yes. I carved them. Sort of a gruesome reminder of some of my past mistakes."

She wanted to ask what kind of mistakes he had made. She would assume "mistake" meant people he had used the knife against, maybe even killed. Except that the drawings were of gentle, upbeat images. A rose bouquet. A sunburst.

Brodie picked up their empty plates, ignoring her curiosity. She had pushed too hard. He was escaping again.

He's escaping.

A tiny pinprick of pain twitched behind her eyes.

Slowly, silently, she rose to her feet and followed Brodie into the kitchen. She paused in the archway, not wanting to reveal her presence yet. Brodie grabbed the edge of the sink and stooped over, his shoulders sagging with the weight of a huge, unseen burden.

BJ started forward, her fingers outstretched toward his lonely, weary back. *Poor Brodie. So out of place. He doesn't belong here.*

The ache behind her eyes sharpened. She needed to call to him. *Brodie. Help.*

She called with her mind, but he couldn't hear her.

Pain spasmed behind her eyes, making her dizzy with its intensity. She gripped the butcher block in the center of the kitchen, riding the waves of nausea spinning the room around her.

It's nothing.

As soon as the thought entered her mind, the

world righted itself. The pain vanished. She could breathe again. Her eyes focused with a strange clarity that brought everything into sharper view.

Brodie still stood with his back to her, too caught up in whatever was bothering him to hear her approach.

Three steps away from him. Two. She had to do it.

She reached upward. Metal flashed. She tightened her fist.

Some little sound or sixth sense must have alerted Brodie. He straightened just as she brought the dagger down, shifting her target. The deadly edge glanced off his shoulder blade, ripping through cotton and skin, but missing the muscle and vulnerable organs beneath.

Her yelp of furious determination drowned out Brodie's startled gasp. The knife became a living, wicked thing in her hand. She raised it to strike again.

But Brodie's reflexes were too swift for her. He twisted around, snatching her wrist and wrenching her clean off the floor with his other arm. Pinned near his waist, she thrashed against him, kicking and twisting.

He has to be stopped!

"BJ!" He snapped her wrist that held the knife, knocking the weapon to the floor. "Bridget! Look at me!"

Somehow he contained her struggles with one arm cinched around her. He cupped the back of her neck and forced head back. "Bridget, darlin', it's Brodie. Look at me."

Bridget. Nobody called her Bridget unless she was in trouble.

"I have to stop you." Her protest faltered and her body weakened.

Dimly, her mind rallied to try and place herself in her surroundings. She was floating in the air. No, she was trapped against a wall.

"Bridget."

Someone called her name again. She felt herself falling. Her feet touched something solid. She grabbed on to whatever she could reach to steady herself.

"That's it. Hold on to me, darlin'."

Her handhold shifted. Then she blinked. She could see already, couldn't she? Yet her vision was clearing. She blinked again and found herself staring at the handle of a dagger. Someone had ripped the leather wrapping to expose a jagged zigzag carving.

"BJ? Bridget, honey, are you with me?"

The soothing deep rumble of Brodie's voice penetrated the fog in her head. Her fingers curled tightly into his soft cotton T-shirt. She lifted her gaze up the pulsing column of his throat, across the angle of his jaw, to find both tender reassurance and something downright predatory in his murky gray eyes.

"What happened?" she whispered.

"You had another episode." His words were

gentle, but the wildness in his eyes meant something else.

"Obviously," she said. She collapsed against him, feeling spent, grateful for his unyielding strength beneath her cheek. Her fingers loosened their grip, but cotton stuck to her right hand. Confused and curious, she tried to see the gummy stuff that made it sticky. But Brodie's hand fanned over hers, capturing it flat against his chest.

"Don't worry about it," he warned, brushing his lips to the crown of her head.

"What?" She tugged her hand within his grip, feeling a surge of panic rise in her throat. "What did I do?"

She leaned away from him, suddenly fearful that he held her so tightly, suddenly mindful of the throbbing pain in her right wrist.

Then she saw how his shirt sagged in front, how a large tear exposed the skin of his right shoulder. Bile churned in her stomach. "What did I do to you?"

"I'm all right."

With a quick twist of her hips, she freed herself from Brodie's hold and moved to his side. She glimpsed his back before he could turn it away from her.

"Oh, God, no." He let her look when she stopped him with her hand on his arm. The wound was already healing, but the bloodstains on the back of his shirt and her hand told her exactly what had happened. "I tried to kill you."

Julie Miller

He shook his head resolutely at her bald statement, capturing her jaw between his meaty palms when she would have looked away. "No. An evil creature manipulated you into stabbing me. It wasn't you."

A vague image flitted through her mind. "I had to get rid of you," she murmured distantly.

"No." His touch grew firmer. "He wanted to get rid of me."

The image wouldn't leave. She could almost make it out. "I tried to fight it. I knew it was wrong. I tried to fight."

She started shaking, like an addict coming down off a high. "How can you forgive me? I could have killed you."

Brodie lifted her onto her tiptoes, dipped his head, and ground his mouth over hers. He thrust his tongue between her lips, uninvited but welcome. His kiss was rough, hard, basic. It blotted out every thought in BJ's mind except the man before her. His raw passion erased everything but her own need to respond to him.

She answered with softer kisses of her own, anchoring her hands at his waist, rocking with the elemental desire he stirred in her.

When he removed his mouth, she whimpered in protest. He rewarded her by brushing his lips across her cheek, blazing a warm path to her ear. BJ arched her neck, giving him access to the sensitive spot behind her earlobe.

She purred in response. "I would never knowingly hurt—."

Immortal Heart

He silenced her apology with his lips. "Don't think about it," he whispered.

BJ had a hard time remembering what she shouldn't be thinking about. Brodie's kiss left her feeling bruised and feverish, soft and gooey inside.

"Did Damon call you?"

His question felt out of sync with the rhythmic heat pulsing through her. He released his hold on her, but didn't let her go far, taking her by the hand and leading her to one of the kitchen chairs. He sat, pulling her between his legs and onto his lap.

For the first time, they faced each other on the same level, eye-to-eye. He caught both her hands in one of his, rubbing the pad of his thumb across her wrist.

"I hurt you." His eyes shadowed with regret and harsh reprimand.

"You were defending yourself."

His grip on her tightened, not enough to hurt, but enough to reveal his frustration. "I don't understand why he'd want you to kill me. He knows it can't be done."

"What are you talking about?"

He lifted his gaze to hers. "Was it Damon?"

What was his hang-up with Damon? "Why do you keep saying that? It was Rick on the phone."

He shook his head, looking as confused as he made her feel. "That's what you said earlier. It just doesn't make sense."

"You think Rick's call triggered the episode?"

"I don't know. I'd have bet money something in that call was the cause, but I can't see Chambers knowing how to do this to you."

"How long was I out this time? Before I tried to get rid of you."

His gentle fingers tipped her sagging chin back up. He wouldn't let her feel any remorse for what she had done to him. "Just a few minutes. You carried on a normal conversation. We talked about your dolls. You asked about my knife."

A vague memory flitted through her head. "I needed a weapon."

"You asked if I had a gun."

BJ felt the heat seep from her body. What was he implying? If he had given her a gun instead of the knife, would he now be lying dead in her kitchen?

His grip tightened around her shaking hands. "Don't worry about it. You can't kill me."

"I can if I'm out of my head. If I don't know what I'm doing."

"No. I mean I won't die."

BJ just stared at him for a moment, wondering if a man of considerable strength of will really could hold death at bay. Did he believe that strongly in his invincibility? Could she believe in it?

No matter what Brodie said, she had done a terrible thing. She picked at the ripped material of his shirt, trying to cover his shoulder with the tattered ends. "Did I hurt you? Was there a lot of pain?"

"At first. But it went away pretty fast. Once adrenaline kicked in."

She appreciated that he didn't lie to her, but his honesty sparked the same compassionate concern she had felt earlier. "So with all the marks on you, you felt pain?"

"But I beat every last one."

"How?"

Brodie sat so silently and so still that she began to think he hadn't heard the question. His eyes darkened like shadowy steel. "Immortality."

BJ just stared at him, wondering if her hearing had been affected by the last episode.

"Immortality?" she repeated, making sure she hadn't imagined his answer.

"Yes. I'm an immortal."

The look in his eyes was just too serious. BJ burst out laughing. "Oh, really?" Her laughter softened to a nervous giggle. "So just how old are you, then, big guy?"

"Forty. But I've been forty for almost eight hundred years."

Her laughter erupted again. She leaned back against his arm at her waist, blinking away the moisture in her eyes. Gradually, she became aware of the darkening of his expression, of the rigid set of his powerful shoulders, of the fury in his eyes. Her hand flew to her mouth to stifle the laughter that wouldn't cease, the laughter tinged with a note of madness in it now.

She hugged her arms around together, shielding herself from the man who shielded her. She forced the laughter down her throat. "Please, don't do this to me, Brodie. I have enough doubts about my own sanity. Don't make me think you're crazy, too."

Abruptly, Brodie stood, shedding her from his lap. She would have landed on her backside if she hadn't caught the edge of the table to steady herself. Brodie straightened to every intimidating inch of height in front of her.

"I'm going to change and get some fresh air."

He strode past her, proud and aloof and distant once more.

"Brodie?" Her outstretched hand touched nothing but air.

He froze and turned, nailing her with such a look that she pulled her hand back. "You need to rest. Take some time to get that head of yours back in order. When you can think straight, and listen and reason, we'll talk. I need to know about Chambers's phone call and anything else that might have triggered the episode, and specifically about how you can be programmed to carry out different functions."

His words sounded solicitous enough, but the unforgiving set of his shoulders and the glittering ice in his eyes informed her she had lost whatever ground she had made with Brodie. She was no longer of personal interest to him. When he strode out of her sight, he carried her

Immortal Heart

distrust with him like another visible scar.

Forget what she had done with the knife. She had laughed in his face and called him crazy.

Some wounds even Brodie Maxwell couldn't heal.

Chapter Seven

BJ kept her distance from him the rest of the day. He made it easy for her, snapping whenever she tried to speak, even at something so simple as the announcement she had dinner ready.

Brodie didn't know why her reaction to his immortality should upset him so. From the start, he had known she was a woman of facts and science. Her knowledge of abnormal things was limited to science fiction movies. She probably knew how the special effects were created. She could probably create monsters and magical illusions on her computers.

Brodie knew monsters and magic were real. He was living proof of concepts BJ couldn't possibly grasp unless she were willing to give in to the idea that not all things in this world had a rational explanation.

She hadn't minced words with him. She felt as if she were fighting off insanity. He knew her initial response to him had been as a protector, someone to ward off the imminent threat of madness. Now she thought him unstable. She didn't trust him.

He had seen such sorrow in her eyes, true remorse for stabbing him. Brodie could see that she cared about him on some level, but not to the terrible, dreaded degree that he was learning to care about her.

He should be relieved that she doubted him. A little distrust and distance might keep her safe. But it hurt. It hurt him in his gut to know that she feared him. To know that the closeness that had sprung up so naturally between them had vanished the moment he told her the truth.

He could hear her at the far end of the house, playing with the dog on the back porch. She had walked a wide path around him today, and avoided eye contact as though she might turn to stone should their gazes ever meet.

Brodie tugged his shirt off over his head and tossed it onto his duffel bag. He rubbed his hand over his jaw, feeling the raspy stubble there. He needed a shave. Hell, it might actually do him some good to look in a mirror. The reflection of his own ugly visage always reinforced how different he was, how necessary it was for him to remain unattached.

He walked into the guest bathroom and unpacked his shaving kit. He filled the sink with hot, steamy water and began softening up the mug of soap with his shaving brush. He took several minutes to prepare his skin before removing the safety cover from his straight-edged razor. He tilted his chin up and stretched his neck before carefully laying the sharply honed blade against his throat. He worked slowly and methodically. Not that he was afraid of a few nicks, it was just a challenge to find the undamaged skin among all the scars.

A transformation in reverse unfolded each time he whisked away a bit of the cream. With half his face and neck covered in white, he looked almost normal. But gradually the monster revealed himself, showing the mirror and the man what he truly was.

Then he saw her. She stood behind him in the doorway, her gaze locking on his in the mirror. She looked relaxed, leaning against the door frame, but the tension in her wide green eyes revealed the truth about how hard the day had been for her.

"I knocked, but I guess you didn't hear me."

Her voice sounded even enough. But he heard her breath catch and saw that her gaze had gone from the mirror to his back. Not many men in history had gotten the drop on him to attack him from behind, but there were scars there too, including the new one on his shoulder blade that she had put there.

Immortal Heart

Brodie automatically reached for his shirt, but came up empty. He'd left it in the bedroom, on the other side of BJ. He couldn't retrieve it without brushing past her, possibly touching her, putting the deformities he wanted to hide right in front of her eyes.

He opted instead to drape a towel around his neck. It didn't cover much, but the ends of it in the front at least masked the scar over his heart. The brand that held subconscious meaning for her. He could hide that much from her.

He spoke to her reflection. "You need something?"

"Yes." BJ stepped into the bathroom, hugging her arms protectively. "I need to apologize."

Coming to him took courage. Seeking him out, and accepting blame for what was as much her fault as his took some real guts. He had quickly grown to admire BJ's tenacity, but there was more involved here. This was taking a chance. This was making herself vulnerable so that he could take the same risk. Something hard and full of rage crumbled inside him.

"I shouldn't have laughed," she said. "There are things in this world I don't know about. But I'm pretty smart." Her full lower lip curled into a timid smile at the understatement. "I want to understand."

He wiped traces of soap from his face with the end of his towel. Before BJ had any chance of understanding, she had to believe in him. She had to trust that he would never lie to her.

Brodie continued to face the mirror, afraid of what her tell-all eyes would say to him if he started speaking of curses and spells and punishment beyond imagining.

"BJ. I don't lie. I've been around way too long to keep track of what I said to whom, so I stick to the truth. And I'm not crazy. I've never been granted that kind of reprieve."

He could see she didn't like the preamble he had given her. She rubbed at her upper arms. He wanted to do that for her, chase away her chill with his own hands. But she had to want him to touch her again. He wouldn't force himself on her, even if it killed him a little more inside to stand by and watch her suffer when he could give her comfort.

She decided to believe him, though he could tell the decision wasn't firm. "Okay. So you've been around for eight hundred and forty years."

"Eight hundred and twenty-one."

She did the math quickly. "You were born in 1176."

"You can quiz my history. I've seen a lot of it firsthand."

She backed up to the doorjamb and leaned against it. "No. I want to take this a little bit at a time. You really believe you've been alive since the twelfth century?"

"I know I have."

She turned from him, stepping into the bedroom. "What I think doesn't matter. It's real for you, so I have to accept it."

Immortal Heart

Brodie suspected she was talking more to herself than to him, but he followed her as far as the door and responded anyway. "My dagger was forged in 1214. It's the only possession that's traveled with me through time. You could take it to a lab and have the carvings carbon-dated for authenticity. I made one about every two hundred years. But artifacts and mortal wounds that heal themselves won't convince you. You have to take a leap of faith and just believe me."

BJ looked at him then. Those spruce-flecked eyes that told him more than he had a right to know looked at him and revealed that maybe, just maybe, she did believe him. She didn't want to, her eyes expressed that clearly, too, but on some level that her rational mind could live with, she believed.

Her eyes also reflected guilt. "I shouldn't have laughed when you told me."

"You just came through a traumatic experience."

She shook her head. "Maybe I can't kill you. But I can hurt you. I seem to be pretty good at it. I'm sorry."

Brodie shifted his weight at her apology, caught off guard by the relief sweeping through him, uncomfortable admitting how much he needed to hear those words. He didn't want to be that vulnerable to her. His gaze darted to the rumpled T-shirt on his duffel bag. The need to cover himself grew stronger. She could see in-

Julie Miller

side him. She could see his pain. He could at least hide the physical evidence of his torture from her eyes.

BJ's gaze followed the same path. She looked at the shirt, then at him. What he read in her eyes shook him down to the core.

He saw need. Raw physical need.

To touch and be touched. To hold and be held.

Her gaze on his torso, covered with nothing but scars and a bit of towel, sparked an echoing ache in his belly. Moments ago he had been self-conscious, fearful of showing her his ugliness. Now her bold gaze on his naked skin awakened a hunger in him, a powerful need that went beyond sexual tension. She made him think of the years he had denied himself any meaningful contact with a woman.

Tonight, in the spacious guest room that suddenly seemed too confining, he wanted her. To touch. To hold. To fill.

And damn his self-restraint all to hell, she wanted him, too.

He cleared his throat in a strangled rush. "I'd better check the grounds before we turn in."

"You've done that already."

He glared at her, remembering how his cruel look had pushed her away from him in the kitchen, and strode over to his duffel bag to grab his shirt. This time she didn't frighten as easily. She beat him to the shirt and snatched it behind her back before he could reach it.

Immortal Heart

"Give me the damn shirt!" He stood inches from her. Much too close for his peace of mind, much too far for his desire. She clutched the shirt behind her, thrusting her breasts upward, teasing him. Not like that first night, not in a calculated seduction. She didn't have to do anything to entice him now.

He was sick with want for her. He craved her eager mouth beneath his. He lusted for her healing touches. He needed her to need him.

"Dammit, BJ! I'll leave half-dressed then."

But his legs wouldn't move. His harsh words sounded determined, but his body wouldn't respond.

Her shoulders sagged a little. Her gaze riveted on a neutral spot beside his shoulder. She held out the shirt with one hand, dangling it like a peace offering.

"No. Don't leave. Please don't leave me."

Her voice, hesitant and waifish, nearly convinced him to stay. But he grabbed the shirt anyway.

Then she touched him. A single finger on the horizontal gash above his waist. A simple touch that was no less fearless because it was shy. Brodie knew he was lost.

"What happened here?"

He looked down at the top of her soft, tawny curls. She didn't really want to know, did she? But she waited patiently, expectantly. So he told her.

Julie Miller

"Swordfight." He spared her the gory details. "French Revolution."

He couldn't see her face, so he couldn't tell how she accepted his answer. He sucked in his breath and kept still when she moved her hand and touched a forked mark on his ribs.

"And this?"

"Hostage in Lebanon." He heard her gasp. He dropped the shirt and captured her hands when she moved on to the lightning bolt that defiled the skin over his heart. "You don't want to know these things about me."

She tipped her head back, her eyes bright with unshed tears. "I marked you like an enemy in battle. Like a kidnapper torturing you."

He cupped her jaw in his palm, tracing the velvet arc of her bottom lip with the pad of his thumb. "No, darlin'. Like a woman being used. You didn't attack me. Some evil-minded son of a . . ."

He hoped he felt the beginning of a smile beneath his thumb. He softened his voice, dropping it to a low-pitched rumble. "I don't blame you. I won't let you blame yourself."

Lowering his head, he dropped a plain, chaste, reassuring kiss on the tip of her upturned nose.

"Hold me, Brodie." In a move as guileless as it was provocative, BJ slipped her arms around his waist and pressed herself against his stomach. His already aching nerve endings blazed into sheer male awareness at the feel of her

Immortal Heart

womanly curves softening against him. He rested his hands lightly on her back, afraid of crushing her if he gave in to his physical desire.

"I feel safe when you hold me. Sane." She snuggled nearer. He bit the inside of his mouth, struggling for self-control as she spoke. "I feel right."

She made him feel totally irrational. She made him feel crazily, stupidly ordinary, and absolutely, incredibly male. With BJ, he wasn't a monster, he was a man. And BJ was a woman.

His woman.

His loving, willing, eyes-wide-open woman.

Desire at its most elemental level erupted in a wave of stark, physical need. Brodie dipped an arm behind her knees and scooped her up into his arms. He sought her mouth with savage intensity, demanding a response. After the initial shock of his swift attack, she opened her mouth beneath his, welcoming, beckoning, giving him what he so desperately needed.

She laced her fingers about his neck, clinging to him with a ferocity matching his own. The side of her breast pushed against him. He heard the telltale moan so like purring in her throat.

Suddenly it became very necessary to feel skin against skin, to know her heat matched his own. He carried her to the bed, sat on the edge, and turned BJ so that she straddled him on his lap. She gasped as he pulled her to him, letting her feel the strength of his need through their clothes. Her heavy-lidded eyes looked boldly

Julie Miller

into his while she imprinted her womanly core against him.

His own eyes drifted shut as his body savored an adolescent rush of heat.

Her breath caught and panted, her growing urgency spawning a wild need to see and touch. Her fingers fumbled with the top buttons of her shirt, but Brodie saved her the trouble, capturing it by the hem and yanking it over her head. Her bra, cotton and lacy and sensibly pretty, followed the jersey to the floor.

With unerring accuracy, he covered her breasts, filling his hands with the weighted globes. "Beautiful, darlin'," he whispered. "So beautiful."

He bent his head, burying his face between them, teasing the curve of one breast with tender reverence. BJ tilted her head and leaned backward, anchoring her fingers to his shoulders. Brodie answered her unknowing invitation by closing his mouth over an extended peak, laving the rose-colored bud into a pebble-hard bead. He repeated his actions on the other side, sucking and nipping until her nails scratched him and her hips twisted against him, seeking release.

His own need had built to such a pitch that he could hardly tell her she would be protected, that she wouldn't get pregnant, she wouldn't get hurt.

He fell back onto the bed, pulling her on top of him, enjoying her like that for a moment be-

Immortal Heart

fore rolling over. It had been some time since he had undressed a woman, and by the time he had her naked and had stripped his jeans and shorts, he was a frustrated, impatient man.

But BJ was a woman to be treasured, not bullied or used. So he pulled her partially beneath him, draping his leg over both of hers, propping himself on his elbows above her, raining kisses along her jaw and neck. He tasted the tang of salt from her pores and the heat of passion burning beneath her skin.

He wanted to bring her to the feverish pitch that consumed him. He stroked her breasts, her belly, her thighs, the sandy thatch of curls in between. She put her hands on him, caressing his shoulders, his chest, his arms. Touching him with her eyes as well, touching him deep in his soul as no woman had for eight centuries. Healing him with her brave, gentle touches and cognizant, caring gaze.

Only when she breathed his name in that honey-husky whisper did her move on top of her, nudging her apart with his knee, settling himself into the cradle of her hips.

He wondered if he was too big for her. If he would crush her with his weight, or harm her with his size. She took his indecision away by grasping him by the buttocks and thrusting her hips upward.

"BJ, darlin'." He groaned as he entered her. Slowly, an agonizing bit at a time. She closed around him, hot and tight.

Too tight.

Fierce male exultation and cold, mind-numbing fear mingled with the discovery that he was her first. Brodie froze as waves of age-old warnings shouted in his mind. He raised his head, fighting for the strength to control himself, cursing the urges that made it so difficult to dampen his need.

BJ sensed his hesitation.

"What's wrong?" She clutched at his shoulders, looking as unsteady as he felt. "You said we didn't need protection. You can't carry or contract an illness, you can't father children."

"You're a virgin."

BJ paled. Then a rosy flush crept from her chest up her neck and into her cheeks.

She looked so stricken, so hurt, so afraid *she* had done something wrong. Then she tilted her chin up defiantly, grasping for a confidence he had taken from her with his indecision. "Isn't it a little late to change your mind?"

He strained with the exertion of holding back. He willed his body to do the proper thing, but everywhere her skin touched his, he was betrayed by a base desire to possess her totally. "This isn't right. You're an innocent. I shouldn't be the one."

She dug her nails into his skin. "I want you to be the one. I never wanted anyone else. I know what I'm doing. I'll remember this. I want you, Brodie. Please say you still want me, too."

He was humbled in the presence of her generous gift. His body surged with the desire to give her what she wanted, to find his pleasure in hers. Was it really better to shatter the self-confidence she so tenuously held on to? He should bear the guilt, not BJ, not his beautiful sweet BJ.

"More than anything, darlin'. More than my next breath." He kissed her thoroughly, wiping her mind clean of the self-doubts he had put there. He rocked his hips against hers and heard a sharp gasp.

"Did I hurt you?" Good God, if he had, he'd . . .

"No." Her breathless reassurance stopped that train of thought as quickly as the recognition of little fluttering tremors surrounding him deep within her.

She lifted her knees and gathered Brodie fully inside. Her nails bit into his shoulders, and he gladly absorbed her pain until it subsided. Then her bewitching little hands slipped down his back and trickled across his spine.

"BJ . . ."

Her honey-husky voice hushed him. "You make me feel like a beautiful, desirable woman."

He framed her head in his hands and felt the power rising within him. "You are a beautiful, desirable woman. No one's ever turned me inside-out as quickly as you can."

"I know the feeling."

She rocked beneath him in a rhythm so natural, his body immediately answered the call. Thoughts and praises faded as instinct and need took over.

"Forgive me, darlin'," he gasped above her. "Please forgive me."

Then he could no longer speak. He sank into her embrace. She hugged her arms around him, hugged him with her legs. Even as she arched against him with a wild, keening cry, she held him close.

Brodie tumbled over the precipice right after, knowing a completion with BJ so astonishing it robbed him of reason.

In that instant, he knew he loved her.

When he regained the ability to breathe normally, he rolled his weight off her and tucked her to his side. She snuggled against him, feeling small and warm and infinitely right. He curled his arms around her, holding her close even after the steady rate of her breathing told him she had dozed off.

Brodie looked down in wonder at the brilliant, generous woman who had given herself to him.

He loved her.

He couldn't imagine a more horrible thought.

An innocent. Good God, another innocent dead!

Brodie cradled the scrawny lifeless body in his arms. He used to be just an annoying kid whom Brodie had kind of adopted. The stupid kid had

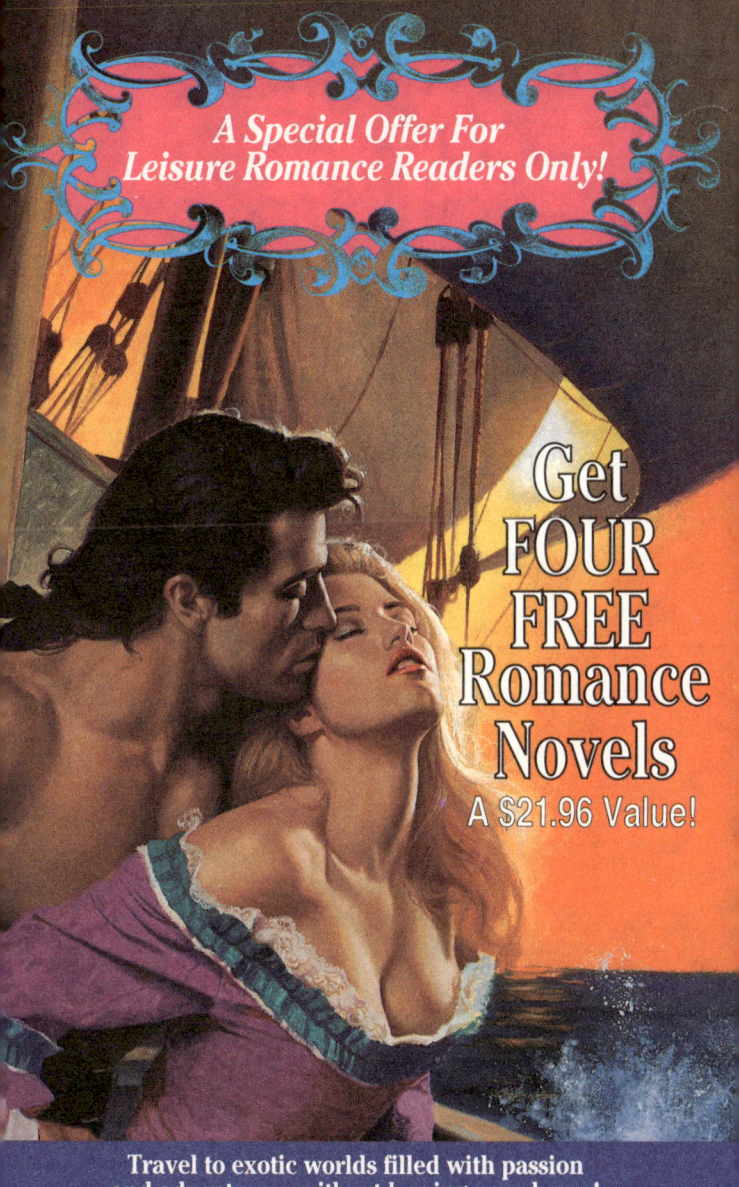

*A Special Offer For
Leisure Romance Readers Only!*

Get
FOUR
FREE
Romance
Novels

A $21.96 Value!

Travel to exotic worlds filled with passion
and adventure —without leaving your home!
Plus, you'll save $5.00 every time you buy!

Thrill to the most sensual, adventure-filled Historical Romances on the market today...

FROM LEISURE BOOKS

As a home subscriber to Leisure Romance Book Club, you'll enjoy the best in today's BRAND-NEW Historical Romance fiction. For over twenty-five years, Leisure Books has brought you the award-winning, high-quality authors you know and love to read. Each Leisure Historical Romance will sweep you away to a world of high adventure...and intimate romance. Discover for yourself all the passion and excitement millions of readers thrill to each and every month.

Save $5.00 Each Time You Buy!

Each month, the Leisure Romance Book Club brings you four brand-new titles from Leisure Books, America's foremost publisher of Historical Romances. EACH PACKAGE WILL SAVE YOU $5.00 FROM THE BOOKSTORE PRICE! And you'll never miss a new title with our convenient home delivery service.

Here's how we do it. Each package will carry a FREE 10-DAY EXAMINATION privilege. At the end of that time, if you decide to keep your books, simply pay the low invoice price of $16.96, no shipping or handling charges added. HOME DELIVERY IS ALWAYS FREE. With today's top Historical Romance novels selling for $5.99 and higher, our price SAVES YOU $5.00 with each shipment.

AND YOUR FIRST FOUR-BOOK SHIPMENT IS TOTALLY FREE!
IT'S A BARGAIN YOU CAN'T BEAT! A Super $21.96 Value!

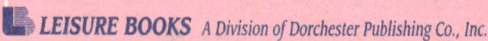

LEISURE BOOKS *A Division of Dorchester Publishing Co., Inc.*

GET YOUR 4 FREE BOOKS NOW — A $21.96 Value!

Mail the Free Book Certificate Today!

Free Books Certificate

4 FREE BOOKS

A $21.96 VALUE

YES! I want to subscribe to the Leisure Romance Book Club. Please send me my 4 FREE BOOKS. Then, each month I'll receive the four newest Leisure Historical Romance selections to Preview FREE for 10 days. If I decide to keep them, I will pay the Special Member's Only discounted price of just $4.24 each, a total of $16.96. This is a SAVINGS OF $5.00 off the bookstore price. There are no shipping, handling, or other charges. There is no minimum number of books I must buy and I may cancel the program at any time. In any case, the 4 FREE BOOKS are mine to keep — A BIG $21.96 Value!

Offer valid only in the U.S.A.

Name _____

Address _____

City _____

State _____ Zip _____

Telephone _____

Signature _____

If under 18, Parent or Guardian must sign. Terms, prices and conditions subject to change. Subscription subject to acceptance. Leisure Books reserves the right to reject any order or cancel any subscription.

A $21.96 VALUE

4 FREE BOOKS

Get Four Books Totally FREE — A $21.96 Value!

▼ Tear Here and Mail Your FREE Book Card Today! ▼

PLEASE RUSH
MY FOUR FREE
BOOKS TO ME
RIGHT AWAY!

Leisure Romance Book Club
P.O. Box 6613
Edison, NJ 08818-6613

AFFIX
STAMP
HERE

Immortal Heart

come back to see why his big buddy wasn't at the scheduled rendezvous point. Now he was dead, his heart holding a piece of shrapnel from a shell that should have killed them both.

Another firebomb exploded outside the shelter, showering Brodie with dust and bricks. Somebody yelled outside, the exact words getting lost in the screams and confusion. But he knew the voice. Brodie stooped and slung the young teen across his shoulders, picked up his rifle and went out into the streets to find Colonel Ramsey.

Thousands of strings of light dangled in the night sky, followed by flashing bursts of fire when they hit the ground. Dark-haired civilians in bare feet and tattered veils scurried from building to building, dodging the hail of bombs and bullets.

This escape had been doomed from the start. And Brodie knew it was his fault. Five men in, twenty men out. Only the twenty hadn't been where they were supposed to be. The twenty men were really twelve. The twenty men included the boy and Zora.

Zora with the raven curls to her waist. Zora with the tiny lines of suffering marring her exotic beauty. Zora who came to him in the night with silent passion, stealing away before dawn.

Zora who had saved herself by betraying them all.

"Maxwell! Del Rio's got a truck two blocks south. Get Murphy and anybody else you can round up down there now!"

"Yes, sir!" Brodie took off at a loping run, con-

Julie Miller

fident Jonathan Ramsey would keep the enemy busy long enough to give his men time to get out.

Brodie zigzagged down the street, avoiding parked cars whose gas tanks could explode, pushing confused civilians back into the relative safety of their shelters. An old man stopped him, rattling off questions in the native language Brodie couldn't understand.

"C'mon, old man." Brodie grabbed him by the upper arm and hurried him into a building with thick walls and little glass. "You'll be safer here."

The man squatted against the wall, wringing Brodie's hand and spouting something that sounded like gratitude.

"Chief!" Brodie whirled around when he heard his rank called. Murphy stumbled through the doorway, his leg shattered and bleeding. "Cloud cover's too heavy to get air support. We have to get out now before they get lucky and shell the airfield."

"Right." Brodie dropped his rifle next to the old man and moved the kid's body to one shoulder. He got hold of Murphy under his arms and took the brunt of the weight off his wounded leg. Together, they rounded the corner of a burning building and found Sergeant Del Rio. The sarge helped Murphy up to the front seat while Brodie dumped the kid's body onto the bed of the truck.

He did a quick head count. Three American bodies, one foreign national. Seven surviving hostages. Murphy, Del Rio. Ramsey and Echohawk arrived moments later. Only one missing.

Immortal Heart

Zora.

"Brodie!" Blessed faith propelled her out of the shadows and into his arms. She was alive! He clutched her tightly, pulling her toward the safety of the truck.

"No!" She struggled out of his grasp. "I only wanted to apologize and wish you luck."

Flashfire lit the sky. Brodie swore when he saw her face. "This is how they treat their informants?"

Bruised and bloodied, she had paid in full for revealing their plans to the government security force. "Zora. Come with us. I'll keep you safe."

She shook her head. "I must stay. My work is here. I am so sorry about your comrades."

She touched her fingers to his face. He heard a muffled thud. She fell against him. Lifeless. Shot in the back.

"No!" He tilted his head and screamed his rage.

"Chief! Get in here now!"

Suddenly the street was alive with gunfire. Holding Zora's body like a shield, he pulled the dagger from his fatigues and gutted the soldier who charged him. The truck growled to life behind him.

"Chief!"

Government soldiers closed in. He took out one more, feeling the sting of a bullet graze his ribcage. He held his ground until her heard the answering report of gunfire behind him. A grenade exploded, scattering the soldiers for a moment.

Brodie dropped Zora's body, tears clouding his

vision. He had gotten her killed. He'd listened to her stories in the dark of the night and grown to care about her suffering. He wanted to help her. But he'd only gotten her killed.

"Maxwell!"

Brodie obeyed the colonel's command and ran toward the truck. He caught it and hoisting himself onto the bed, he took a rifle from Echohawk and resumed his duty as a United States Marine.

He couldn't see what he fired at. The tears ran too freely. He had killed another innocent. Good God, how many innocent people had to die before his punishment would end?

Never again, he swore. Never again.

Brodie jerked awake instantly. His heart thudded in his chest. Moonlight poured across his naked body through an open window, glistening on the sheen of cold sweat that enveloped him.

His nightmare vision had been real. Hundreds of times in the past he had lived through similar nightmares. Innocent people dying because he cared. He had saved a few lives along the way, too. Jonathan had always liked to argue that one with him. But somehow they didn't seem to count for much when faced with the knowledge that one more person, one more innocent, had died because of him.

Slowly, Brodie collected himself. He wiped the sweat from his forehead and looked down at the woman sleeping beside him. BJ lay curled in a ball, facing him. He had thrashed so during

Immortal Heart

his sleep that he had uncovered himself and pulled the sheet down to her waist.

The moonlight touched her skin, giving her an ethereal glow that disappeared in the shadowy cleft of her breasts. The tempting sight sent heat rushing to the lower part of him. But another, gentler warmth settled in his chest. Her plain face, profiled where she lay on the pillow, was relaxed in calm, serene beauty. She must be both physically and mentally exhausted to have slept through his nightmare. He touched her cheek, brushing back a love-tossed lock of hair.

She had been wild and free, with a touch of ladylike shyness that had been missing from her programmed seduction two nights ago. This real BJ was better. Definitely better.

No wonder he fancied himself in love with her.

Brodie berated himself silently. Honesty ruled him as much as his sense of justice and fair play did. He loved her. Period.

Nothing was fair about that.

He pulled the sheet up and tucked it under her chin. The sweet memory of her soul-healing apology and the humanizing lovemaking that followed was blanked by the memory of a dark set of eyes.

Eyes branded into his heart for all eternity. Evil. Vindictive. Without remorse.

Brodie had done an unforgivable thing. He deserved to be punished. But the innocents he

Julie Miller

encountered didn't deserve to be a part of his punishment. BJ didn't deserve it.

"I can't do this, darlin'," he whispered, brushing her cheek with a kiss. "Forgive me."

Ignoring the urges of his body and heart, Brodie slipped off the bed, dressed silently, and left the house. He ran deep into the night.

BJ opened her eyes when she heard the outside door click shut. She gently traced the warm spot on her cheek where Brodie had kissed her goodbye.

I can't do this, darlin'.

Did he know he used the endearment? If he did, did it mean anything?

BJ wished she could reclaim the sweet dreams of a few minutes ago. After loving Brodie, she had drifted into contented sleep, her body feeling sore but deliciously whole. Sheltered by Brodie's big body, warmed by his fiery need for her, she eased into the most restful sleep she had known in weeks.

But Brodie's groans and feverish twisting beside her roused her. She wondered what demons tortured him so.

She had nearly reached for him when he went deathly still. He was awake, dealing with whatever torment had plagued his dreams.

I can't do this, darlin'.

Brodie's voice was filled with anguished regret. Regret over taking things so far with her. He thought she had more experience. She

Immortal Heart

hadn't pleased him the way he had so thoroughly pleasured her.

BJ knew computers. She knew math. She knew abstract thinking and deductive reasoning.

She didn't know men.

Brodie's scent lingered on the sheets, drawing her attention up to the pillow beside her. She touched the hollow indentation where his head had rested.

Empty.

Her bed was empty. Her heart was empty.

And the man who could fill that emptiness had kissed her good-bye and run away into the night. The man who claimed he could never die had killed the bud of light and hope blossoming to life inside her.

BJ curled up into a tight, tiny ball, burrowed into the pillows and accepted the pain and loneliness Brodie had fleetingly chased away back into her life.

Chapter Eight

BJ wondered how she could have lucked out twice. She stuck her fingers into the dog carrier on the seat beside her and scratched Duke's inquisitive nose.

As the cab sped toward its destination, BJ replayed the past few hours in her mind. Brodie had lifted her to the very top and plunged her to the very bottom last night, with his glorious lovemaking and his sad, regretful words. She felt as if she had been waiting her whole life for him to find her, to make her feel like a womanly treasure, not just a clever prize.

Her body still trembled with the memory of his rough, tender hands on her body, drawing fire out of her with every caress. She could close her eyes and remember how he had claimed her

Immortal Heart

so fiercely, so possessively.

He restrained himself patiently until her first moments of pain had passed and her body adjusted to the intimacy. Then he led her on a new journey, one filled with pleasure and sensation so exquisite that it robbed her of conscious thought. He banished the cruel, cold shadows that erased clear thinking, and filled her world with warmth and light, with protection and love.

Love.

In spite of her limited experience with men, BJ had no idea how she knew it, but she knew that Brodie loved her.

After he left, sleep became an elusive state. She returned to her own room, dressed in jeans and an oversized shirt, crawled into bed and pretended to be asleep when Brodie checked on her.

She waited a long time before silence filled the house and she guessed he had finally fallen asleep. She stacked her stuffed animals under the covers, a childish trick to make it look as if she were still in bed, then carried her shoes and tiptoed past Brodie's closed door. She picked up a miniature remote phone and left through the back door, loading Duke into his carrier and taking him with her. She walked down to the gate and called a cab. Then, suppressing a stab of remorse, she changed the entry codes to her security system. If Brodie should wake and find her gone, she wanted to delay him as long as possible.

Because she couldn't see him again. She absolutely couldn't bear to look into his icy, pain-filled eyes and hear him spout some noble garbage about how last night had been a mistake. How he could only serve as her bodyguard. How it wouldn't be right for a battered, cynical guy seven hundred ninety-one years her senior to have a meaningful relationship with an abnormal genius influenced by random mind control.

His words might make sense. She didn't want to hear them.

So, like a calculating coward, she snuck out of the house with her most reliable friend and left to find someone who could set her world right once again.

"Morrisey Institute, ma'am." BJ paid the driver, adding a generous tip for coming out so early.

The outer doors to the complex were still locked, but the guard on duty knew her and let her in. "Is Doctor Morrisey in yet, Tom?"

"I believe he stayed the night in his penthouse. I can call the top floor, if you like."

"I'd appreciate that."

A few minutes later, BJ stepped off the elevator and crossed the hall. She had just reached for the bell when the door opened. Damon, dressed in his pajamas and a silk robe, drew her immediately into his arms.

Immortal Heart

"What's wrong?" She clung to him for a moment, letting him rock her back and forth like a child. "Did that beast you hired do something to hurt you again?"

BJ stiffened. Beast didn't sound right. She shouldn't let Damon insult Brodie that way. Yet she did hurt, more than she thought she could possibly stand. She pulled away and looked up into his dark, adoring eyes. She nodded. Then he gathered her to him once more while the tears burned down her cheeks.

A blanket of humidity masked the trees in a blurry haze as soon as the sun rose above the horizon. The same oppressive heaviness suffocated the air in Brodie's chest, strangling tightly around his heart.

He knew what he must do. Last night, he prayed to the stars and the moon, and finally to the God that had forgotten him, prayed for a chance to have what he knew he never could.

Happiness. Contentment. A woman's love. BJ.

Now, she slept in her bed, hugging herself, curled in that little ball looking lonely and afraid and so damned vulnerable that it had taken every bit of his considerable strength to close the door instead of crawling into bed with her and taking her into his arms.

He stood over the stove, cooking a hearty omelet filled with vegetables and ham. Not because he had any appetite, but because BJ would need to replenish herself after all he had put her through last night.

When he was done, he arranged the eggs on a tray with some toast and juice. But he hadn't quite worked up the courage to wake her and face those tell-all green eyes this morning. He knew they would reflect hurt and confusion, maybe accusation, or even worse, guilt.

He had taken her innocence and left her. She should wake in the morning, sheltered in a kind man's arms, treasured in a good man's heart. But all BJ had was him, a sorry excuse for a man who had taken what she so tenderly offered and then abandoned her.

Though it pained him to know he had hurt her, he also knew she would get over it. She was young, bright, funny, and inexplicably caring. She would find another man who could give her all the things she deserved.

She could never survive Brodie's brand of loving.

Forcing that fact to the center of his attention, Brodie picked up the phone and punched in the LadyTech office number. He was quickly transferred to Emma.

"Brodie!" The guarded panic in her voice momentarily shifted his concern from BJ.

"What's wrong?"

Emma breathed deeply to regain calm authority. "I think I found what BJ's stalker is really after."

"Emma, wait, before you tell me anything,

Immortal Heart

you should know that I can't—"

She cut off Brodie's carefully worded resignation.

"He made her do something criminal."

He didn't want to hear this. He didn't want to get drawn into helping BJ any further. "What happened?"

"Rick was working on a program last night. He discovered that LadyTech is tapped directly into Takahashi Telecommunications. The program is buried too deeply to be legit."

"You have a deal with Takahashi. Isn't it normal to have a computer link?"

"We interfaced only long enough to check the software we installed. I watched BJ cancel the program myself. The only reason we would still be connected is to glean or feed information into or out of Mr. Takahashi's systems."

Brodie rubbed the back of his neck. He didn't like the sound of this. All his protective instincts rose to the surface. The warnings that tingled through his nervous system when he prepared for battle made him edgy. "What else?"

"Rick got curious, so he looked for other hidden programs."

"What did he find?"

"We're tapped into a banking office in Lucerne, Switzerland, and a defense strategy system in Falls Church, Virginia."

The flatness of Emma's voice belied the fear she must be feeling.

"Can Chambers erase the programs?"

"Not without triggering notice at the other end. Right now they're so intricately interfaced, they're impossible to detect. If he should make a mistake, someone could trace the line back to us, and criminal charges might be filed against BJ. She doesn't need that right now. How could we explain that it wasn't her fault?"

BJ certainly didn't need another guilt trip right now. Brodie ran his tongue around the sour taste in his mouth. "Are you sure Chambers didn't write the programs? He's got a grudge against BJ."

Emma sighed, weighing the idea. "Do you think I should call him on this?"

Brodie considered BJ's lack of expertise in judging people. "No. I'd better talk to Chambers myself."

"I'll back you in whatever you decide to do with him."

More trust. Damn. Did he have to become everyone's enemy in order to save BJ? He concentrated on his scars. He concentrated on the rage against injustice that stalked his soul. "Emma, I'll talk to Chambers, but you need to find somebody else to finish this job."

"I thought you were making progress."

"I should have stayed in my hole where I belong. BJ will be safer without me."

"But you care about her," she protested. "I can see it when you look at her. I can see how she's changed with you here."

Care? Hell. What did he know about caring?

Immortal Heart

He only knew killing. "I can't stay with her! Find somebody else to take care of her."

He ground the words between his teeth, knowing he had to make this decision, hating that somebody else would get the privilege of protecting BJ.

"Tell me how to reach Chambers. I'll drive BJ in so you can keep an eye on her until you hire someone else."

Brodie jotted down the information he needed, roughly silencing the protest Emma wanted to add. He hung up the phone and stared at the cooling breakfast on the counter beside him. Something else caught his eye.

BJ wasn't the neatest housekeeper, but she kept everything clean. That's why the wadded up ball of ripped paper looked out of place tucked into the corner by the splashboard. He unwrapped the note, remembering the grim message he had received in the LadyTech parking lot.

But that threat didn't make him pale the way this set of scribbles did. The paper matched the notepad beside the phone. The writing looked like a child's, heavy-leaded with jerky lines.

He could make out three letters, B, R, I. Whatever else followed was obscured by a raggedly drawn lightning bolt.

Brodie touched the cotton covering the brand on his heart. During yesterday's episode, BJ must have tried to piece together some kind of clue before succumbing to the trance. For a brief moment, she knew what the mark meant. B-R-I, Bridget.

He flipped through the pages of his notebook, looking for a name and a phone number. He didn't have many friends in the outside world, but there was one man he could call on who might be able to explain the significance of the note.

Brodie placed the call, wrote down the address, dumped BJ's cold breakfast in the garbage, and went to wake her.

He found her still snuggled up in bed, in the same position as when he had checked her earlier. "Beej," he called softly.

When there was no answer, he knelt beside her bed and reached out to gently shake her shoulder. The moment he touched the soft shape, his concern changed into absolute fury.

He flipped back the covers and sent pillows flying. He grabbed an offending furry elephant and squeezed the animal until cloth ripped beneath his fingers.

He ran to the front door, but the damn thing was locked. His large fingers felt awkward as he punched in the security code. Nothing. He tried again.

He didn't bother a third time. He ran through into the kitchen and out on the back porch. He didn't waste time with the door there, either.

Brodie jimmied a window open and cut the screen with his knife, cursing his size, gravity, and BJ as he climbed through the window and

Immortal Heart

dropped to the ground below. He circled the house and jumped into his Explorer, gunning the engine to speed down the drive toward the front gates.

He pushed the accelerator to the floor. No sense wasting time figuring out new codes. The steel chain links came up quickly. Without blinking an eye, he crashed through the barrier, stomped on the brake, and spun the vehicle onto the road.

He didn't bother calling anyone. He didn't need to search. There was only one place BJ would go.

The one place she shouldn't.

"Duke!"

The headstrong canine leaped out of BJ's arms, snarling at Damon. Quickly, she snatched him by the collar and picked him up.

"Bad dog!" Normally, BJ used a calm tone of voice to command Duke. This time, though, the command sounded stern and harsh. "Damon, I'm sorry. He doesn't behave this way when I take him to the LadyTech offices."

"You know I don't like animals. I only tolerate that dog because he's so dear to you." Damon's clipped tones elicited tiny growls in Duke's throat.

"He doesn't growl at you when we're at home." BJ pondered her pet's odd behavior while she loaded him in the carrier. "Of course, I usually put him out when I have company."

Damon pulled a handkerchief from his back pocket and blotted the beads of sweat from his forehead. "He probably senses your tension. Animals pick up messages from the people around them."

"I suppose you're right. He can't stand Brodie at all."

Damon refolded the handkerchief, looking cool and immaculate once more. "That illustrates my point. Obviously your security guard causes you a great deal of stress. I tell you again, you should fire him. That stress might make you even more susceptible to those blackouts."

BJ fell into a moody silence, absently stroking Duke through the front grate of the carrier. After comforting her through a solid bout of crying, Damon had fed her a continental breakfast, and gently prodded the story of the past few days out of her. She had given him a bare-bones version, leaving out the part about sleeping with Brodie.

But Damon could easily guess that she had developed feelings for Brodie, and that the main emotion she felt this morning was a deep, fatiguing hurt.

He had been sympathetic at first, giving Brodie the benefit of the doubt. After all, BJ was inexperienced in relationships. She might be confusing gratitude and a false sense of security with something deeper and more meaningful.

But when she gave the details about stabbing Brodie, Damon hardened into the ruthless, despotic executive she knew he could be. The gentle father figure vanished, replaced by a strutting, fuming tyrant.

"Doesn't that tell you anything?" he finally said, sounding accusatory. "How could you possibly hurt someone you care about? Your subconscious is trying to tell you that you can't trust him."

"Brodie said someone else planted the idea in my head."

"Of course, he'd say something like that." Damon sat beside her on the couch, drawing her hands into his. "I know you don't want to hear this, but isn't it possible that Brodie Maxwell is the man stalking you? At the very least, he could be working for someone. Who is in a better position to keep an eye on you or to trigger your episodes?"

BJ shook her head, refusing to believe that Brodie intended her harm. "He wouldn't hurt me like that."

Damon arched an eyebrow. He saw more than she wanted him to. "But he has hurt you."

BJ withdrew into the corner of the sofa after that, curling her knees up to her chest and hugging her arms around them. Damon's words left her feeling unsettled, unsure where to turn, whom to trust.

She thought she trusted Brodie. She believed in his intrinsic honesty, and in his devotion to duty, helping Jonathan Ramsey and anyone within Jonathan's sphere of influence, including her.

But a man could lie in other ways. He could lie by bringing a woman's heart and body to life with rough, needy touches and gruff-voiced praises, and then abandoning her while he thought she slept. He could lie by sharing bizarre secrets from his past, but hiding those that plagued his dreams. He could lie by swearing to protect her from an unseen evil, yet strike a painful blow himself by making her feel something he could not feel in return.

Maybe Damon was right. While he went into his den to make several phone calls, BJ cuddled with Duke, trying to make sense of what she felt for Brodie. Compassion, certainly. A healthy appreciation for his angular physique and secretive, icy eyes. An indescribable need to be held by him, to feel his gentle strength surrounding her.

Damon had always been a pillar of strength for her. They had weathered some bitter times in their relationship, but the love was always there. Brodie evoked many of the same emotions. But he was too different from anyone she had ever known to say the emotions were exactly the same. After just four days, surely love couldn't be counted among the things she felt for Brodie.

Damon returned, leaving her undecided. He called her confusion a criminal act for which he held Brodie responsible. But he would do something about it.

"I've called in some of my closest friends. Discreet colleagues who will work with me to help you."

"How?"

"Let them talk to you. See if they can piece together what's happening inside your head."

"Like one of your think-tank projects? I don't think so." BJ's internal defenses shot up instinctively. She started when she felt Damon's hands on her shoulders.

"I can give you something to relax."

"You know I don't like to take anything stronger than aspirin."

His fingers massaged the knotted muscles in her neck and shoulders. "Bring Duke with you. And I'll be there to monitor everything."

After a great deal of patient coaxing, Damon had talked BJ into accompanying him down to the fifth floor, which was divided into small offices and observation rooms with picture windows made of one-way glass.

Damon escorted her off the elevator, down a long hallway, and into a small generically decorated office. BJ skipped over the dark paneling to the fourth wall, where a one-way mirror rose from waist level to the ceiling. Through the glass, BJ saw four men and one woman dressed in white lab coats, sitting in a semicircle around a leather-covered examination table. The fancy upholstery and arrangement of pillows at one end didn't make it look much like the daybed someone had intended.

BJ stopped in her tracks. Her breath came in shallow, uneven gasps. "I can't do this."

Damon turned her away from the window, wrapping his hand around Duke's muzzle to control the dog's snarling. "Of course, you can."

"Duke doesn't even like this."

Damon smiled indulgently. He tapped his finger on the tip of her nose in a gesture one might use with a small child. "My dear Bridget. I won't let anything happen to you. You are too precious to me."

For an instant, BJ's mind went blank.

"Do you understand?" She heard Damon's voice in the distance.

The shadow blinked and then was gone.

BJ rubbed at her right temple, knowing everything one moment, knowing nothing the next.

"What are you doing to me?" she asked, frowning.

"It's nothing." Damon squeezed her shoulder, his eyes filled with concern. "Are you all right?"

BJ had to think a moment. Was she all right? "I guess."

She let Damon turn her toward the door adjoining the two rooms. "Let me introduce you to my friends."

The names escaped her, but their professions registered. Psychiatrist. Mathematics professor. Private detective. Neurotechnologist. Registered nurse.

An odd combination, but Damon reminded her that a true think tank contained a diversity of individuals. He never assumed that only one field of expertise could provide answers to his questions.

She clutched Duke in one arm while she sat on the end of the table, drawing her legs up pretzel-style. The nurse arranged the pillows behind her so she could lean against the wall. With deft hands, he taped suction cups in the vee of her elbow, at her temple, and over her heart.

She watched him hook her up to machines to monitor her heart rate, pulse, and the electrical activity in her brain. BJ sat silently, quelling her misgivings because Damon had such faith in her.

This whole setup felt wrong. Everything felt clinical, sterile. Hostile. But Damon winked at her, giving her a small morsel of encouragement. The psychiatrist asked Damon to move to the adjoining office to observe the session.

"Promise you'll be there?" BJ requested, giving in to a moment of panic.

"I promise." He kissed her brow, then left the room.

Duke settled in her lap, fortifying BJ with his calming presence. She forced a game smile for the others in the room. "So what do you want to know?"

"Name the resulting states of the dissolved Soviet Union."

"Huh?" BJ slowly answered. "Latvia, Estonia, Lithuania."

Before she reached the fourth in the list, they launched a bombardment of questions.

"Calculate the probability . . . Quantum theory . . . Which president . . . In what year . . . A combustion engine . . ."

The answers to each wove themselves into a maze inside her head. Each time she spoke, someone shot a new question at her. Duke grumbled in her lap. Her muscles tensed.

"What is the faulty logic of this statement?"

"Wait a minute!" she snapped. "Damon! What the hell are you people doing? What does Chester A. Arthur have to do with me?"

Damon reentered the room, coming quickly to BJ's side. The nurse checked printouts from the machines.

Damon pushed BJ back to her seat when she tried to get up. Though his hands were firm, his voice was gentle. "Shh, relax, Bridget. I'm sorry we panicked you, but the barrage of questions is per my instructions. The random questions distract you, they remove you from the immediacy of your situation. Concentrating on the answers allows them to access your subconscious mind without you putting up any conscious barriers. It's nothing to worry about."

It's nothing.

A fuzzy part of her brain thought she could

understand Damon's logic. But a smaller, distant part of her began slipping backward in time.

"You know what this reminds me of."

His fingertips on her lips shushed her. "I won't let them hurt you."

Damon backed to the door and left her. She pulled Duke up to her chest and nuzzled her cheek against him. She leaned into the pillows and focused her tattered nerves, attempting to keep her mind in the present.

But the passionless faces swam before her. They swirled into another set of faces. History. Math. Computers. Shadows. Symbols. Stalkers.

"I don't believe you, Bridget. Where did you get the answers?"

"I didn't cheat. I figured them out. It's not that hard."

"Don't lie to us. You're a clever girl. But you can't fool me."

"Make it stop." She barely recognized her own voice.

Past and present blended into one. Duke's growl rumbled through a thickening fog. BJ curled against the pillows. She wanted her daddy. Her chin bowed to her chest. The questions kept coming. She answered what she could, but soon the words turned into static. The faces blurred into black and white and shades of grey.

Why didn't Damon stop this?

Julie Miller

A helpless, confused child, she called to him. Reaching through the years. Reaching through the darkness. Calling for the one person who could snatch her away from her terror.

Chapter Nine

"Where is she?" Brodie repeated the question through clenched teeth, doing his utmost to remember that the security guard was not at fault. He pinned the guard by the neck with his forearm, getting closer and closer to doing real physical harm.

Bent backward over his own desk, the guard didn't waver in his loyalty to Morrisey. "I can't give out that information."

"Then I'll find her myself. Sorry." Brodie added the quick, flat apology while at the same time he adjusted his forearm and applied pressure to the guard's neck. Within a minute, he passed out, unharmed, but temporarily out of Brodie's way.

Brodie dumped the unconscious guard back

in his chair and rifled through the papers on top of the desk, looking for some kind of directory. A blinking light on the computer screen beside him caught his attention: Level Five—Off Limits. Experiment in Progress.

"Level five it is." Brodie jogged past the elevators, opting for the stairs, in case the guard recovered and activated some kind of security lock down.

He took the stairs quickly. His was breathing hard by the time he reached the fifth floor fire door, more from fear and anticipation than from exertion.

The door opened into a labyrinthine layout of short hallways and offices. He tapped his fist against one wall, confirming his suspicion. Thick, soundproof. It might delay him, but it wouldn't stop him. He'd break down every door to locate BJ. He had a gut feeling her sanity, if not her very life, depended on him.

One by one he pushed doors open, methodically working his way through the maze, checking every corner and closet that would be big enough to hide BJ.

The barking alerted him first. Faint and muffled, it grew in intensity as Brodie trained his ears to the sound and followed it. Flattening his back against the wall, Brodie slipped around one corner, catching a glimpse of a blond-haired man in a lab coat disappearing around the next turn. The man shuffled ahead at a furtive pace, carrying a bundle of some kind in front of him.

With long, silent steps, Brodie positioned himself behind the man. In one swift, sure move, Brodie captured him in a headlock. "Where is she?" he whispered.

The man said nothing.

"Where?" Brodie jerked a little harder, lifting the man off his feet. The bundle yapped and fell to the floor. In a flurry of twisting and shaking, Duke emerged from the rolled-up blanket.

Brodie turned the man and shoved him against the wall, holding him up by the lapels of his coat. "Where?"

Duke's high-pitched bark echoed the question. But Brodie knew they wouldn't get any answers. One look into the man's wide, unseeing eyes told him that. Brodie dropped the man flatly to his feet.

Brodie repeated the same maneuver he had used to neutralize the guard at the front desk. He let the man slump to the floor.

Brodie looked down at his last, best hope. "Show me BJ, boy."

The dog backed toward the wall, growling, keeping the unconscious body between them. His impatience flared briefly before Brodie dropped to his haunches. This wasn't the time to vent his temper. As much as he and the dog disliked each other, he needed Duke's help.

"I'm on your side, pal. I love her, too."

Brodie developed a quick respect for the intelligence of poodles. The dog hesitated an instant, as though evaluating his motives and sincerity. Then Duke gave an arrogant little humph of a bark, climbed over the prone body and trotted past Brodie.

Brodie followed the small black trailblazer.

Duke moved unerringly through the corridors, tracing his mistress's scent. He stopped at an unmarked door and scratched at the base. Brodie tested the knob and found it locked. Duke continued scratching while Brodie wedged his knife between the door and jamb, forcing the lock.

Duke squeezed through the opening as soon as he could fit. Brodie entered the empty office a step behind. The darkness in the office made the light from the adjoining interior room seem that much brighter.

Brodie looked through the glass and swore viciously. BJ huddled on top of a tall table, her knees drawn up to her chin, her arms wrapped in the hem of her shirt and clutched between her legs and body. She chanted the same word over and over.

His name. Brodie.

She rocked back and forth, staring at a spot on the floor. Wires connected her to a whirring machine, which spat out a steady stream of zigzagging graphs. This sinister reproduction of her childhood nightmare could serve no purpose but evil. Her terror filled the room and seeped through the glass.

Immortal Heart

That bastard had done this to her. A rage swelled inside Brodie so powerful that he knew he could commit cold-blooded murder. His palms itched with the desire to strangle that madman.

Duke clawed at the connecting door, snapping him back to sensibility. Getting BJ out of this cruel asylum should be his primary concern. Brodie tried the handle and found it had been bolted from the inside. He pounded on the connecting window.

"BJ! Can you hear me?"

Duke tipped his head back and whined in chorus. BJ's staring eyes blinked. "Duke?"

Her breathy plea galvanized Brodie. He scanned the outer room for something big and hard enough to break through the glass. He picked up the executive chair from behind the desk.

Three more people in lab coats sat in the room with BJ, as still as plastic mannequins. Why didn't she run? Why didn't she tell them off the way she seemed to take such pleasure in putting him in his place?

A fourth person, a woman, showed him an answer he didn't want to see. With precise, mechanical movements, she set a bottle on a medicine cart, then raised her hands to the light and tapped a syringe.

"No!"

Brodie lifted the chair like a battering ram and bashed the window, splintering it in a spi-

191

der web of tiny cracks. The unflinching woman looked over her shoulder at the sound, fixing glazed eyes on Brodie. Just as slowly and purposefully, she turned away.

"Stop it!" He smashed the glass a second time, breaking an arm off the chair. "BJ, fight her!"

The woman pushed up BJ's sleeve and swabbed her arm with a gauze pad. In halting slow-motion, BJ pulled her arm away and sank back into the pillows. Two of the men rose and advanced, seizing BJ by either arm, dragging her to the edge of the table.

"No!" Frightened into raw fury, Brodie hurled the broken chair across the room and kicked at the window. Once. The glass bowed. He kicked again, shattering the window, raining splinters of glass in the other room.

Brodie climbed across the divider, knocking interfering bits of hanging glass out of the way with his fists. In a single stride he reached the woman, grabbed the syringe out of her hand and crushed it beneath his boot. Thankfully, the contents had not yet been injected into BJ. Uncaring that his adversary was a woman, he flattened his hand over her collarbone and shoved her across the room.

The two pasty faced men holding BJ released her and came at him. One raised his fist, the other charged his midsection. Brodie deflected the punch with his forearm, then staggered backward when the second man hit him. He shifted his feet and regained his balance, slanting a blow at the first man, catching him at the juncture of neck and shoulder, dropping him to the floor. He raised his knee and toppled the second man with a thrust to the solar plexus.

Brodie charged the clear path to BJ. She climbed up on her knees and reached for him. Her questing fingers touched the corner of his mouth, tracing a scar, seeking something familiar.

"Daddy?" she called to him in a fuzzy voice. "I wanna go home."

"It's Brodie. You're safe."

He clutched her around the waist, binding her to him, only marginally reassured by the warmth he felt through her clothes. With rough, urgent fingers, he pulled the electrode pads off her skin, cursing the red marks left behind.

"Brodie." She pronounced his name as if she were deciding whether she liked the sound of it on her tongue. The lack of recognition concerned him. This was clearly an episode. But what purpose did it serve? Why take her back to her darkest fears? His rage at this unjust cruelty was so profound that it blinded him to the third man advancing from behind.

The blow to his unprotected side knocked him forward. He curled an arm around BJ, cushioning her from his crushing weight. His side ached, but it didn't slow his reflexes. When the attendant attacked him again, Brodie jerked sideways. He jabbed with his elbow. He felt the give beneath his arm, heard the pop.

The man landed on the floor, holding his bloodied nose, shaking his head. Waking up.

"They're all in some kind of trance," he muttered. He captured BJ's face in his hands, seeking clarity in her deep green eyes. "Are you with me, darlin'? Did they hurt you?"

She reached for him, burrowing her face against his neck. "Damon will take care of me. He promised."

Brodie swept BJ into his arms, afraid to ever let her go. He carried her over the partition into the outer room. Duke barked joyously, jumping up and down at his feet. He strode out the room and down the corridor toward the stairwell.

Duke's growl warned him before he turned the last corner. Brodie stopped in his tracks, face to face with Damon. Three armed security guards backed him, including the one from the front desk. Their guns were drawn and aimed at Brodie.

Damon waved his hand to his men. "Lower your weapons. I don't want to risk hurting her."

The guards obeyed, but Brodie didn't relax. "Snap her out of this. I know you're controlling her somehow, but she doesn't deserve this."

"Where are you taking her?" Damon's smooth drawl scraped against his ears. BJ murmured Brodie's name in a groggy voice and snuggled closer. The tension in her muscles seeped into his arms as she struggled to beat exhaustion and find restful sleep. Brodie would protect this woman at any cost. He'd trade his life for hers if he had one to give.

He'd burn in hell if for her sake if he could just take this sorcerer with him.

"I'm taking her home. Away from this madhouse you've created."

"She's known nothing but pain and confusion since you entered her life." Damon's eyes turned black, mocking. "She came to me because you hurt her. She is an innocent in so many ways. Easily taken in, easily hurt. She mistook your pitiful sense of duty for something more meaningful."

"You bastard."

"She hears nothing now because I wish it so. Your condemnation of me means nothing to her." Evenly modulated laughter rolled in Damon's throat. "She trusts me more than you, warrior. You saw to that yourself. I'm helping her. I'm getting you out of her system. Taking her back to a time when you didn't exist for her. A time when she would turn only to me for help."

"You can't leave her like this."

"I don't intend to. She's of little use to me as a child." Damon snapped his fingers. His silver ring flashed before Brodie's eyes. He steeled his hold around BJ, shielding her from a sorcerer's curse.

Brodie felt a subtle change in BJ's body. A release, perhaps. She grew a slightly heavier, relaxing into true sleep.

"She'll remember nothing of this when she wakes up."

"Then why torture her?"

Damon waved his hand over his shoulder. The three guards dispersed, walking past Brodie without acknowledgment, as though he and BJ and Damon were invisible. Brodie pitied men who were so easily influenced.

"A child's mind is much easier to control. I'm merely reinforcing my influence. Apparently you've become quite a distraction." Damon stroked the back of BJ's hair. Brodie turned her out of reach. "It pains me to see her question my advice."

"Let me put you out of your misery."

Damon scoffed at him. "If I stood here and let you run me through, you could not kill me. I must strike the blow or provide the means to kill myself. So it was written ages ago. And I have no intention of committing suicide or allowing anyone else to turn my hand. Not with the modern world at my fingertips."

"You can be beaten, sorcerer. I'll find a way."

Damon folded his arms together, nonplussed by the threat. "The last time you tried to destroy me, you took the life of an innocent young woman. History seems destined to repeat itself."

Brodie shifted BJ in his arms, damning the amount of guilt a man's soul could stand. If only guilt could kill him. He'd have been peacefully buried centuries ago. But guilt didn't kill. It tortured. It punished. It forced others to pay a price that should be his.

"When will it end?" He rasped the words past the tight constriction in his throat. "Does BJ have to die? Doesn't her death punish you as well as me?"

"Don't play your strategy on me, warrior. The sacrifice that frees you must be willingly given. Bridget would not betray me. Loyalty means everything to her. And if she should stray . . ."

The sorcerer thumbed the signet lightning bolt on his ring, twisting it around his finger. "She's still mine, warrior. When I'm done, she'll see you for what you truly are."

"You're the monster."

Setting his shoulders in grim defiance, Brodie walked toward the stairs. When he reached the door, Damon spoke. "She won't believe you, warrior. She'll never believe the truth."

Brodie tried to form a prayer. For BJ's sake, he tried to reach the God who struck down evil and cherished the pure of heart. She lay so still in his arms, a sweet woman-child charmed into malevolent sleep.

Brodie straightened to every inch of his massive frame and turned around. He had been raised to fight. He had taken a blood vow to protect those who could not protect themselves. Even against an indefatigable enemy, he could do nothing other than fight.

"Let her go, sorcerer. You're killing her. Her body may live, but her mind and spirit—you're killing her from the inside out. I won't let you do it."

"I'll let you play your game for now, warrior. Protect her as best you can. You'll suffer that much more when all this is done. She'll forgive me. But will she do the same for you when you finally walk away?"

The immortal phantom, the devil's own brother, laughed. The black sound wove its way into Brodie's soul, haunting him as he descended the stairs.

"Go on, boy. I'll let you out later." BJ pulled the door shut behind Duke. She stretched her arms over her head and sighed wearily. She turned and looked at Brodie, working over the stove.

His big body dwarfed the dimensions of her spacious kitchen. Yet he seemed to fit. His presence added warmth and security to her home, giving the security of his strength, his sense of honor, and his knowledge. More important than anything else, he had answers to her questions.

"Brodie?"

Anxiety and fatigue had ground her nerves into a tangled pulp. Her sleep on the ride home had been fitful at best. Even though her eyelids felt like lead shutters, she refused to close them now. She feared the nightmares she recalled might be real. She never wanted to visit that dark place again, that foggy place in her mind

Immortal Heart

where shadows blocked the light, and where love didn't matter.

Brodie led her into the living room. "Let's sit where it's comfortable. I want you to drink this."

BJ accepted the cup and saucer he gave her and sat on the sofa. She sniffed the steam rising from the cup, liking its sweet smell. "What is this?"

Brodie settled at the far end of the sofa. "Cambric tea." He hesitated a moment, and a wistfulness softened his hard expression. "My mother made it for me when I was a child. It's warm cream blended with weak tea, extra sweet."

"An old family recipe, hmm?"

A dusky light glittered in Brodie's eyes at her sorry pun. Would she ever see him laugh or smile? Did it make any difference? Certainly she found little to smile about lately.

Brodie fixed nothing for himself. He just sat there, watching her, a lonely sentinel ensuring the safety of those in his charge. BJ sipped the tea. Its heat trickled down into her belly, soothing her from within. But goose bumps tickled her skin.

"Why did you leave me?" She barely heard the words herself, but Brodie understood the underlying question clearly enough.

"You didn't do anything wrong."

His gruff, deep voice washed over her with the same effect of warmth and comfort as the tea he had prepared. With that small morsel of encouragement, she lifted her gaze to his. "You thought last night was a mistake."

Tortured fires blazed behind the ice in Brodie's eyes.

"Last night was a priceless gift I will cherish the remainder of my days."

BJ swallowed a large gulp of tea, scalding the delicate lining of her mouth. "Of course," she rattled off in wild sarcasm, "last night was so beautiful, you couldn't stand to be around me anymore. Emma must be paying you good money to protect me."

Brodie pried the cup and saucer from her hand and set it on the table. "Emma's not paying me a dime."

He caught her trembling hands in his. BJ could only stare at the battered fingers that held hers so gently. "Then I'm a charity case. You must have owed Jonathan an enormous favor to do so much for me. Just what exactly does a security consultant's list of duties include? Did you log last night in your little notebook?"

"You can't really think that."

His index finger nudged her chin up. The canyons and crags of his face couldn't mask his eyes. The ice had melted. Dark pools of gray reflected concern, kindness, and what? Loneliness? Need?

Her defenses eroded along with her self-pity and her wounded pride. She felt the same loneliness, the same need. He rubbed his thumb across her bottom lip. She felt the caress all the way to her toes.

"This message keeps flashing on and off in my head that says you're using me. That I shouldn't trust you. But in here . . ." She tapped her hand over her heart, retrieving a very different message.

Blindly, she reached for him, going up on her knees to match his level. She turned her face into his neck, hugging him tightly.

"I love you, Brodie." She whispered the words against his musky, beard-roughened skin.

"You can't." His hard hands bit into her shoulders, pushing her away.

"But I do."

He held her at arm's length, scowling at her as if she were crazy. "How can that be? He said—"

One moment, he bruised her with his grip and disbelieving eyes, the next, he had fallen back onto the cushions, gathering BJ into his embrace. She sprawled on top of him, snug in the cocoon of his arms, battling for breath as he rained hard, hungry kisses on her eyes, her cheek, her throat before claiming possession of her mouth.

BJ, raw with stress and fatigue, put up no resistance. She accepted the brush of his tongue, the brand of his lips. She opened her mouth when he begged entrance, welcoming him with the taste of love unencumbered by pretension or self-reproach.

He ran his hands down her body, tracing the flare of her hips, cupping her bottom and pulling her up to meet the deep thrust of his tongue. BJ squirmed on top of him, adjusting her rounded contours to the flat planes of his body. A groan rumbled in his chest, a feral call answered in the tightening rush of heat between her legs.

Brodie finally came up for air, tearing his lips from hers and nuzzling the curls at her temple. "It's too soon for you. We should stop. You need your rest."

He panted the husky words into her ear, thrilling her with unmistakable desire. She started to ease herself into a less intimate position, but he tightened his arms around her.

BJ rode the rise and fall of his chest, relishing the protective way he tucked her head beneath his chin and stroked her back. He was an incredibly tender caregiver. He championed her troubles with the dedication of a true knight. If she could rally enough patience, if fate gave them enough time together, she could soften his heart and find the key to unlocking his soul. He could learn to love her in return. Hope's fiery tendrils eased down her spine, soothing her in ways his mother's tea could not.

His voice rumbled beneath her ear. "Do you remember anything from this morning?"

As far as declarations of love went, Brodie's left a lot to be desired. Still, she cast aside the nigglings of doubt that threatened her contentment. The touch of his hands. His gentle strength. His fierce kiss. They all told her a message his words did not.

The pressure on her back increased. "I'll be sent to hell, if I ever die. You should hate me. I should make you hate me."

"What are you talking about?" It took an insistent struggle for him to allow her to pull away far enough to prop herself up and see his face. She cradled his damaged jaw in her hands. She looked beyond the scars, beyond the inflexible mouth, and saw the knight behind the harsh facade.

"You are a beautiful man, Brodie Maxwell. Whoever did this to you ought to burn in hell." Heat pricked at her eyes, too dry and weary to shed any more tears. "You have the soul of a true knight. The spirit of a warrior. The honor and kindness of a real gentleman. How can I not love you?"

Brodie turned and pressed a kiss into her palm. "I do not deserve such a lady."

"But?" The dreaded word hung unspoken in the air.

Brodie sat up, spilling BJ onto his lap. He plumped a pillow behind him, then pulled her securely into his arms. "The sorcerer who did this to me gave one unspeakable antidote for lifting the curse."

His heart thumped in his chest, beating a staccato syncopation to his halting words. BJ thought her own heart had stopped beating. "How?"

Long, hushed moments ticked by. BJ leaned against Brodie, squinting away the sleep that tried to claim her.

"Someone I love must sacrifice her life for mine."

The unadorned statement didn't shock her as much as the next words that floated down to her ears.

"I love you."

He quickly shot down BJ's foolish, fleeting notion of hope and happily ever after. "That's why I can't stay with you. I won't risk your life. I'll stay until the sor . . . until I know you're safe. There's someone I want you to talk to. After you rest, I'll take you to him."

"Who is it?"

"Someone who can help."

"You're helping me." She tried to recapture the closeness, physically and emotionally.

"Darlin,' I can't do this alone. Hawk might be able to see a clue I'm missing. He might know a way to battle mind control."

The living room spun around her. BJ closed her eyes to ward off the dizzying sensation. The vertigo attack of panic came from the inside, from a frightening place she thought had been left far behind her.

"He's a shrink, isn't he?"

Brodie's palm framed the back of her head, slowing her spinning universe. "Counseling

Immortal Heart

psychologist. But he has other skills I'm more interested in. He's Native-American. A shaman."

"No."

"Darlin,' I'll be right there with you."

"No," she repeated more forcefully, burrowing against him. "I know you mean well, but I won't be picked apart. Damon's experts couldn't find anything wrong. Damon cares about me and couldn't help. I'm not about to let a stranger play with my head."

Brodie swore under his breath. "Damon's experts damn near killed you! Don't you remember? I carried you out of there myself."

BJ frowned. This intimate, heart-exposing conversation had gone off on a very weird tangent she didn't understand. Damon had tried to analyze and erase the demons in her head, but had failed. Whatever she was up against was more powerful than scientific experts. They didn't deserve censure. Brodie's continuing jealousy and distrust were unwarranted. Damon had failed, but not for lack of trying.

"Can we change the subject?" Compromise seemed to be out of the question. She wished her faith in Brodie could be absolute. She wished she didn't feel so compelled to defend Damon.

"Beej." Gently, but firmly, he slipped his hands around her shoulders and started to push her away.

BJ clenched the folds of his shirt between her

fingers, holding on, knowing already he was slipping away from her. A shadow of desperation clouded her voice. "You'll stay, right?"

"Look at me." BJ tilted her chin until she could see his eyes. She wanted to weep at the powerful emotion she saw there.

"I love you more than the twenty lifetimes I've lived. I'll love you for twenty more beyond this one. But I can't stay with you. The people I care about die, BJ. Violently. Needlessly. They die. You deserve to see your eightieth or ninetieth birthday. To live a full life and die a peaceful death."

He trailed his fingers along her cheek, his touch matching the regret in his voice. "I can't give you that. I destroyed what that sorcerer loved. And his curse has made damned sure that I'll never have what I took from him. I can't sire a child with a mortal. I can't grow old with you. All I can give you is a few days, maybe a few hours. Then I have to go. I'll have to fight here long enough to help you through this. I have to do what's best for you. The longer I stay, the less I can guarantee you'll be safe."

BJ flattened his palm against her cheek, holding him close. "You know who's responsible, don't you?"

He nodded. "Maybe my friend can help you find a way to fight this."

"Why won't you tell me who you suspect?"

"Because I've never met anyone like you before. I doubt I ever will again. I don't want to spoil these few precious hours I have with you. They'll have to last me through eternity."

Knowing he would eventually leave spoiled her contentment already. Yet, when his mouth bowed to hers, she gave herself willingly. He kissed her until she thought her heart would burst with poignant sorrow. She clung to him, loving him until he pulled away with a reluctant sigh. He tucked her under his chin and rocked her in his lap.

"Sleep, darlin.' Nothing will hurt you while I'm here."

Gentle, cleansing sleep pulled her into a loving embrace. But in the haze before losing consciousness, she heard Brodie's final words.

"Nothing except me."

Chapter Ten

Long after midnight, Brodie finally drifted to sleep with BJ tangled in his arms. He had tried to move her once, but she stirred and grew restless. He shed his shirt, boots and belt, and pulled her back into his embrace, lying with her on the sofa. Telling himself he did it to help her sleep, not admitting he did it for his own selfish need to touch her and keep her safe.

"Hey, big guy." BJ's honey voice and sweet lips nuzzled against his ear. She hugged him from behind the chair, slipping her arms around him and leaning forward to look over his shoulder. The kitchen was dimly lit in the wee hours of the morning. Brodie knew such utter contentment, it humbled him. The place felt right. The time felt right.

Immortal Heart

The woman felt right.

"How's the little guy doing?"

Five tiny digits latched onto Brodie's pinkie, tugging on the bottle he held in his hand. The baby's luminous blue-green eyes lit with delight when BJ popped her head over Brodie's shoulder. The baby sucked greedily, content in his father's arms.

"He's perfect, of course." Brodie smiled proudly. "Strong like his father. Smart like his mother."

BJ nipped at his ear, zinging a charge like lightning through each nerve ending. "You're not prejudiced at all, are you?" she teased.

He angled his head and caught her mouth in a brief, searing kiss of promise. "Want to make another one?"

He loved her ready response to him. Her eyes couldn't mask her hunger. Nor did they hide the beckoning little gleam that made him feel he was the only man who could sate her desires. "When he goes to bed, so should we."

"If you insist."

Suddenly, the perfect, peaceful tableau shattered with the crash of glass. Brodie leaped to his feet, laid his son in BJ's arms, and ran through the house to find the cause of the noise.

Danger pricked his senses into keen awareness. He felt his knife in his hand. Foreboding made the air heavy. The evil was in the house. He felt the curse around him, sucking the life and love from his world.

Julie Miller

He kicked open the first door, finding dank stone walls draped with European tapestries. Clarinda lay on the canopied four-poster, coughing up blood and barely conscious. Jakob was shrouded on the floor at the foot of the bed. Bryndan and Nestor shared the trundle, looking pale, unconscious, near death.

"No!" Brodie roared, slamming the door to the past. BJ was with him now. He had a future here.

This was some damn spell of memory. The sorcerer clutched him in his grip, mercilessly replaying the nightmares of Brodie's past.

He butted his shoulder against another door, desperately seeking escape from his dream prison.

He found himself outside, in the rolling hills of the British moors. Lynelle rode ahead of him on her dapple, her long golden hair falling loose from its pins. She laughed over her shoulder, urging her mount into a gallop. Despite her skirts, she sat astride the saddle, as skilled a horsewoman as she was a lover.

Brodie reached for her, remembering what lay ahead, calling her name. Just as before, the horse stumbled. Lynelle sailed over his neck. She landed on the rocky ground, her body twisted at an unnatural angle. He knew before he reached her side that she was dead.

"BJ!" Brodie called to her, fighting for consciousness. He wanted her to free him from this nightmare, he wanted her to take the baby and run far away.

Immortal Heart

Only there was no baby. There was no wife. This was not his future.

Abruptly he landed in the streets of Beirut. Missile fire studded the smoky air with light. Zora ran to him, apologizing, saying her good-byes. The shot thudded through her. She sagged in his arms. Dead.

Brodie ran as hard as his legs would take him. He crashed through the gates of BJ's estate and bolted up the drive. When he cleared the trees, he saw the house in flames.

"BJ!"

He tore through the house, hoarse and breathless and full of dread. Instinct took him to the computer room. BJ sat in a rigid, straight-backed chair, holding the baby in her arms. Wires attached their scalps to a wall lined with monitors. Golden stars and jagged lightning bolts blipped across the silvery computer screens.

And he was there, laughing. Gauzy white robes billowed behind him. His delicate, brave daughter stood to one side, arms stretched beseechingly toward her father. "No, Father. No more."

The sorcerer looked at her, then the baby, then BJ. Finally he lifted his black, mocking gaze to Brodie and smiled. He raised his hand before his face and twisted the ring on his third finger.

Flames exploded and Brodie lost everything he had ever loved.

Brodie screamed. He screamed and cried and begged for mercy.

The scream woke him.

He jerked into consciousness as if someone had fired a gun next to his ear. Brodie swiped at his forehead, mopping sweat, feeling disoriented. The warmth that had lulled him to sleep had disappeared.

BJ was gone. The coolness of his skin indicated she had been gone for some time. It had all been a cruel trick, a nightmare distraction to keep him from protecting BJ.

"BJ?"

At the second anguished wail, Brodie hit the floor running. Maybe he had never screamed at all. Maybe his nightmare hadn't ended. He pulled his knife on his way through the kitchen, dropping the sheath as he sped toward the sound of sobbing terror.

Unfailing instincts carried him through the darkened rooms to the back porch. He slipped noiselessly through the open door, scanning each corner and beyond the windows into the night. No sign of forced entry. He had come through the only opening that wasn't locked tight. Still, the room felt violated.

"Duke. C'mon, sweetie. C'mon."

A sniffle punctuated each plea. At the far end of the porch BJ knelt on the floor, her shoulders quaking with undisguised pain.

Tucking his knife through a belt loop, he moved toward her, speaking her name so that his barefooted presence wouldn't startle her. She lifted her head, and Brodie knew from the haunted look that shadowed her tearstained eyes that BJ had suffered another episode. He gave her a few moments to recognize him fully before moving any closer.

"Who would do this?" she whispered through teeth clenched as tightly as her fists.

Brodie shifted his gaze to the tiny black bundle lying in front of her. He lowered himself to one knee. He wanted to touch her, to comfort her. But he didn't dare risk giving in to the urge while his emotions were out of control. The exterior of his big, scarred body was nothing compared to the violence roiling within him.

He hovered momentarily at her shoulder before checking Duke's inert form.

BJ hugged her arms around herself. "Why would someone want to kill him? How could he possibly hurt anyone? All he ever did was love me."

Duke's belly was cool to the touch. But something stirred beneath Brodie's fingertips. Perhaps the erratic beating of the dog's heart, perhaps his miniature lungs struggling for another breath.

"He's alive."

BJ's tight little gasp echoed the dog's. "But he isn't moving."

Brodie pushed to his feet. He grabbed a cotton afghan off a wicker rocker and wrapped it around Duke's body. BJ still hadn't moved.

"Call the vet. I'll drive him to the emergency room."

"Will he be okay?"

He lowered his tone and spoke more firmly. He didn't want to frighten her unnecessarily, but he needed her to stay in control and make the call. "Go, darlin'. Do it."

With an tentative nod, BJ got up and went into the kitchen. Brodie turned on a lamp and checked Duke again. The little animal who hated him so made his big hands feel clumsy, but he felt no broken bones or wounds. The problem must be internal.

Brodie inspected Duke's food dish and found the remnants of a white, grainy powder mixed with the crumbs of dogfood.

"Brodie?"

Brodie stood while she paused in the doorway. Her eyes looked clear. BJ was with him again. She knew his name, knew her surroundings. But his relief was tempered by the stricken pallor of her skin.

"Did you reach the vet?"

"He'll meet us at his office."

Brodie stepped toward her. The dog might be a nuisance, but he'd never wish any harm to the cur. The little fluff ball helped save BJ at the Morrisey Institute. Brodie intended to repay the favor. "We'd better hurry."

"I poisoned him." She stopped him at the door.

"You know damn well you didn't. You're crazy about Duke."

"I did it."

She uncurled her left fist and held it up. Three

tablets sat in the midst of the same white dust he had found in Duke's dish.

"Aspirin with codeine for my migraines. I never used them. There were only a few left in the bottle. How could they make me kill . . . ?"

A sob choked off Duke's name. Momentarily forgetting the dog's need, Brodie knocked the pills out of her hand and pulled her forward.

She came willingly, unresisting when he wrapped his arms around her and pressed her cheek against his chest. He accepted BJ's aching pain when she wound her arms about his waist and aligned her body more closely to his. He felt each sob that wracked her body. He felt her tears burning his skin.

"I tried to kill Duke."

Rage that pushed the limits of his control churned inside Brodie. Abruptly, he took her by the shoulders and pushed her away. He heard her dismayed gasp. Her fingers snatched the air, trying to return to his embrace.

He forced gentleness into his touch and cupped her face between his hands. "You aren't responsible for this."

"I had the pills in my hand."

"No!" She flinched at the undisguised fury in his voice. He brushed a curl behind her ear, and continued to stroke her temple, atoning for his harshness. BJ's hands settled at either side of his waist, steadying herself.

Brodie worked to control his anger. If he told her what he knew about Damon Morrisey, he could send BJ over the edge. How could he protect her from an enemy she refused to acknowledge? Drowning in the depths of her blue-green eyes, though, Brodie silently swore he would never hurt her with his words or his actions.

"You didn't do this. Whoever is controlling your mind is responsible for poisoning Duke, not you."

"But why would they want me to hurt him? He doesn't have anything to do with my ideas."

Panic crept back into her voice. "There was no phone call this time. How did I get programmed for this? How could they make me hurt something I love?"

He felt her desperation in her fingers digging into his skin. He stopped the madness overtaking her the only way he knew how.

Lowering his head, he closed his mouth over hers, grinding her soft lips against her teeth. The punishing assault brought a startled cry to her throat, but he paid no heed. His goal was to blot out the fear and self-doubt that transformed this smart, sassy woman into a frightened creature barely capable of standing on her own two feet.

Surprisingly, her lips parted, inviting him inside. He responded to her welcome by softening his touch. He slid his hands down to the small of her back, pulling her against him. Her fingers brushed his chest, reaching upward to anchor themselves around his neck. BJ clung like she needed a lifeline. Like she needed him. She tilted her head to the side and he angled himself above her to plunder her sweet mouth with his tongue.

Unlike the fire that had ignited between them during their previous kisses, this mating was pure and holy. A comforting contact that nurtured both their souls. Brodie savored her healing touch, and tried to give her some solace in return.

But his skills lay not in trading comforts, but in taking action. BJ would never forgive herself if Duke died. Reluctantly, Brodie withdrew. He hunched himself down to her level, and brushed the pad of his thumb over her kiss-swollen bottom lip.

"We need to get to the vet's office, darlin'. Throw on some jeans and your shoes. I'll get Duke and meet you out front."

His gentle command met with a calmer, more rational response. "I'll get your shirt and boots, too. You take care of Duke, please."

Brodie watched her disappear into the kitchen. Only moments before, in his charmed, tortured sleep, he had sat in that kitchen with her, living the sweetest dream of his life. Holding their son, loving BJ, sharing a life together.

But cruel reality had turned the exquisite vision into a nightmare, reminding him how useless it was for him to care.

With an angry shake of his head, Brodie picked up Duke. Even wrapped in the afghan, the tiny dog barely filled his hands. Duke whimpered in his unnatural sleep, reminding Brodie of the dog's mistress and her shaky trust in him.

Brodie's territory had been violated tonight. BJ and Duke weren't really his family, but he couldn't quell the fiercely protective instincts that crowded his head and put murder into his heart. He cradled the dog in his arms and headed for the garage.

"I want to see your friend. This Hawk you think can help me."

Brodie uncurled himself from one of the tiny chairs in the waiting room. BJ had stood at that window for over an hour, arms crossed in a protective hug, staring at the reds and oranges of the dawning sun.

Other than the clinical exchange she had shared with the veterinarian upon their arrival, she hadn't spoken a word. Brodie maintained a respectful distance, understanding the intensity of her sorrow, knowing exactly how it felt to be responsible for hurting someone you loved, and knowing that no words could ease the guilt that consumed all else.

She turned and faced him, tilting her chin and looking at him with a clear, steady gaze. "It's stupid to let a phobia keep me from seeking help. Especially when this is the result of my stubbornness."

He followed her gaze to the door of the emergency room where the vet and an assistant worked with Duke. "It's not stubbornness, Beej.

It's called self-preservation. After living through the childhood you described to me, you have every reason to be afraid."

She shrugged her shoulders and looked at him. "Maybe if I had gone to a psychiatrist sooner, I could have avoided this."

"A psychiatrist can't help you with what you're up against."

"Dammit, Brodie, you talk in riddles!" She thrust her fingers into her hair and shot past him, pacing the length of the room. "You know more than you're telling me. Maybe if we work together, we could figure this out. But no, you've got some old-fashioned notion that you're a knight in shining armor who has to protect me."

She planted herself in front of him, grateful and defiant at the same time. "Well you can't protect me. You've tried, and I love you for it, but you can't."

She made a fist and pounded her chest. "I need to do something. As soon as we know about Duke, I want you to take me to your friend. I'll answer his questions or get hypnotized or do whatever it is he wants."

Brodie reached for her, but she pulled away.

"I have to get this monster out of my head! You have to tell me those secrets you keep hiding."

A weight that seemed like hell settled around his shoulders. The desperate, pleading light in BJ's beautifully expressive eyes resigned him to telling the truth. But maybe he could buy a few more hours of her love. Maybe she didn't have to hate him just yet.

"I'll tell you what I know. But after you talk to Hawk."

"Why wait?" Her gaze grew skeptical.

Briefly, Brodie wished this mission was taking place even a hundred years earlier, back in a time when he could tell a woman to accept what he said without argument. But this wasn't the 1800's or the Middle Ages. This was the modern world where women spoke their minds and asked questions, where they served on the front line in the same battles a man did.

This was BJ's world, and part of what made her so special was the honesty and tenacity she wouldn't have expressed a century ago. She deserved an explanation. Maybe if the evil that stemmed from his time hadn't reached across the centuries and clutched its talons into BJ's mind, he would find it easier to respect the demands of a modern woman.

Carefully, he put together his explanation. "I'm afraid the information might upset you. I'd rather wait and tell you afterward, in case it affects Hawk's ability to help you."

"Okay." She agreed to the compromise, and something in her eyes shifted. Her resolution remained firm, but now she opened herself to her need. Her need for him.

She swayed forward and Brodie caught her, wrapping her tenderly in his embrace. "Anyone else would have put me away in an asylum by now."

"In my natural time, you would have been chained in the tower. If nobody had beheaded you yet for that smart mouth of yours."

Her laughter reverberated against his stomach. She leaned back against his arms and gave him one of those beautiful, bright smiles that made him feel human. "I'm just lucky, I guess."

The smile vanished and the mood was broken when the door swung open. "Ms. Kincaid?"

BJ clasped his hand and squeezed it tightly, waiting for the vet to speak.

"Is he okay?"

The vet's kind countenance took in both BJ and Brodie. "Fortunately, you acted quickly and kept him from going into shock. We pumped his stomach, and yes, I think he's going to be fine."

Brodie pressed her hand in return, sending up a silent thank you that fate had made a rare, favorable decision in his life.

"I want to keep him until tomorrow for observation, but I think he could use a friendly tummy rub."

"Of course."

BJ's relief was a palpable thing. When the vet held the door open for them, Brodie stayed put. "You go ahead. I don't want to get him agitated."

The door swung shut behind them, leaving Brodie alone in the waiting room. With the immediate crisis over, he turned his thoughts to other matters. Why would Damon want BJ to kill the dog? Was it simply a show of power? A reminder that he still controlled BJ's mind?

What kind of game was Damon Morrisey playing? He used BJ's skills to tap into computers undetected around the world. Her pirated ideas could make millions on either the legal or the black market. Those things made sense. The lust for power was an entity that fed upon itself. The more Damon accumulated, the more he wanted. He could control his employees, control his protégée. With BJ's technological capabilities at his command, he could spread his influence throughout the world.

But why turn BJ into a killer? Damon must have recognized Brodie immediately as his daughter's slayer, so he would have known BJ could never succeed in killing him. Yet he programmed her to try anyway. And why go after the dog?

Brodie stalked to the window, symbolically looking for some inspiring light on the subject. Duke had as much spirit as a Doberman, as much intelligence as a German shepherd. His diminuitive size did nothing to diminish his loyalty and devotion to BJ.

He remembered the first time he had met the mutt. How the tiny thing had attacked his boot and wedged himself protectively between BJ and himself. He remembered the growling and the snarling, despite BJ's assertion that he was normally a very good-natured pet.

Brodie snapped into intuitive awareness. Duke sensed that he was different. Unnatural. Immortal.

Duke would have the same reaction to Damon. And BJ just might believe the truth if Duke backed it up. Would a sorcerer as powerful as Damon Morrisey really fear that a noisy dog might give him away?

If that were true, it could only mean one thing. Damon's control was slipping. He was no longer the all-powerful sorcerer who could kill a man with a mere suggestion of thought, a flick of his hand. Damon was covering his bases. He was afraid.

He could be beaten.

Brodie bought BJ breakfast at a real sit-down restaurant, an ordeal he would not have endured a week ago. Customers stared at him, the waitresses whispered to each other behind the counter. The busboy who brought them their water spoke to BJ, but never made eye contact with him.

For once, Brodie didn't mind being a sideshow. He didn't really feel like one with BJ sitting across from him, sharing silly stories about her adventures with Duke. He could listen to that husky-honey voice for hours without tiring of it. And even if she couldn't speak, he'd still know her thoughts. Her eyes showed him everything: relief, love, anticipation, apprehension.

Julie Miller

She listened to him intently, looking beyond the scars.

She worked a miracle in that restaurant that morning, easing the tension in the people around them, allaying their fears and curiosity just by being with Brodie.

But now that they were alone again, heading across northeast Kansas on Route 36, she had grown quiet, withdrawn. He reached across the seat and captured her hand. "Sleepy?"

She offered him a reassuring smile. "Just thinking." She looked out the window again. "There's not much out here but cornfields, is there? These rolling hills seem to go on forever."

"The land is fertile," he said. "Don't be fooled by the desolation. This area is rich in history. The Pony Express came through here. This highway generally follows the Oregon Trail."

"Let me guess. You were a wagon train master in the 1880's."

Brodie shook his head. "I worked as a guard for the Overland Express Stage Company. We followed the same route to Sacramento."

BJ laughed. "You know, that is really a bizarre thing to say while you're driving a late-model, four-wheel drive with a six-cylinder engine. But I believe you."

They rode in companionable silence for several more minutes before she asked, "This Indian friend of yours, is he immortal, too?"

Brodie answered the question with the same seriousness in which it was asked. "No. He's a

Immortal Heart

friend from the Corps. First Lieutenant Echohawk. Communications and reconnaissance. I never did know his first name. We just called him Hawk."

"He probably doesn't get much business up here, does he?"

"They may be spread out, but a lot of his people live in this region of the country. There are several reservations in the area. He counsels all kinds of problems—juvenile delinquency, marriage, depression. He did a lot of work with local farmers a few years back when the agricultural industry was going broke."

Brodie paused and thought about the man he had served with. On special missions, they had depended on each other for survival. They still contacted each other from time to time, mostly to inquire about leads on Jonathan Ramsey. Yet Brodie knew very little about the man himself.

"I don't know his reasons, but I think the solitude up here suits him."

"Do you trust him?"

He felt her gaze, sensed the trepidation in her fingertips. He slowed the Explorer as they reached the outskirts of Marysville, Kansas. "In battle, I always acted as if I were mortal. I kept my head down and took the same precautions the other guys did. It made me a better soldier, I think, to pretend a bullet could take me out, too. I served with good men. I trusted them. I trust Hawk to take care of you, too."

She seemed to relax with his reassurance, but

he suspected her relief was only skin-deep. When he pulled into a parking space in front of Hawk's office, she stiffened up again. Brodie cut the engine. He leaned across the seat and caught her chin in his palm. She faced him without resistance.

"I'll be with you every step of the way," he promised.

BJ smiled crookedly. "I'm counting on it."

He kissed her briefly yet surely, liking the flush it left on her cheeks better than the pallor that had been there before.

The front door opened before they reached it.

"Brodie."

"Hawk."

Brodie shook hands and introduced BJ. The Indian was lanky and tall the way Brodie remembered, but he had let his sleek black hair grow to shoulder length. The familiar mystery still glittered in the obsidian eyes that studied BJ.

Hawk spoke to Brodie, though his gaze never left BJ. "I see the shadows in her eyes. Come in. Let's see what I can find."

He moved aside for BJ to enter first. She glanced up at Brodie, waited for his approving nod, then set her shoulders and determinedly stepped inside.

Chapter Eleven

"Are you sure hypnosis is safe?"

"This isn't true hypnosis. I just want to relax you enough to recall some hidden memories."

BJ decided that she liked Hawk, though Brodie's ready trust went a long way to dispel the anxiety building in her as the counselor asked her a series of questions regarding her episodes. His voice was soft, gentle, mesmerizing. But his words were succinct and to the point. He was kind and patient, but he didn't waste any time with common pleasantries.

Brodie hovered in the background of Hawk's office, a comfortable, masculine room replete with Native-American artwork and artifacts. Hawk sat in an easy chair draped with an Indian blanket while BJ curled in the corner of his hunter-green couch.

"I'd like you to lie down, BJ. Make yourself comfortable."

After a second's hesitation, she complied. She plumped a pillow at one end of the couch and stretched out on her back.

"Close your eyes and listen to the sound of my voice."

For several minutes, Hawk led her through relaxation techniques, mentally erasing the tension from her limbs. But as muscle after muscle of her body relaxed, her mind tightened and clouded with all the old fears.

BJ shot up to a sitting position. Her limp body struggled for balance following the abrupt movement. "I can't do this."

Hawk's dark eyes were a stark contrast to the icy familiarity of Brodie's pale gaze. Hawk's eyes were kind, but the security, the special cherishing gleam she needed was missing.

Brodie appeared instantly at Hawk's shoulder. "I'm right here, darlin'."

Hawk must have seen the connection between his guests, and smoothly altered his approach. "Brodie, sit with her."

"Will that distract her?"

"I don't think so."

BJ slowly expelled the panic she held in check. The cushions sagged beside her, taking Brodie's weight. She turned on her knees to face him. Brodie held out his hands and she took

Immortal Heart

them, adjusting her grip within his, absorbing his strength, finding her own strength in the presence of his love and support.

"Shall we try this again?"

BJ nodded, concentrating on Brodie's face. The ugly hollow beneath his cheek throbbed with the beating of a vein. His hard mouth pressed into its perpetual horizontal line. And his remarkable eyes shone with faith in her and trust in Hawk.

This time, as Hawk spoke, everything within her relaxed. Brodie's grip never slackened, his gaze never left hers. But somewhere along the line, BJ slipped away from her surroundings. She sank into something soft while the line between the outer world and her inner mind blurred and disappeared.

After several moments of fuzzy incoherence, a wall threw itself up inside her head. As solid and imposing as brick and mortar, the blank oblivion prevented her from seeing what lay on the other side.

"Must get through." She heard the voice, knew it was hers, but it came from such a distance that she knew she had left the substantive world and entered a plane of ethereal existence.

The image of a fractured lightning bolt floated past. Then again.

Bridget. It's nothing.

"No. You can't turn me away this time. I have to remember."

Physically, BJ tensed her muscles. Mentally,

she summoned her strength to push past the impenetrable wall.

"I've seen you. I know what's on the other side. I will remember."

It's nothing.

"Stop saying that! I know you're there. I'll find you."

Then BJ saw herself running. She pushed her way through hazy darkness, running on a cloud, running from the light toward the dark abyss.

It's nothing. Turn back.

BJ pushed forward, her breath coming in short, painful gasps. "Not this time."

A chink opened in the wall. Blurry halos of light flashed behind the nothingness. BJ touched the wall, wedged her fingers through the crack.

"Let me through!"

Lightning flashed, momentarily blinding her. A silvery circle floated before her eyes. *It's nothing* echoed in her ears.

"No!"

With Brodie's strength flowing through her, she wrenched the opening even wider. Light spilled through, bathing her in a new level of reality and awareness. Then she was through. With the finality of a slamming door, she was on the other side, the darkness behind her.

Gradually the light took shape and form. She watched herself from an unseen place. She sat in her office at the computer. It was late, judging by the number of lights she had turned on in the room. Duke dozed by her feet. Her fingers flew over the keyboard, programming new data.

She looked over her own shoulder at the screen, hoping to discover some truth that would help her. She noticed the shadow that fell over her from behind, but the BJ at the computer did not. Duke growled, alerting the other BJ. But it was too late. Long hair swung into her line of vision just as the rubber cudgel slammed into a precise spot at the juncture of BJ's neck and skull.

The other BJ slumped onto the keyboard. Duke leaped to her defense, but got kicked aside for his troubles. The other BJ moaned in dazed awareness as a needle pricked her arm. A black-gloved hand reached around her and dialed a number on the phone.

"She's ready."

The assailant hung up and pulled the other, reeling, BJ to a sitting position. When he was sure she'd remain upright, he pointed her face toward the computer monitor.

The data she had put there blipped to black. Then a clear screen appeared. She watched, transfixed, as the image of a lightning bolt surrounded by a silver circle appeared on the screen.

The assailant picked up Duke and tossed the snarling dog into the closet. When he returned, his face came into focus. His smiling, handsome, greedy face came into focus.

Julie Miller

Rick.

The BJ who watched the scene tried to step forward. "Why are you doing this?" she asked when her feet wouldn't move.

Rick glanced with satisfaction at the computer screen. A program of words and symbols unfolded before the staring BJ's eyes. "Why are you programming me?"

The other BJ stared, unblinking, falling under the spell. Rick punched up the other computer and sat in front of it, slipping in a diskette and typing in a set of commands. After several minutes, he shut off the machine and placed another call.

"It's done." He waited while someone spoke. "I understand."

He cradled the receiver, then crouched on the floor beside BJ. He turned her chair toward him and whispered in a condescending, menacing voice. "Bridget?"

The other BJ blinked once, then focused on Rick.

"Bridget, you will remember nothing. You will do as you are instructed and then you will forget. If you try to fight this, you will hear 'It's nothing.' And you will forget. You will forget tonight and anything else I tell you. It's nothing, Bridget."

He turned her chair back toward the computer and stood, laughing smugly behind her. "You think you're so smart. You're making this too easy, little miss brainiac. You'll pay for your

Immortal Heart

arrogance. I promise, you'll pay."

He reached past her and punched a button on the keyboard. "Good night, Bridget." He laughed. Then he disappeared before the other BJ shook herself into waking awareness.

BJ felt the same pain the other BJ felt. She rubbed at her own temple just the way the other BJ did. "I must have dozed off." She muttered in sync with the other BJ. "Man, what a headache."

Barking interrupted both BJs.

"Duke? Duke. He knows. He knows everything." BJ faded from the scene in her office.

Blackness closed upon her, rushing at her with the speed and power of a freight train. She ran wildly, trying to beat the shadow before it consumed her.

"No!" she shrieked. Tongues of evil lapped at her heels. She pushed herself harder. "Brodie!"

The shadow expanded, cutting off all the light. She didn't know where to turn. She spun frantically, lost in the vortex. An eerie chill touched her, making her jump. "Brodie!"

She started to shake, violently, back and forth. "BJ! I'm here. Come to me, darlin', come back."

Suddenly she was falling, spiralling downward through the black void.

"BJ!"

Then she slammed into consciousness, abruptly opening her eyes. Brodie hovered above her, shaking her by the shoulders.

Abruptly, gratefully, she recognized where she was. Not in the shadowy place. In the afternoon light. With Brodie.

She flung her arms around his neck. He caught her squarely against his chest, crushing her in his protective embrace.

"It was so awful," she whispered.

"I know, darlin'. We heard. We could imagine."

BJ remembered Hawk was there with them and modestly slackened her hold. But Brodie didn't release her entirely. Instead, he shifted her onto his lap, wrapping his arms loosely around her. She snuggled securely against him, glad for the shelter that kept her demons at bay.

Hawk wore a grim expression. His eyes gave her no clue to what he might be thinking.

"Was I any help?"

"Yes." His answer told her nothing.

She would have pressed him further, but a yawn forestalled her question.

"You must be exhausted." Hawk got up and crossed to his desk as though the session was over. "Rest for a while. I think you'll be able to. I have some questions for Brodie."

"But what about Rick Chambers? And the symbol I saw? The same one is on Brodie's chest."

Hawk waved aside her questions. "I want you to sleep if you can. You'll be safe here. I need you rested and rational before we can continue."

Immortal Heart

"All right." Reluctantly, she agreed. She couldn't remember the last time she had slept well for any length of time. Brodie was with her to keep her safe. Hawk sounded as if he thought he could help her.

She lay back on the sofa. Brodie tucked the Indian blanket around her and brushed a gentle kiss across her forehead.

"I'll be within shouting distance if you need me."

"Okay." Her smile encompassed Brodie and his friend. "Thanks, Hawk."

"Don't thank me yet. We'll get some coffee down the block and return within an hour. Sleep well."

BJ nodded, already drifting into sleep. Answers were within her reach now. Already she could think of one way to help herself. But exhaustion claimed her before the plan could be put into motion.

"What aren't you telling me?"

Brodie looked at his companion over the rim of his coffee mug. The man would make one hell of a cardplayer, thought Brodie. He never revealed more than he was ready to share.

Brodie set down his mug and waited for Hawk to do the same. "I know who's responsible for the brainwashing."

Hawk released a tight breath. "But you haven't told BJ."

"I don't think she'd believe me. I know she

wouldn't want to. And I can't explain it in any rational way she could understand."

"Perhaps you'd better explain to me." Hawk fingered his mug with deceptive detachment. "I sense the presence of the Dark Ones in BJ. There is evil at work here. Something not of this world."

Brodie hesitated. "You believe in such things?"

"I am a shaman. My people believe in the forces of light and darkness." Hawk rested his elbows on the table and leaned forward. "When we first met in Nam, I sensed you were an Ancient One. You transcend the parameters of normal human existence."

Brodie wasn't shocked so much as relieved at Hawk's intuition about him. He leaned back in the booth seat. Other than Jonathan and BJ, he had told no one of his immortality. Not in this century, anyway. But Hawk knew—or at least suspected.

Regaining his composure, Brodie leaned forward and matched Hawk's stance. He could speak freely now. He trusted Hawk to believe the truth.

"In 1216, I served as a knight for the villagers of Camber-on-Avon. In a revolt against a feudal lord, I inadvertently killed his only daughter. As punishment for my mistake, I was cursed by the lord.

"That sorcerer lives today," Brodie said, "And he has replaced his lost daughter with BJ."

Immortal Heart

Hawk's eyes narrowed. "Her father?"

Brodie shook his head. "Her mentor. BJ was orphaned at a young age. She's known him for thirteen years, and credits him with turning her life around, giving her purpose. She believes he loves her."

"Does he?"

"How could he? She's bright and caring and funny and generous beyond reason. But he's taking away all that in the name of vengeance or greed or . . . I don't know."

"So you believe BJ is controlled by magic, not posthypnotic suggestion?"

Brodie heaved his shoulders in a massive shrug. "I don't know. Maybe both. That injection bit she described throws me. Maybe that's how magic works in the modern world. I can't explain Rick Chambers attacking her. I told you about him. His motives hinge strictly on personal gain and professional jealousy."

"Is it possible that he's being manipulated by the sorcerer as well?"

"I thought of that. Damon certainly possesses the power to influence minds. That whole research center of his is full of automatons who have no clue about what he's doing to them."

The two men paused to sip their tepid coffee. "What do you want to do?" asked Hawk.

"I was hoping you could remove the spell from her mind."

"Under normal circumstances, it would be risky."

237

Brodie swore softly. "Then there's nothing we can do?"

"Only BJ can undo the magic that consumes her. Or the sorcerer who placed the spell." Brodie waited expectantly while Hawk deliberated. "BJ must discover the evil for herself, if she is to believe that this father figure you speak of is responsible."

"How do I help her do that?"

"Let her pursue the tangible leads. Rick Chambers. The computers he tampered with."

"How can she do the work without succumbing to any suggestions? She could forget the answer the moment she finds it."

"You'll be there. That symbol, combined with her given name are what control her. Find out how. She has a very strong determination to fight this. And she has you for an ally." Hawk's features creased into a smile. "I know I always felt safer knowing you were covering my backside."

Brodie responded with an echo of a laugh. He dug a couple of bills out of his pocket and tossed them onto the table. "Coffee's on me since you won't let me pay for your help."

"You can return the favor sometime."

"I'll do that."

Hawk stood and the two men walked side by side out of the coffee shop down the sidewalk to Hawk's office.

"Are you in danger? An old enemy is usually the toughest."

Immortal Heart

The question surprised Brodie. He assumed he'd be invincible as always. And a few more scars couldn't make any difference. After a moment's consideration, he answered. "The only way Morrisey could hurt me is through BJ."

Hawk gripped Brodie's shoulder and gave him a sympathetic squeeze. "Then, my friend, you can be devastated."

Hawk's parting wisdom haunted Brodie all the way back to BJ's house. He climbed out of the Explorer and opened the temporary gates, which repairmen had installed earlier in the day.

Devastation.

After eight hundred years of losing the people he loved, and denying his love to any who might save him, Brodie thought he might have grown immune to heartbreak. Clarinda and her sons had filled a special void in his life. He had cared deeply about Lynelle, Jane, and Zora.

But his love for BJ felt different. Destined. Somewhere in his knight's soul, he knew he had spanned the centuries searching for his true lady. The one woman to whom he would pledge honor and devotion above all others.

Bridget Jacoba Kincaid was that woman.

One small, nameless part of him was glad he had been cursed through eternity. How else would he have met his lady of the computer world? His lady of the baggy clothes masking generous curves to be revealed to him alone?

His lady of the teasing and laughter and life-affirming smile?

He gladly accepted his curse for the opportunity to know BJ Kincaid.

But what about afterward? What about when she stopped believing in him? What about when she turned away and put him out of her life for the remainder of her days?

What would happen to him then?

Devastation.

Then he truly would be cursed, living forever with the memory of what once had been his. Long after BJ was gone, he would still love her.

BJ must have sensed his mood when he shut the gates behind them and returned to the Explorer. Her chatting stopped. Her plans for running a diagnostic of LadyTech and her own private computer systems, her idea of breaking into Rick Chambers' private files, all evaporated into pensive silence.

The somber mood followed them into the house. He checked the security while she went into the kitchen to phone the vet and ask about Duke's condition. A while later, she joined him in the computer room, where he stared, immovably, at the blank screen. He would always associate technology with her. As eons passed and the status quo changed, he would think of BJ, knowing that her brilliance played a part in the evolution of technology.

"What's wrong?"

The inevitability of losing her made Brodie

interpret her innocent question with shades of despair. He turned to see her leaning against the doorjamb, her arms crossed beneath her breasts, lifting them toward him in innocent invitation. Her eyes were smoky, with flecks of blue darkening the bright green fire.

He started at the top and traced her figure with his gaze, memorizing each curl, each curve, each nuance of personality that was BJ. His body felt parched for what he could not, should not have. He slid his tongue across his dry lips. Her gaze instantly darted to the tiny gesture. The matching need that flared in her eyes washed over him like a cooling, healing caress.

He was a starving soldier, wandering through a desert without hope for eight hundred years. BJ was his fortress, the home of welcoming love and acceptance he had finally reached. But like the most inept of young knights yearning to return to safety too quickly, he led the enemy straight to her door and sealed her fate. Maybe he himself was the real enemy. For if a sorcerer's magic didn't destroy BJ Kincaid, then he most certainly would.

But knowing what could happen to BJ didn't stop the wanting. It didn't stop the need.

"I love you." He ground the words between his teeth, a raw promise of devotion.

Her chin lifted a fraction. Fear flickered through her eyes. The blunt intensity of his need consumed the room's atmosphere with a daunting force.

Throw me out, darlin'. Get me out of your life. His conscience rang inside his head but found no voice.

Just when he thought she would politely refuse him, just when he thought she would supply the conscience he lacked, trust blossomed in her eyes, replacing the shadows of fear.

"What's going to happen to us?" she asked.

He imagined the quiver in her voice revealed the same futile desire he battled to repress.

"I can't give you what you deserve, BJ. I can't promise you any tomorrows."

He held his breath while she processed his words, giving her the opportunity to turn away, but desperately wanting her to say that nothing but the two of them together mattered.

"You wake up day after day for eight hundred years, and you honestly believe there are no tomorrows?" Her eyes gleamed with a surprising look of worldly knowledge and sheer determination. "Between your experience and my ingenuity, we can make tomorrow happen."

He almost believed her. He could almost see the future through her eyes, a future filled with hope and promise. Almost.

Then she came to him, never giving him the chance to doubt what he felt in his heart. He swallowed her in his arms and pulled her up to his chest as she laced her fingers around his neck and held on. Her mouth met his halfway,

Immortal Heart

ready to welcome his tongue. Her lips moved hungrily beneath his, instinctively compensating for the stiff side of his mouth. Her sweet, sassy tongue entwined with his, making him feel like both a gifted and a giving lover.

He reached down and squeezed her bottom, pulling her higher and anchoring her against him with one hand. She wrapped her legs around his waist, fitting herself snugly against his thickening heat. The surrendering moan he elicited from her answered the victorious call deep in his own chest.

She dug her fingers into his shoulders when he tipped her back over his arm to plunder the beckoning curve of her neck. He neared the sensitive hollow at the base of her throat, felt the warmth of her pulse hammering beneath her peachy skin. He nudged apart the placket of her shirt and nuzzled even lower. When he reached the first button of resistance, he growled his frustration and shifted to take the tip of her breast into his mouth, clothes and all.

The cotton barriers of shirt and bra couldn't hide her instant reaction to his touch. Her fingers raked his shoulders, clawing for grip, scratching for balance in a world that reeled around them.

"Brodie," she gasped her need for him. She gripped him tighter with her legs, twisting her hips in search of release. The delightful friction aroused a painful need. Brodie throbbed with torturous pleasure. His legs tingled and grew weak.

He set BJ down, smothering her protest with a hard, searing kiss. While holding her prisoner with his mouth, he searched for the buttons of her shirt. The damn things proved too tiny and uncooperative, so he grabbed a handful of material and tugged. Buttons popped, cloth ripped, and without apology, he moved on to the clasp of her bra. The thread binding the hooks in place surrendered easily to the strength of his hands.

He pushed aside the offending material that kept her from him and gave up her mouth only to step back and use his gaze to caress the rose-tipped peaks that filled his hands so perfectly.

His admiration was short-lived, though. BJ drove on with reckless abandon, unbuttoning the front on his jeans and pulling down his shorts and pants, freeing him. She wrapped her fingers around him, her unabashed assault robbing him of the ability to do anything more than feel.

With rough, clumsy hands, he stripped off her shorts and panties, and retreated to the recliner, pulling BJ with him. He positioned her on top of him, with her knees bent at either side of his legs. Her gaze sought his for steadying reassurance as he reached beneath the hanging drape of her shirt and covered her breasts, holding the ripe treasures in his calloused palms.

"I'm sorry I can't make this absolutely perfect." He offered the husky apology, then watched her catch her bottom lip between her teeth as he slid his hands over the indentation of her waist and settled them on the generous flare of her hips.

Locking his eyes onto hers, he pulled her forward and down, teasing her sensitive core with the hot tip of his manhood. He felt her heaviness there, her slick, waiting readiness for him.

"Trust me," he rasped. "This will be more comfortable . . ."

With a bold advance, she slipped herself over him, leaving him senseless. She sank around him, her sweet, honeyed folds surrounding him entirely.

Brodie gritted his teeth and tried to hold back, clenching, gasping, yet straining for release.

"No. Don't stop." Brodie barely heard her, but BJ communicated in ways that didn't need words. She tightened around him and rocked her hips in sensuous rhythm, binding them together through a wild march that defied both time and an immortal enemy.

He threw his head back and closed his eyes, humbled by her symbolic acceptance, reveling in her willingness to give everything to him. He snatched at her thighs, pulling her closer, straining in counterpoint to her sensual rhythm. Brodie drove himself upward, echoing her triumphant cry as he erupted into her.

When they returned to earth, BJ collapsed

against him. He freed her legs and gathered her comfortably into his arms. She lay half on top of him, half tucked to one side. Her hand spread possessively over the middle of his chest, not put off by the scars beneath her palm. She nestled her head contentedly against his shoulder.

He loved this calm aftermath filled with serenity as much or more than the fiery passion they had shared.

"Tired?" He broke the peaceful silence, finally regaining a bit of his own strength.

"Exhausted." He felt her smiling against him. "But happy. We got kind of carried away, hmm?"

"Darlin', I'm sorry. I behaved like an animal."

She pressed her fingertips against his mouth. "Don't spoil this for me. You made me feel you needed me to make you whole. I feel that way about you. I believe anything is possible when you're with me."

He assimilated her statement. "I don't think I've ever felt emotions so powerfully as I feel them around you."

"Is that good or bad?"

Her drowsy murmur reminded him just how vulnerable BJ really was. Intelligence and determination aside, she could be hurt too easily. Her trust, rarely given, could be shattered with the flicker of a shadow or misspoken word. Brodie brushed his fingers through the curls above her ear and hugged her a little more tightly. "I don't know, darlin'. I honestly don't know."

Immortal Heart

Then, with a reverence befitting a woman of BJ's grace and generosity, Brodie stripped off the remainder of their clothes, lifted her into his arms, and carried her to her bed, where he intended to take his time showing her the depth of all he felt for her.

Sometime later, in the indefinite hours of early morning, BJ roused herself from a deep, contented sleep. She kept her eyes closed, savoring the memory of Brodie's furiously needful, then tenderly reverent lovemaking. She snuggled up to her neck beneath the top sheet and quilt, not wanting to lose the peaceful warmth that turned her muscles to mush, yet energized her with a womanly confidence.

The first chill swept over her naked skin and she snapped open her eyes, only now aware that she was completely alone.

She checked the other pillow and found it plumped and unused. It made her think Brodie had never been with her, had never cradled her tenderly in his arms, had never used his lips and hands and body to lead her slowly and completely through the most beautiful night of her life.

Had it been a dream? Had last night been a trick of her screwed-up mind? BJ rolled onto her side and pulled her legs up into a fetal position, hating the little nigglings of self-doubt creeping in to spoil her contentment.

Though inexperienced in such matters, she

felt reasonably sure that the aches in her body were real. The emotions Brodie had aroused in her were real enough. Maybe she should trust her body and heart instead of her mind.

BJ believed Brodie needed the reassurance of two hearts joining as one as much as she did. He pledged to protect her. He treated her with care and respect. He allowed her a power over him so she didn't feel frightened or intimidated by his size and appearance.

Yet forces beyond the grasp of either of them controlled their destiny. More than love was at stake in her relationship with Brodie. She finally accepted the evil curse that had dictated the choices in his life for nearly eight centuries.

BJ heard him in the kitchen making coffee. Whether or not she trusted the reality of last night's passionate affirmation of love, this morning he was avoiding her.

"Damn the man," she muttered, clutching the other pillow and hugging it against her stomach.

Brodie loved her. She knew that as surely as she knew her own love for him.

But he believed that loving her guaranteed her sure death. He could give her one beautiful night, but he refused to promise her any future beyond that.

BJ lay there in the creeping light of dawn, mulling over Brodie's fear that the people he loved would always die. She considered his declaration that the only way to release him from

Immortal Heart

immortality was for the person he loved to sacrifice herself.

How did one make such a sacrifice in the modern world? Throw herself in front of a bullet? A bullet couldn't kill Brodie. Would that really be a sacrifice?

She wanted to free him of his curse, to free him to love her without reservation. He had granted her the power, if not the permission, to do it. But how? Sorcery seemed destined to keep them as separate as night and day.

He could leave her, or she could die and leave him. Was that really a choice?

Either way, the only victor would be the evil that wanted them apart.

Chapter Twelve

"We've got work to do."

BJ tried to sound more confident than she felt. The resolution that had carried her through an awkwardly silent breakfast and drive into the city started to fail her when they walked through the doors at LadyTech.

Brodie seemed relieved that she hadn't pushed any kind of closeness or heart-to-heart talk that morning. But she also sensed the concern in him. The distance she had placed between them was respectful, not cold. But distance was unnatural for her. Even against a threat such as Brodie imagined himself to be, she had never kept her distance.

But for Brodie's sake, she would do it. Despite the protests of her heart, despite the hope that cried out against logic, she would remove the personal overtones from their relationship. She'd make them boss and bodyguard once again—even if it killed her.

Today, she didn't find the play on words all that amusing.

"You track down Rick. Keep him occupied for about an hour. I want to dig into his files and see what I can find."

Brodie grasped her elbow, then pulled his hand away as though he regretted touching her. Not wanting him to feel the sting of a rejection that didn't exist, BJ stopped and looked up at him.

"Will you be all right?" That sinfully sexy voice rumbled with concern from the depths of his chest.

BJ reassured him with a smile. "I'll let Emma know what we're up to. She can keep an eye on me.

"Rick's generally in the warehouse playing a pick-up game of basketball this time of morning."

"I'll find him."

Brodie nodded curtly, then turned and strode through the station carrels toward the warehouse door. BJ watched him over the tops of the movable walls, already missing the strength of his broad shoulders. With his regal bearing and easy gait, he must have been quite a dashing member of some king's court all those years ago, before scars and time and heartache had taken their toll on his body and soul.

Would he have loved her if they had met in the thirteenth century? Would he even have noticed her? BJ considered the man beneath the harsh exterior. Honesty, loyalty, and a sense of right and wrong etched on his very heart made up the true man. Sir Brodie Maxwell might not have paid Bridget Kincaid any heed back then. But if she needed his help, if she asked him to protect her—in the Middle Ages or on the eve of the twenty-first century—she knew he would sacrifice his love, his honor, even his life, to keep her safe.

Could she be brave enough to do the same for him?

Only after the door closed behind Brodie did she dash up the grand staircase and head toward the executive offices.

"I can't wait to string him up myself." Emma paced inside the door, maintaining a lookout position while BJ investigated the files Rick had buried deeply within LadyTech's computer system.

"Subliminal suggestion." Shock blended with stunned fury when BJ hit paydirt and broke the code that let her into Rick's files.

"What are you talking about?" Emma stopped her pacing.

"Just a minute. Let me isolate the screen." When BJ found the picture she wanted, she

Immortal Heart

froze the image on the monitor. "Tell me you see that, too."

Emma stood behind BJ and looked over her shoulder. "It's a lightning bolt inside a circle."

BJ leaned back, knowing profound relief. "This is the symbol that triggers the episodes."

She pounded her fist on her desktop, scattering several teddy bears onto the floor. "Damn! He's been controlling me over the computer lines. This is my forte, and I didn't even see it. He's got to be tapped in at home, too. He talks to me or calls me, and programs me like my own damn computers."

Emma gave her a consoling smile. "Hang in there. You have to stay calm and rational to beat this."

"You're right." Frustration churned in BJ's stomach. "I just want to know why. What did I ever do to Rick?"

Emma remained calm. "Probably nothing. Greed and jealousy feed upon themselves. Maybe he had this planned from the moment he joined the company."

BJ sighed. "You know, he's a clever enough technician, but I never thought he was innovative enough to come up with a scheme like this all on his own."

"Forget him for now. Did you find the files I mentioned?"

"Yes." BJ cleared the screen and called up the sequence of hidden files she had uncovered. "He's tapped in to Takahashi, all right. And the

Swiss bank account. And some place in the Cayman Islands. I think I can disengage the connections without calling attention to LadyTech. That is, if I can find them all."

The lines scrolled by with ominous abundance. Then a name caught her eye that made BJ lean forward and type in a quick series of commands.

"Oh my God."

Shadowy memories fluttered across BJ's consciousness, teasing her memory, but vanishing before she could latch on to them and understand.

"What is it?" Emma's concern matched BJ's.

"He's tapped into the Morrisey Institute." BJ glanced up at Emma. "There's an open net between LadyTech and Damon's lab."

"Is he stealing data from Morrisey Labs, too?"

"No." BJ paused, trying to make sense of the implication on the screen. "He's transmitting our stuff over there."

"A mole? Rick Chambers is a mole for the Morrisey Institute? They're a research institution, we produce market-ready products. What's the connection?"

BJ frowned with skepticism, too, though not for the same reason. "Somebody who works for Damon must be in on this, too. The feed for the subliminal symbols comes directly from the Morrisey labs."

Brodie's blatant, mutual dislike and distrust of Damon immediately crowded her thoughts.

Immortal Heart

But Damon would never do anything to hurt her. Even if his attempts were occasionally misguided, he'd always taken care of her. He'd always loved her.

Still, she felt compelled to say it out loud. "Damon wouldn't do this to me."

Emma squeezed BJ's shoulder. "Of course not. But maybe Damon can help us out from his end, since you know what to look for now."

"Right." BJ started for the phone, but never reached it. A knock at the door indicated her hour was up. Brodie had returned.

She stood to face her enemy while Emma crossed to the door and opened it.

Rick stood in the doorway, his retreat effectively blocked by Brodie's imposing presence behind him. Rick fell back on the abrasive bravado that had won him few friends in the past. He stepped inside, pointing a finger at Emma. "I want you to arrest this man for harassment.

"You're fired." Emma smiled smugly at Rick's open-mouthed reaction. Then she winked over her shoulder at BJ. "I'll let you and Brodie handle it from here."

Rick gaped stupidly at Emma when she walked past him, out of the office. BJ almost pitied the man when Brodie ushered him inside and shut the door. Rick looked different from his usual, immaculate self. Sweat beaded his forehead and hairline. Damp, wrinkled workout clothes clung to his skin. His hair hung

255

loosely over his shoulders, falling out of its usual ponytail.

"I want my lawyer."

"That's not an option." When Brodie spoke, Rick jumped closer to BJ. Not that he'd find an ally in her, but she couldn't blame him for being intimidated.

"I found your files, Rick. What you're doing is illegal. LadyTech won't be a party to it." She watched him struggle to regain some of his composure.

Gloating triumph lit inside her, feeling unnatural, but she seized upon the strength it gave her. "I also had an interesting bit of memory recall yesterday."

Rick's eyes blazed darkly.

"I remember you attacking me and shooting me full of something. I remember you planting the trigger to a posthypnotic suggestion."

Found out, Rick's face turned a variety of colors as he worked through his emotions, pale white, sickly green, angry red, then finally a challenging flush of pink. He crossed his arms in a pose of cocky confidence. "So what are you going to do about it? Arrest me? Worry the rest of your life that I can punch a button anywhere in the world and tap into your head?"

BJ felt the first waver in her own confidence. Rick seized the weakness and stepped toward her, but was stopped by Brodie's hand on his shoulder. Rick smiled and acquiesced. Brodie released him.

Immortal Heart

"Prisons have computers, too. I can control that arrogant brain of yours anywhere, anytime I want."

"I can erase your programs, Rick."

He laughed, a sick, disgusting sound. "They're your programs, Beej. You're the one who cracked the security lockout in Washington. You're the one who reorganized the accounts in Bern. I'm just a guy a little smarter than you who can make you do whatever I please."

BJ hugged herself, fighting the urge to crumple into her chair. She looked beyond Rick to Brodie. The vein that betrayed his intense emotions throbbed beneath his scarred cheek. He was holding back, allowing her to control this confrontation. His silent support gave her the strength to continue.

"I'm cognizant now. I know how you're doing this. I can fight it."

"Can you?" Rick glanced at Brodie, then moved past BJ to a neutral corner of the office. She turned, not willing to leave her back exposed to him. "I want you to guarantee me there will be no criminal prosecution. And I want that position in Tokyo."

He smiled at her, rubbing his hands together. "Or I'll never release you from the mind control."

The floor spun beneath her feet and rushed up to greet her. But she fell against the sturdy wall of Brodie, who gripped her by the arms and supported her until she could think clearly again.

"Shut up, Chambers." She had never heard Brodie sound so menacing before. Even she trembled within his gentle hands. "You're not controlling her. You're as much a victim of this game as she is."

"I'm no victim," Rick countered. "None of you will believe that I'm the genius here, not little miss brainiac."

"Where did you learn about posthypnotic suggestion? You're trained in computers, not psychiatry. Think, Chambers."

Brodie's muscles bunched in controlled fury behind BJ. Rick looked shaken. BJ's thoughts whirled in confusion.

Brodie charged ahead, relentlessly. "You don't remember where you learned it, do you? Because you didn't. You're nothing more than a pawn in a cruel, sadistic game, being manipulated just as completely as BJ."

"You don't know what you're talking about."

"*You* don't know what you're talking about." Brodie released BJ and stalked toward Rick. Rick fell back a step. "You're being used by a sorcerer who's put you under a spell. He can control people's minds with a flick of his wrist and a whim. He's using you."

"Who is he?" BJ's question drowned out Rick's. "Brodie, what are you talking about? I remember what happened."

Brodie turned and looked down at her, his

Immortal Heart

eyes bristled with such pain that BJ went to him. But he pulled his arm away at her touch.

"Do you remember what happened two days ago when you saw Morrisey?"

BJ admitted a surprisingly vague recollection. "I talked with him most of the morning. He brought in some experts to interview me."

"After that. Do you remember?"

The look he gave her was so pointed and forceful that she felt compelled to lower her gaze. For Brodie's sake, she tried to remember the details. But the harder she concentrated, the more elusive the memory became. She remembered going down to the interview room. She remembered Damon nixing her protests. She remembered . . .

Nothing. Her recollection of that day ended with Damon tapping her on the nose, or some such silly, loving gesture. She couldn't recall a single question the so-called experts had asked her.

What she did recall was a sensation of panic, of hopelessness and fear. What she couldn't remember was why.

"Do you remember my carrying you out of there?"

Brodie seemed so angry with her. Or was the anger directed at himself? Or at Rick?

"I don't remember leaving."

"Because he cast a spell over you."

"Rick?"

"No, dammit!" Brodie's voice rattled the furniture. "This won't stop when you put Chambers away! This will go on forever until you confront him!"

"Who?" His unfair attack sparked her own anger.

Brodie suddenly hunched his shoulders and lowered his voice, making himself smaller, trying hard not to scare her. "I didn't want to tell you. I don't want to hurt you."

BJ waited with a sinking heart. "Who do you think is behind this?"

"Damon Morrisey."

The name hung in the air while BJ processed it. Facts jumbled like pieces of an unworkable jigsaw puzzle in her head. The glimmer of understanding that toyed with her got pushed aside by her denial of the one thing in this world she could not accept.

"Damon?"

"He's a fellow immortal. He's using sorcery, not science, to control you."

"Damon?" BJ repeated dumbly.

Rick's laughter bounced through the room. "This is my scheme. I don't know how thoughts get through that muscle inside your head, Maxwell, but this one's obviously out of left field."

BJ heard the insult, but didn't respond to it. She was too caught up in the turbulent plea for forgiveness etched in Brodie's grim features.

Rick walked right past them to the door, unimpeded. "I planned all this. You can attribute it to my brilliance, not hocus-pocus. My pass-

Immortal Heart

port is in order. Let me know when to pack my bags, Beej."

When he left, BJ had no clue. The shock finally eroded and emotional self-preservation galvanized her. She put the distance of the room between them before facing Brodie. "Rick Chambers is behind this, not Damon. Just because you hate the man—"

"The man isn't human. He's a sorcerer. He's the same damn sorcerer who did this to me!" He took a step forward but halted when BJ threw up her hands and retreated. "I knew him the moment I saw his eyes. You never forget the eyes of a man who has no conscience, a man who kills for sport and uses people because it feeds a sick need for power and control."

"You're crazy. I thought I was messed up, but you're crazy."

His cheek throbbed with some emotion so powerful that it scared her. For the first time since she had grabbed his foot and looked up at his towering figure, he truly frightened her.

"I'm not crazy. I'm cursed. And the bastard who did this to me is using you to replace the daughter I killed."

BJ circled toward the door, knowing it was a useless gesture to try and run from Brodie. But she seized upon the false security the outlet gave her.

"It doesn't make sense, Brodie. I might buy that you're eight hundred years old, but not Damon. If he is a sorcerer, he can't be the one you talk about. There's no logic to it." She grasped at a slim thread of reasoning. "He would know that my death could free you of the curse. But if he's the one tapped into my brain, he wouldn't want me dead. I'm too valuable a tool. You just said he thought I was his daughter. It doesn't make sense."

"He's insane, BJ. Logic doesn't apply here. He didn't count on me being hired to help you."

BJ stared at Brodie. She just stared while she battled the emotions threatening to drive her mad. Bewildering hurt. Defensive anger. Impossible love. Betrayal.

But who had betrayed her? Brodie? Damon? Everyone?

A morbid calm washed over her. "If Damon really is a sorcerer, then you're the one using me."

"No." He jerked as if she had slapped him.

BJ jammed her hands into the pockets of her shorts. Her emotions skittered in wild disarray, but her mind stayed lucidly sharp. "Yes. You're the one looking for vengeance. You're just like all the others who see me as an opportunity. You're using me to get to him."

"I love you."

She shook her head. "Damon raised me. I was a freak, an oddity. He turned me into a human being. He accepted me for what I am. He's my family."

"Emma and Jasmine are your family. They're the ones who truly care about you. Believe me, darlin', he has groomed you for this mental takeover from the moment he met you."

"This is the little secret you wouldn't tell me, right? I finally figured you out, big guy." Resolutely, she walked toward him, knowing her accusations hurt him as he had hurt her.

"If Damon really is your enemy," said BJ, "then why didn't you just get rid of him when you found out who he was? Don't you immortals chop off each other's heads and gain some incredible power?"

"He can only die by his own hand. Unless he's responsible for his own death, a suicide, or he gets caught in his own trap, he'll be seeking power and vengeance throughout eternity."

BJ laughed. The crazy sound came out of her throat, but it didn't sound like her own voice. "You know, you had me believing you were immortal. I was even trying to figure out how I could release you, how I could make a sacrifice and save you. But I don't have to worry about that. You're insane. I finally fall in love with a man I think understands me and I find out he's insane."

Brodie grabbed her, hauling her off the floor up against his chest, pinning her with hands that bit painfully into her arms. "Dammit, BJ, listen to me. I have never lied to you. I give you my word that what I'm saying is true."

"Your word means nothing to me." Now, she could see the monster others saw. The beautiful eyes were a lie. They weren't windows into a tortured man's soul. They were icy barriers that hid the truth. "Damon is no sorcerer. I'll prove you wrong. And then I want you out of my life."

After a moment of pained disbelief, Brodie dropped her. She recovered her balance with as much dignity as she could muster and walked to the door.

BJ closed it behind her and nearly fainted as shock caught up with her. She could commit Brodie to an institution. She should probably commit herself.

She staggered down the hallway, bearing the weight of a pain that consumed her thoughts as completely as the mind control had. Brodie had to be wrong. He just had to be.

How could he claim to love her? How could he make her love him, and then tell her such outrageous lies? She should hate him for betraying her so, for attacking the stable foundation of her life. She should hate him with the same intensity with which she loved him. She had risked her trust. Shared her secrets. Given her heart and body to the strange giant with the distorted features and ravaged soul.

She should hate him. But she didn't. She couldn't.

She might be able to get Brodie Maxwell out of her life. But she could never get him out of her heart.

Chapter Thirteen

BJ moved through the remainder of the afternoon in a haze of pain and confusion. Brodie hovered at a protective distance, close enough to keep an eye on her, never close enough to touch her. He limited their conversation to perfunctory statements regarding where he could find her next if he needed to step out of the room.

She had hurt him badly. She could tell by the invisible barrier he erected around himself. He stood cold and aloof, his eyes always watching, yet revealing nothing.

BJ felt small and insignificant, even at this distance, truly a powerless pawn in a madman's cruel game. But who exactly was the madman here? Her heart screamed at her to believe in

Brodie, who had comforted her, rescued her, taught her to love. But logic would not allow it.

She wanted Rick Chambers to be the only choice, not just the obvious one. Brodie claimed Damon was responsible. But she refused to accept the idea that the man she loved like a father, the man who had nurtured her so she could get out of a laboratory and into the real world, could have used her to further his own interests for thirteen years.

BJ numbed herself to the pain and concentrated her energies on purging Rick's files from LadyTech's systems. Emma stopped in on her way to pick up her daughter at the sitter's. The strain between BJ and Brodie was painfully evident, judging by Emma's worried frown. When Emma broached the subject, BJ politely excused herself on the pretext of going to dinner.

Normally, BJ didn't avoid her friends. But now she was holding herself together with a tiny little thread. Discussing Brodie or Damon would force her to feel again. And feeling seemed to get her into a lot of trouble. Feeling worked against her ability to see things clearly and to choose wisely where to put her trust.

BJ's reprieve from the pain was short-lived. She escaped Emma's questions only to run into Brodie, himself, in the break room, sipping a paper cup of steaming coffee. By this time of day, the brew from the break room usually resembled primordial goo. But Brodie drank it down, unmindful of how it must burn his

Immortal Heart

tongue and eat away at his insides.

BJ's first impulse was to invite him to join her for dinner and a fresh cup of coffee. He didn't take care of himself properly because he didn't think it made any difference. That was wrong. BJ started to tell him so, but caught the words on the end of her tongue. It shouldn't matter how Brodie took care of himself, not to her, anyway.

"I've purged all of Rick's files," she said instead, struggling against the urge to bolt from the room. She spoke to one of the scars showing above the neckline of his shirt, not feeling brave enough to look Brodie in the eye. "I want to check my home files, too. I'm going to grab a candy bar to keep Emma happy. You can meet me outside and drive me home."

"Fine." A single word. A simple agreement. Yet the rich, rumbling tone spoke volumes. He missed her already. They stood three feet apart, but the distance between them remained unbreachable. BJ lifted her gaze to his, in time to see the icy shutters close down over the turbulent pain that must be reflected in her own eyes.

She missed him, too, but she could conceive of no way to allow him back into her life.

"I'll meet you in the parking lot in about five minutes," she said. She turned from his responding nod, fished some change out of her pocket, and selected the first candy bar she saw out of the vending machine. Without looking back, she left.

Julie Miller

She could be making a huge mistake, alienating Brodie like this. But she shared too much history with Damon, and only a few days with Brodie. Logic dictated that she trust the former, not the latter.

Logic and brainpower had made pretty lonely companions for BJ throughout her life. Emma and Jas opened her to the possibilities of true friendship. Brodie had opened her to the possibilities of love. But the curse of genius still ruled her life. Her innate abilities had been the one constant that endured from the time of Jake's death to the present. Her IQ remained her best reliable hope for the future. It was too hard for her to take that leap of faith and trust her heart instead of her head.

Forcing her mind back to the business at hand kept the indecision at bay. She'd check her system at home for signs of tampering, and then, as her last task, she'd go over to Damon's and tell him the truth about Rick.

As BJ mentally ticked off the list of things she needed to do, another thought came to mind. She had cleaned up LadyTech's main system, but Rick could easily have rigged an independent system with more illegal transmissions of her programs. BJ would have to deactivate those as well, and the most likely place for Rick to set up such a system was in his private office.

Changing directions, she went back down the hallway to the junior executive wing and knocked on Rick's door. No one answered, so

Immortal Heart

she quietly opened the door and stepped inside.

Rick's ultramodern glass and chrome designed office would be spotless, with every piece of furniture arranged just so. She didn't turn on the overhead light. Instead, she crossed to the desk, and flipped the switch on the lamp there.

Light flooded the room. BJ jumped back with a gasp, covering her fluttering heart with her hand. She wasn't alone. "Dammit, Rick, you scared the hell out of me! Why didn't you answer when I knocked?"

BJ's question faded into silence. She could tell from Rick's stark, staring eyes that he hadn't heard her knock.

She circled the desk and slowly, reluctantly, touched two fingers to the base of his neck. She shivered at the sensation of cool, damp clay, and hugged herself tightly. Not since saying good-bye to her father had she seen a dead man. From the open gape of his mouth to the horrific look in his eyes, Rick looked as though he had died right in the middle of a scream, that fear, itself, had killed him.

She saw that Rick's computer was on. No scrolling data, no words, no program. Just a single picture on the monitor. She stared at the screen with the same intensity that Rick must have just before he died.

The cursor blinked in the bottom left corner, at the lower tip of a lightning bolt encircled by a silver band.

Bile burned in BJ's throat as she backed

away. One thought crowded her mind. She wanted Brodie. Despite all that had happened, her first instinct was to turn to him for safety.

She backed to the door, putting the desk between her and Rick's body when she heard the door click shut behind her. Tough, sinewy arms closed around her before she could turn, and a leather-gloved hand clamped over her mouth, muffling her scream.

She twisted and tried to bite her way to freedom, recognizing familiar scents of hair tonic and cologne. The arms jerked her off her feet, tightening like a vise and strangling the breath in her chest.

Smooth, cool lips teased the back of her ear. "Bridget. It's nothing."

BJ screamed against the leather, turning dizzy from her effort. Or maybe the stealth of shadows creeping in made her light-headed. Tears stung her eyes. She squeezed them shut and hot trails ran down her cheeks.

The darkness rushed in, crowding out coherent thought. Where was Brodie? What had she done? What terrible mistake had she made?

Her muscles turned to gelatin while her mind struggled to break free.

"Come with me quietly. No one knows I'm here. Drive me to the lab. I can help you forget all this. I can bring you peace again. Trust me."

No! I trust Brodie!

Help her forget. BJ's head lolled to one side, too groggy to support. She wanted to forget. No, wait. She had to remember. Rick, dead. Brodie, right. Damon, responsible.

Damon.

She fought her way back toward consciousness.

"Bridget. It's nothing."

Blackness consumed her and she knew no more.

Brodie's internal radar alerted him even before the passage of time made him wary. BJ was gone. Damon had her.

He slammed through the offices upstairs, searching for her, knowing where she was, but hoping . . .

At the end of the hall he found Rick Chambers's body. Out of a sense of duty, he checked for a pulse, confirming what he already knew. There were no marks on the man, no sign of a struggle. Just fear. A terror so intense, it killed a man—from the inside out.

He remembered the peasants who had died beside him in Damon's dungeon. Terror had killed them. Damon planted the thought, twisted his ring, and the men died.

With the same compassion that had allied him with those peasants, Damon closed Rick's eyes. He might hate the man for his part in hurting BJ. But no one, not a misguided peasant who threatened murder, nor a greedy technician who stole BJ's ideas, deserved to die so horribly. So helplessly.

No one deserved a sorcerer's vengeance.

Brodie felt for his dagger at the back of his belt. He didn't know what he could do to fight the black magic, but there had to be a way. One way or another he'd free BJ. One way or another.

When he climbed into his Explorer and drove toward the Morrisey Institute, he knew that it was the beginning of the final, most important battle of his immortal life.

"You killed Rick."

BJ's voice filled with accusation. It was the only mode of attack open to her. Damon had muttered something and flashed his ring, binding her to the chair as securely as a set of ropes and handcuffs.

Yet for some reason, he had freed her mind of the shadows. He wanted her to hear this. He wanted her to know how utterly under his spell she had been. And how helpless she would be to escape from his control again.

When Damon laughed, she heard a hollow, ancient sound she had never noticed before. The evil in it chilled her to the bone.

Brodie had been right. Damon was insane. The rules of logic she had clung to so desperately wouldn't help her. So while Damon talked, she listened with half an ear. She pretended rapt attention while she turned her brain to more abstract thought. She sized up each piece of equipment in the lab, the empty cubicles, the power grid, the death chambers.

And she watched Damon. She watched his curious movements as he worked on a computer. She watched the eerie fire that gleamed in his black eyes.

"Chambers served his purpose. But he got greedy. Careless. He thought he could learn from a master. He was a fool, an easy, gullible fool. I needed someone to give me access to you without arousing your partners' suspicions. He tried taking things into his own hands. I knew Brodie Maxwell wasn't a threat, but Chambers got scared. He thought he could persuade you to kill him. Imagine, trying to murder an immortal."

He clicked his tongue and looked at BJ with the once familiar, indulgent smile that now looked condescending and controlling. "He betrayed me."

Damon walked around the console to where BJ sat. With gentle, creepy, fatherlike fingers, he caressed her cheek. BJ steeled herself and tried not to flinch. She didn't want to inflame the unnatural light in his eyes. But when he touched her again, she jerked her head to the side.

He grabbed her chin and forced it upward, twisting her neck at a sharp angle. "You betrayed me."

He released her with the same violence with which he had gripped her, then he returned to the console and began typing again. BJ worked her jaw back and forth, wishing she could use her hands to massage away the cramp in her neck.

This was not her Damon. This was Brodie's sorcerer. BJ tried to formulate some plan of escape. But what did she know about magic? How could she pit her skills against Damon's? She had no other option than to try.

She clenched her throat muscles to keep the quavering fear out of her voice. "How did I betray you?"

Damon looked at her. "You left me."

He straightened and threw his hands out to either side, indicating the vast complex surrounding them. "I gave you everything." His hands dropped to his sides. "And you left me."

"I wanted to start my own company. I never abandoned you. I always thought of you as the father I had lost." She shrugged her shoulders. "Jas and Emma provided me with the opportunity to grow up and branch out on my own."

"No, no, no!" He shook his index finger at her as if she were a confused child. "I gave you every opportunity you needed."

He pulled the chair from behind the console and dragged it over so he could sit right in front of BJ, facing her, his knees touching hers. BJ's leg wouldn't respond to her desire to break the contact.

"You were nothing when I discovered you." She tried to look meek, nonthreatening. But she didn't allow herself to look away. "You were floundering in a graduate program, confined by the strictures of academia. I saw the potential in you. I gave you an outlet for your creativity. I set you free."

"I'll always be grateful for what you did for me."

"You have an odd way of showing your gratitude."

A protesting bite worked its way into her voice. "I never left you. I left my job at the Institute. I still—"

He cut off the rest of her words with a wave of his hand. BJ tried to speak, but she could only make a gurgling sound in her throat.

"Combining my power to control minds with your power to design and manipulate artificial intelligence made us an unbeatable pair. With you to channel my power, I could influence companies, countries, maybe the entire planet."

His skin turned gray, his eyes swallowed the light. BJ sank back in her chair.

"Since you would not stay and join forces willingly, I ensured your cooperation by other means."

He stared at her, accusing her of terrible crimes with his eyes. BJ had no choice but to sit there and absorb the invisible assault. Her soul ruptured, spilling out every fond memory of their past together.

It had all been a lie. Everything that had grounded her, everything that had given her hope and comfort, had been a lie.

When Damon got up and returned to his work, BJ's throat unknotted. She could speak again.

"You never loved me." He didn't respond. "You were a father to me. I was an—opportunity—to you."

Damon smiled at something on his computer screen. "And you will be again."

He walked over to BJ, grabbed her by the upper arm and drew her to her feet. Somehow, her inert body responded to his touch. "How?"

Ego blended with the madness in Damon's eyes. He waved his hand in front of her face with all the flourish of a practiced illusionist. A stripe of silver flashed before her eyes.

"Your ring."

Keeping his hand in front of her face, he slowly turned his knuckles toward her until she could see the round face of the signet ring on his third finger. Hammered out of an ancient silvery metal, the icon mocked her. The jagged slash of a lightning bolt, encircled in silver, glowed on his finger with a greenish, unearthly light.

"And with this ring," he paused to let the traditional words of bonding sink in, "you will be mine forever. I will make you be like me."

She jerked her chin up. "Immortal?"

She thought of Brodie. Of his ugly exterior, hideous reminders of endless torture and suffering. She remembered his eyes, icy gray shutters that tried to shield the outside world from the horrors of his immortal existence. She thought of his love, and how he had sacrificed his own happiness to protect her from the endless pain that followed him through eternity.

"You can't," she said, remembering Brodie gave her the strength to fight. "I don't want your curse. I'd rather die now than live forever as a pawn in your world."

His fingers tightened on her arm until she cried out in pain. "I'm not giving you a choice."

He dragged her over to the console and showed her the screen. BJ read the data and blanched, already suspecting his plan.

"I've programmed a series of explosions that will throw the power grid off line, forcing a meltdown of the Institute's nuclear reactor. We'll perish in the unfortunate incident, and be reborn somewhere else."

"What about the people who work here?! And everyone else who'll die? You'd kill innocent people just to get me back?"

He looked at her with a resolve that told her her concerns were inconsequential. "He took you from me once. I won't let him take you again."

With an insight that rocked her to the core, BJ finally, fully accepted every word Brodie had told her as the truth. Damon was pure evil, without conscience, without any value for human life.

She might well be one of the smartest people

in the world, but she had spent most of her life living like a fool.

"Brodie will come after me. He'll know that I'm alive. He won't let you get away with this."

Damon smiled, a cruel, demonic slash across his features. "I've kept Sir Brodie Maxwell in his place for eight hundred years. He'll never defeat me."

Damon jerked her arm, dragging her toward a rear exit. BJ kicked at his legs, tried to claw at his skin. But he quickly subdued her attacking limbs by snapping his fingers. While her mind reeled in protest, her body dutifully fell in step beside him.

Glass shattered and wood splintered in a furious, thunderous maelstrom behind them. BJ thought the first explosion must have gone off. But Damon whirled around, more surprised than she.

"Let her go, sorcerer!"

That blessed voice, deep and rumbling and full of rage told her that her knight in battered armor had found her. She couldn't turn, but she could well imagine the size and breadth and sheer intimidation of the unleashed warrior.

"Be gone, Maxwell" Damon thrust out his hand. BJ heard a crash. But at the same moment Brodie distracted Damon, sensation returned to her arms and legs. With Damon's focus turned aside, she was in control of herself again.

In a free-fall of renewed vigor, BJ reached for

the first object she could find. A clay pot filled with fake flowers, which someone had used to try and bring life to this sterile building. With all the force she could muster, she hurled the pot at Damon's back. The projectile glanced off his shoulder, doing nothing more than shift his attention back to her.

He turned, arcing his arm in a vicious swing. He never touched her, but a blow rang through BJ's skull and knocked her to the floor. She clutched at her temples, shaking her head and fighting dizziness.

When he turned his attention to her, Brodie hauled himself off the floor and charged Damon. Damon thrust out his hand and muttered. Brodie left his feet and went flying into a computer terminal, crashing with the equipment onto the floor, shattering glass and creating sparks with the discharge of electricity.

One at a time. He can only control us one at a time.

She pushed to her knees and then her feet. "Get his ring, Brodie! If we work together, we can get his ring!"

When she spoke, she succeeded in capturing Damon's attention. She backed away with every step he stalked toward her. "You fool. I can give you everything. We belong together. Forever. Our destiny is together."

BJ backed into the fire door, shaking her head in denial as he advanced upon her. "I don't want what you're offering me. I never cared about anything like that. I only wanted you to love me."

"I do, Arabella. You're everything to me. You're my future."

"Arabella?"

A massive shape loomed behind Damon. Brodie's arm snaked around his neck, cutting off Damon's windpipe.

"She's not your daughter, sorcerer! She's an innocent woman. You've killed enough innocent people!"

As Brodie twisted Damon backward, BJ lunged for Damon's hand. Her fingertips brushed across cold metal, but he jerked his fist into the air, eluding her. At the same time, he uttered a foreign word.

A shockwave drove the three of them to the floor as the ceiling blasted into a million pieces and buried them with debris from the floor above. BJ saw part of the upper floor collapse on the two men, crushing them.

Closer to the wall, fragments of ceiling tile and flooring showered over her, but she was protected from the heavier beams and machinery that crashed down on top of the two men. Rational thought flowed through her with cunning clarity.

Pushing first with her shoulder, then using her foot, she dislodged the bar across the fire door and kicked it open. The building automatically responded with the blaring repetition of a fire alarm. Sprinklers turned on overhead, dousing the sparking machine Brodie had broken and setting up an electrical charge that could blow out the rest of the equipment.

BJ climbed over the mountain of wreckage to the computer terminal Damon had used earlier. Quickly, she accessed the power grid and shut down the surrounding equipment. A flash of insight, a half-formed strategy, led her to type in a second command. One that transferred this console to auxiliary power, keeping it on-line, but free of any subsequent damage that the systems could incur.

Then she climbed back into the debris, pushing over a filing cabinet, knocking aside a broken monitor. She fell to her knees and started digging. When she reached the floor, she found what she was looking for.

Damon's still, dust-shrouded hand protruded from beneath a pile of ceiling beams and wires. BJ lifted the third finger and twisted the ring off. It caught once on the first joint, but with an insistent tug and a heartfelt prayer, it slipped off.

The evil circle burned in the palm of her hand, but the first glimmer of victory coursed through BJ. For the first time in months, or was it years?, BJ sensed the shadows fleeing from her mind. A weight lifted from her as the light rushed in, bathing the darkest corners of her consciousness with sunny understanding.

BJ savored her freedom all too briefly. While she knelt there, ignoring the inevitable, the deathly hand came back to life. BJ recognized the danger too late.

Damon's hand snatched her wrist, gripping with an intensity that could snap her bones.

She screamed a second time when the rubble rose before her like a mountain forming in the dawn before time. Equipment, steel, and concrete fell by the wayside as Brodie emerged from the mountain, still clutching Damon by the neck and dragging the sorcerer to his feet.

BJ scrambled to safety as the two immortals resumed their struggle. Brodie, bigger and angrier, had the advantage of size and strength. But Damon was clever and quick. They each took their blows, staggered by injuries that would kill a mortal man. Explosions rocked a distant point of the complex. And still they fought.

Unable to help Brodie, BJ returned to the computer console and accessed the nuclear reactor. She breathed again when she saw that it was still intact. She pulled up the sequence that would start it on its timed shutdown. Maybe she couldn't do more here, but she could help save other innocent people. She could take that responsibility off Brodie's conscience, and hers.

A metallic crash and a crushing "oomph" sounded behind her. She turned to see Brodie stumbling toward her. He cried out hoarsely, "Give me the ring."

She tried to catch him as he fell forward, but his weight carried them both to the floor. His shoulder was bleeding, and she could see a new cut above his eye. "Oh, God, Brodie."

She touched his face, caressed his wounded shoulder, unable to speak, but communicating her love and concern.

Brodie kissed her on the forehead, understanding and returning her message to him. He pushed himself off her and repeated, "Give me the ring."

BJ unclenched her fist and dropped Damon's ring into his palm. Then he closed his other massive hand over it and began to squeeze. BJ watched the incredible strength crushing, twisting. A vein popped out in his cheek as he poured every bit of strength he possessed into his hands. A silvery light glowed through his fingers, increasing in intensity, trying to break out of his grip.

A flash of movement behind Brodie caught BJ's eye. A bruised arm with the shreds of a silk shirt hanging from it emerged from beneath a twisted I-beam.

"Brodie." She tried to warn him.

Damon rose like a phoenix from the ashes, his face battered and bloodied.

Brodie ignored her repeated warning as Damon limped closer. He concentrated fully on squeezing the life out of the object in his hands. BJ cried out as Damon reached for Brodie.

But she lost sight of him as the light from Brodie's hands exploded outward like a supernova, blinding them all for several moments.

The air in the room swirled and rushed in a frenzy. BJ ducked her head and shut her eyes against the evil, living force erupting from Brodie's hands. It could find no home, no outlet. It raged through the air, sucking up oxygen, clutching for a place to dwell. A discordant cacophony thrummed in her ears, rising in maddening intensity.

And then it was gone.

BJ knew it had been vanquished. The good in Brodie had triumphed over Damon's evil.

Still on his knees, with his head bowed over, Brodie looked down at his hands. They rested, palms up, on his thighs. BJ followed his gaze and saw the newest scars etched indelibly there. In the center of one palm, a red, puckered circle. In the other, a charred round emblem slashed in two by a jagged lightning bolt.

BJ went to him, brushing his hands out of his vision and taking their place. She hugged him tightly, rubbing her soft cheek against his hard one. Then she turned and pressed kisses along that cheek. Along his wounded brow. And finally, she opened her lips over his, loving him with every bit of strength she possessed.

"I am so sorry. I should have believed you. I should never have hurt you."

Suddenly, he came to his senses, crushing her in his arms, silencing her apology with his kiss. "Don't, darlin'," he growled between kisses. "Don't blame yourself for any of this."

"Isn't this touching." Damon's dry voice

shocked them both. Brodie stood up, pulling BJ with him, positioning his body as a shield between her and Damon.

"Your power is gone, sorcerer."

BJ clung to Brodie's waist while she peeked around his bicep. Damon's evil smile encompassed them both. He crossed his arms over his chest in a jaunty pose of arrogance.

"You've destroyed the ring, that's true. But I am still immortal. And so, dear warrior, are you."

Brodie's muscles jerked tensely beneath her hands.

BJ rushed to protect him. "You can't control me anymore, Damon. You can't control Brodie, either."

Damon clicked his tongue. "There are ways besides magic to control a man, Bridget."

She steeled herself against the mind shadows that never came. She truly was free of Damon's spell.

But not Damon's evil.

"What are you talking about?" she asked.

Brodie answered instead. "He's made my existence a living hell for centuries. I'm guessing he plans to keep on punishing me."

Damon clapped his hands together. "I see my pupil's intelligence has rubbed off on you, warrior. You took away everything I loved in that dungeon. You murdered an innocent that day. I see no reason to stop punishing you now."

Brodie's shoulders sagged, and BJ realized that he had accepted defeat.

Chapter Fourteen

"Brodie, no."

BJ tugged on his arm, turning him to face her. She cupped his jaw in her hands and tilted his head down toward hers. His guilt-riddled features nearly broke her heart.

"Don't listen to him." She shook him, trying to rekindle his hope. "You are not a murderer. You've paid for whatever crime you commited a hundred times over."

"I killed her, Beej. I can't deny that." He pulled her hands from his face, but she fought to keep loving contact with him.

"In battle? Accidentally? You don't deserve to suffer any longer." She latched onto the rough lapel of his jacket, then burrowed beneath to the soft cotton covering his heart. "You are a

Immortal Heart

kind-hearted, honorable man. You deserve a better fate."

She could see when the understanding hit him. His frown deepened, his eyes sparkled with a fearful light. "No. I won't let you do this."

BJ grew strong in her resolve. Strong enough for both of them. "It's my choice. It has to be my choice."

"No!"

BJ pulled away from him then and faced Damon. He had smoothed his silvery hair back into place. Arrogance was entrenched on his features once more. He eyed her calmly, but curiously.

"You're bound to release Brodie if the person he loves sacrifices herself willingly?"

Damon never blinked. "Yes."

"You can't change your mind?"

"No. The spell has been cast."

"Brodie's been alive for eight centuries. Hasn't he ever loved anyone before me? Surely someone else has tried to save him."

This time Damon looked over her head up to Brodie. "I killed them all before they had the chance."

Brodie's pain-filled gasp brought tears to her eyes. The enormity of what Damon must have done stunned her. Brodie sagged onto an overturned desk, and dropped his face into his hands. She wiped away the useless tears with the back of her knuckles, wrapped an arm around Brodie's shoulders and smoothed her hand across his hair.

"All of them?" Brodie's rasp carried past her to Damon.

"I was the patient from whom your wife, Clarinda, contracted consumption. A particularly virulent strain she shared with her sons."

"Lynelle?"

"I tripped her horse on the moors. I created the storm that downed the airplane Jane piloted. I fired the bullet that killed Zora. I was the one she confessed to. I let her go so you could watch her die."

Brodie's shoulders shook with untold grief. BJ pressed a kiss to his temple, holding him tightly, loving him with an emotion that was pure and profound.

She knew she must do next.

She pulled away from Brodie, tipping up his chin to capture his gaze and let him read her intent. "This has to stop."

"No."

Ignoring his plea, she turned to Damon once more. "Your mighty institute is crumbling down around us, Damon. But your death chambers are intact. I checked the systems. They're still operational."

"You can't." Damon reached for her, but she jerked away, repelled by his touch.

She dodged Brodie's hands as well, crossing to the main console. She flipped on the power feed to the chambers and listened to the rising

Immortal Heart

hum of power through the connecting cables.

"So there will be no question that this is a willing sacrifice, I'm activating the execution program myself."

Brodie reached around her from behind, pulling her away from the console. His fingers bit roughly into her arms, shaking her. "I won't let you do this! I'm not worth it! Nothing is worth your dying!"

He pierced Damon with a desperate glare. "Dammit, sorcerer! Stop her."

Damon moved in behind her. "Bridget, don't be foolish. Your talents are too great to waste."

"I'm not listening to you anymore."

"Stay with me. I can erase all that's happened. I can make you happy again."

"Happy?" She shook her head, amazed at Damon's total lack of human compassion. "How could I be happy knowing Brodie's still living in the hell you sentenced him to?"

"If you make him mortal, I'll kill him. You'll both be dead, and you will have sacrificed yourself for nothing." She wavered a moment after Damon's threat.

But Brodie remained steadfast, resolute. "There's no point in living if you're gone. Don't throw away your life on me."

Seeing the despair in his eyes, BJ grew implacable, loving him for protecting her, counting on him to remain true to his noble character. He loosened his grip and narrowed his eyes, trying to understand the silent message she sent him.

"Trust me, big guy. I'm doing this."

He reluctantly released her, and she knew he would not betray her.

BJ went to the console and completed entering the program. With the men frozen in shock and grief behind her, she mouthed a silent prayer and typed in the code to her own final subroutine.

S-E-C-O-N-D C-H-A-N-C-E.

"He deserves one," she whispered, and hit ENTER.

She walked to the first chamber and opened the door. A sterile, metallic smell stung her nose, giving her a moment's hesitation. But she wouldn't falter.

Brodie joined her, big and strong and, in her eyes, incredibly handsome. "Promise me that no matter what, you won't stop the program. No matter what happens to me, you won't touch the computer or open the chamber until the program is complete. Promise me."

He caught her up in his arms, lifting her clear off the floor, crushing her in his embrace. His mouth hungrily sought hers, begging her, forgiving her. BJ responded with the same fierce ardor, pouring everything she was into this last kiss.

At last he lifted his mouth and held her tightly. When BJ could breathe again, she whispered in his ear. "If you give me your word, I'll

Immortal Heart

believe it. Promise me you won't try to stop this."

Slowly, he let her slide down his chest and stomach until her feet touched the floor. Then he stepped back, his eyes bleak. "I promise."

BJ smiled up at him and touched her fingers to his damaged cheek. "I love you."

She released him and stepped inside the chamber, closing the glass door behind her. She picked up the wires from the switch box on the floor and sat in the cold chair. Then she unwrapped the electrode cups and placed one on either temple.

The humming sound increased its pitch and BJ knew the program had engaged. Only then did she look up at the man she loved. Brodie pressed his fingers to the glass, never blinking, never taking his gaze from hers.

He wept.

How could his world have gone so horribly wrong? Brodie saw BJ smile reassuringly at him. He should be the one doing something for her. He should stop this madness. But she had made him promise to do nothing. It seemed so vitally important to her, such a small thing to give her while she gave her very life for him.

He tasted his tears in the corner of his mouth, yet he did nothing. Her beautiful smile faltered. Her eyes blinked. She shook her head, trying to remain conscious. He didn't understand how this machine worked, something about bombarding brainwaves, she had said. He only knew it was killing her. Putting her to sleep and leading her quietly to her death.

And killing him in the process.

When this thing had run its course, when his sassy, quirky, loving BJ had gone from this world, he'd turn on the machine one more time and join her. He had no reason to live, no reason to celebrate the blessing of mortal life if he had to bury BJ.

Her watched her beautiful blue-green eyes drift shut for the last time. When she slumped onto the arm of the chair, and gravity carried her on down to the floor, Brodie sank with her. He fell to his knees outside the glass barrier, reaching for her, knowing he'd never touch her warm, sensitive flesh again.

"Darlin'," he whispered, drowned out by the slow, almost imperceptible beep of her vital signs from the computer monitor.

When the beeping deteriorated into one final, unbroken sound, Brodie tipped his head back and howled his grief and rage at the incredible injustice of BJ's sacrifice.

"I can't believe she chose you over me. I can't believe she did this." Damon's smooth voice broke in an uncharacteristic show of emotion.

Damon was an intrusion on Brodie's grief that barely registered. Knowing that she was gone, Brodie clawed at the door handle, trying to reach her.

"She said to let it run until the program

stopped." This time Damon's voice sounded firm, cruelly reminding Brodie of his promise. "It's logging her time of death. Verifying a successful execution."

Now that he listened, Brodie could hear the computer clicking away, still processing the fatal program. Brodie touched his forehead to the door and kissed the glass. "I love you."

The vow came out in a strangled whisper as he finally found the courage to answer her final words.

He knelt there, utterly bereft, completely devoid of feeling. Numbness seeped into his limbs. Grief choked his heart.

Damon quickly got over his disbelief. "Well, my old enemy. You finally have your mortality. You win."

"No." Brodie's voice crackled in a low rumble. His moist gaze lovingly caressed BJ's lifeless form. The spirit that had breathed life back into his ancient, tortured soul would smile no more. His warrior's heart fell with her. Paralyzed. Shattered.

"I lose."

Silence enfolded him, shrouded him in a hazy, unnatural peace.

He was only marginally aware of the flurry of sound rising in chorus behind him. Something big and heavy screeched across the floor. The clicking from the computer console increased it tempo. The noiseless cables started to hum again.

Julie Miller

Brodie struggled to find awareness. An intermittent beep thrummed into his subconscious mind, drawing him into the mortal world.

Or was he hallucinating? Brodie rubbed his eyes and looked again. BJ's eyelids fluttered like a dreamer in REM sleep. He reached for her, but was thwarted by the glass barrier.

Her eyes popped open, dazed, squinting to find focus. He wasn't imagining this. They were real.

"BJ!"

He twisted the handle and flung open the door, crawling on his knees to reach her. "Darlin' . . ."

Her lips pursed to form a word. But her eyes conveyed the message more quickly.

Glancing over his shoulder, he saw Damon advancing from behind. Brodie dove to the floor, covering BJ with his body. A steel pipe whistled past his ear and knocked the metal chair off its floor bolts.

In one swift, sure move, Brodie rolled to his feet and rammed Damon with his shoulder, catching him square in the gut and sending them backward against the computer console. The pipe careened out of Damon's hand and smashed the monitor. Sparks flew, igniting Brodie's jacket.

A fist to Damon's gut winded the older man, giving him a brief reprieve.

Brodie jerked his arm out of one sleeve. But the other sleeve singed his shoulder. He twisted

Immortal Heart

away from Damon, ripping the flaming material off and tossing it away.

A kick to his back knocked Brodie to his knees, the pain bruising his kidney and robbing him of breath. Damon picked up the pipe and raised it like a club over Brodie's head. Brodie jerked to one side as it crashed down to the floor, loosing itself from Damon's grip. The jarring momentum toppled Damon off balance, sending him stumbling toward the death chambers.

BJ had freed herself and was crawling out the open door. She saw Damon headed for her and tucked herself into a ball. Damon tripped over her and fell into the chamber.

Seizing the opportunity, Brodie lunged at BJ, grabbed her ankle and dragged her out of the way. He kicked the door shut and locked it.

BJ scrambled past him and pulled herself up in front of the console. She jerked her hand away from the flying sparks. Only now did Brodie realize how loudly the thing hummed, how his jacket charred on a pile of soaked debris, how puddles gathered at their feet while the sprinklers sprayed water over them.

"I can't shut it off!" BJ shouted over the noise, turning frightened eyes to him. "The electric impulses will flood this entire room. They'll kill all of us if the place doesn't go up on its own first."

Damon pounded on the door, his ineffectual curses muffled by the glass.

Brodie's life had come full circle. This technical fortress falling down around them was not too unlike the inquisitor's dungeon where he first met Damon all those years ago. Once again he was faced with the opportunity to destroy his enemy. This time he wouldn't fail. This time, he would keep the innocent safe.

He pulled the dagger from his belt, his one companion throughout the ages, and jammed it into the door frame, sealing the chamber. He wedged it tightly so that even if Damon broke the lock, he couldn't open the door. And if the screaming madman could break the shatterproof glass somehow . . . by then, it would be too late.

"Let's get out of here!"

He grabbed BJ's hand and ran. He hurdled over the rubble and through the fire door, dragging BJ behind him. Explosions rocked the stairwell as he dashed down two, then three steps at a time. When BJ stumbled, he pulled her to his side and half-carried her so their pace never slackened.

Plaster and bits of metal fell on top of them as the explosions built upon themselves, growing closer and closer together as one blast triggered another.

Brodie and BJ hit the ground floor at a dead run, losing the race with billowing smoke and lapping flames. Steel and concrete collapsed around them as they ran through the last door into the cooler air of the night outside.

Immortal Heart

They ran until they hit the parking lot and passed the circle of fire engines and ambulances lining the curb. Fire fighters and paramedics hurried around them, shouting commands, helping dazed employees who had escaped the burning complex.

A crowd gathered around them, but Brodie wasn't aware of a single person besides BJ. She fell against him, winded from their run, sucking in big gulps of air. Alive. Blessedly, beautifully alive.

A paramedic stopped and examined BJ, leaving her with a mask and a small tank of oxygen. Brodie sat on the asphalt and held her in his lap while she breathed the reviving air, rocking her and thanking God that she was safe.

After several minutes, she removed the mask. "Damon?" she wheezed, "Do you think?"

He wrapped her more tightly in his arms. "He's gone. I can feel it."

Her fingers clutched at his shirt. "But he's immortal."

"His prophecy came true. Damon died by his own hand. In a machine, in a complex, that he designed and built. He got caught in his own death chamber."

"I helped build it."

He loosened his hold at the remorse in her words, and tipped her chin up. "You never shared his evil intent."

He followed her gaze to the dying buildings. "It's strange. I don't feel any grief. A little guilt, maybe. But I don't miss him."

Brodie thought of some of the deaths he had been responsible for. Even in the heat of battle, even to save another, it always hurt to know he had taken a life. "You may once the shock has worn off. You did love him. Don't feel guilty about that."

"It does hurt to lose the man I thought he was."

"Which brings up another point."

She turned in his lap. "What's that?"

"I lost you. I watched you die." Brodie shook with the admission. "How did you come back to me?"

BJ smiled. Brodie wished he could smile in return. Despite dusty clothes, an ash-smudged face, and wet, debris-caked hair, BJ looked absolutely lovely with that smile.

"When I activated the computer, I pulled up a sub-program to revive me in the chamber after my death. It was a failsafe I had programmed into the system when I still worked for Damon. I found the execution program when I was shutting down the reactor and it gave me the idea."

BJ paused a moment to catch a healthy breath. In her heart she thanked God for those extra I.Q. points, and for the insight to remain true to her values in spite of the pressure from Damon all those years ago. She reached up and touched the man who had helped her find the courage to believe in herself again.

Immortal Heart

"I hoped I could cheat death. To be clinically dead long enough for Damon to release you. The curse didn't say I had to stay dead, did it?"

Brodie's grim face provided no answer and her feelings of triumph diminished. She'd ridden a euphoria of mind over magic. But were they really free? "My second chance at life subroutine was never tested. I'm glad it worked."

"Me too." Brodie gathered her in his arms and kissed her. When he finally lifted his head, her eyes were ablaze with passion, her lips swollen and branded by his kisses. "I've never suffered the way I did when I thought you were dead."

"I'm sorry. But I had to try. I couldn't bear to see you hurt any more."

With a virile power that he attributed solely to her, Brodie rolled to his feet with BJ in his arms. He carried her across the lot to his Explorer.

He set her inside the driver's door and climbed in next to her. He tucked her to his side and drove them home.

After securing the front door, he carried her straight to the bathroom. He set her down and gently stripped off her clothes. His fell into a pile with hers.

Brodie took her by the hand and led her into the shower, adjusting the water until it sluiced warmly over their bodies. He washed her gently with his hands, shampooing the grit from her hair, rinsing the grunge and memories of this fateful night from her skin.

When he had finished, she took the soap and began to wash him. With gentle, arousing tenderness, she ran her hands along his flanks, over his shoulders, down his arms. He hunkered down so she could wash his hair.

She pressed her palms against his temples and massaged her fingers across his scalp. He closed his eyes to receive her tender comfort. While his eyes were closed, she moved nearer. She pressed her warm, womanly body against him, fitting soft curves against his hard contours. His arms went around her and held her close. She kissed the new scar over his brow, the immovable corner of his mouth. As he straightened, her lips traced a tender path down his neck, across his burned shoulder, over the marks on his chest.

Her hands slid with the water down over his buttocks. She massaged the muscles there, flattening her breasts against his stomach with bewitching innocence. Her gentle touches calmed him, renewed him. She filled him with strength and need.

Brodie tipped her head back and swept his tongue into her mouth, drinking in the warm welcome there. She accepted his fierce need and matched it with her own. She clung to his waist, stretching up on tiptoe to accommodate him more fully, maddening him with the feel of her smooth, peachy skin rubbing against his thighs and stomach.

His need for this woman overwhelmed him.

Immortal Heart

In her presence, he felt reverent and humble, yet fiery and out of control all at the same time.

"Brodie." She whispered his name and stroked his back. Her honey-husky voice called to the need inside him.

"Darlin'." He gave her his pledge of love in that single word. Then he shut off the water and carried her into her bedroom.

He was only vaguely aware of things flying across the room as he tossed back the top covers and laid her on the crisp white sheets. She wound her arms around his neck and he propped himself on top of her. She accepted him, wanted him.

She seemed small and fragile beneath him, but her spirit was strong, her need as a powerful as his own. Brodie succumbed helplessly to the pressure of her fingers and settled himself over her, inside her.

BJ looked up at him, her eyes wide and loving. Brodie took her mouth and savored her sweet, sassy kiss. He slid his hands down her damp sides to the swell of her hips. Then he reached beneath her and pulled her fully around him. She gasped and arched into him.

Together, with love and passion and a desperate, final promise, they soared to that spot where lovers become one and the love that consumes them becomes a thing greater than themselves.

* * *

Julie Miller

In the aftermath of the most beautiful night of her life, BJ woke up alone. She knew before her eyes adjusted to the late morning light that she would spend the rest of her life waking up alone.

A fluid, languid feeling of utter contentment flowed through her, the glowing physical response to Brodie's loving. But it contrasted sharply with the twisting ache in her gut, the ache of abandonment and heartbreak.

They had come together three times that night, each time with a passion more desperate, more final than the last. She had lost him. She loved him with all her heart, and she believed in her soul that he loved her. But she had lost him.

She knew before she rolled over and found the regal purple iris placed on the indentation of Brodie's pillow. She knew before she opened the envelope with her initials scrawled on the front. Brodie had left her.

And this time, he wasn't coming back.

She sat up in bed, pulling her knees up to her chest and tucking the covers around her naked body. She sniffed the fragrant flower, loving the unique choice better than a traditional rose. She kept it in her hand while she opened and read his note.

My darling BJ—
I love you more than I ever thought possible. You've given me the blessed gift of your

healing love and trust. You've humbled me with your generous loving, and awakened my soul with your life-loving smile. Know that I do what I feel I must with a heavy heart.

If you are alive, then I cannot be mortal. I do not trust that destroying the ring or killing Damon has freed me. The scars still cover my body as proof of my sentence. As long as the curse plagues me, I am a threat to you.

I don't think I could bear to watch you die again for my sake. I love you too much to allow anything to happen to you because of me.

Live a long, happy, healthy life.

Forever yours, Brodie.

A teardrop fell and smudged the corner of his name. BJ wiped it dry with the pad of her thumb, not wanting to spoil her last communication from Brodie.

She lay back on the pillow, clasping the note and the flower to her bosom and letting the tears stream unheeded down her cheeks. She would do nothing to track him down. Nothing to convince him to come back to her. For Brodie's sake, she would let him go. She would accept the loving farewell of her noble, honorable knight.

Chapter Fifteen

Several weeks later

BJ's pain had transformed itself into a numb emptiness. Before Brodie freed her, she had functioned for months without the full use of her mind. Now she moved through her days in a similar fashion, functioning without the full use of her heart.

Jas and Emma had listened to the details of her fantastic adventure, accepting her explanations of immortality, evil magic, and the vengeful cost of cheating death. Their support was unflinching, their loving friendship unconditional. But it wasn't enough to ease the hurt.

She slept badly, longing for Brodie's strong, secure presence to keep the loneliness at bay.

Immortal Heart

She didn't eat particularly well, sustaining herself mostly on homemade bread and milkshakes. Emma fretted over her like a mother with a sick child, making her take naps at the office, often inviting her home to eat a well-balanced meal.

BJ thrived on her work. With meticulous perseverance, she tracked every program she had written, consciously or not, from scratch to insure there were no remnants of Damon's evil, invasive plan.

Then she poured herself into writing new programs. Games mostly. Anything positive, uplifting, anything that might lift her out of the endless sorrow.

Today was no different. She had opened the windows to let in the cool, biting autumn breeze. Even with the heat turned down, she found it warm in her baggy jeans and oversized sweater. Duke was curled on the sofa, burrowed in a pile of heart-shaped pillows. BJ munched on a soda cracker while she clicked the mouse and scrolled through her latest game, checking for anomalies.

She heard a knock on her open door and looked up, summoning a slight smile when Emma greeted her.

"How are you doing this morning?"

"About the same, I guess." BJ saved the game and shut off the computer, joining Emma on the sofa. She scooped Duke into her arms and sat. "I can't seem to shake this flu."

Julie Miller

Emma opened the brown bag in her lap and pulled out a plastic bottle. "Here's the lemon-lime soda you asked for. But honestly, I don't think it will settle your stomach."

Emma hesitated. BJ grimaced at her motherly frown. "What else do you have in that sack? A doctor's prescription?"

Emma reached inside and pulled out a narrow white box with a drugstore label on it. She handed it to BJ. "It's a pregnancy test. You have the same symptoms I had with Kerry. You're tired all the time. Your stomach's on edge. You're eating a strange diet."

An aching hurt awakened inside BJ. She opened her mouth, then clenched her jaw, not sure how to explain. "Em, I can't be pregnant."

"Are you sure?"

BJ closed her eyes and remembered that last night with Brodie, a beautiful, healing touching of souls. It should have been a fresh beginning for them. Instead, it became a poignant farewell.

"Brodie is the only man I've ever been with. He can't father children. Because he's immortal, he can't get me, a mortal, pregnant. Because he's immortal, I'll never see him again."

A tide of nausea shifted in BJ's stomach and she reached for the soda. Emma pushed the box into her hands instead.

"Take the test."

* * *

Immortal Heart

Brodie tossed another log in the stove, trying to chase away the chill that would never leave him. He scratched at his beard, feeling more and more like the hermit of the hills with each endless day that passed. He crossed to the window of his cabin, nestled on a remote peak in the ancient Ozark mountains.

For years he had treasured the solitude here. Normally, he appreciated the scenery. This morning, fog shrouded the golds, reds, and oranges of the hillsides, insulating him further from the outside world. Today, the isolation aggravated his loneliness instead of giving him peace.

In the distance he heard the crunch of gravel. A tourist must have gotten lost and missed the sign that labeled his long driveway a private road. Nobody came this far off the main road unless they couldn't read a map or had an ulterior purpose. Nobody had been here in months, not since Kel Murphy dropped in to tell him Jonathan Ramsey's widow needed help. If only Brodie had known how much keeping a promise would cost him.

With defensive instinct, he reached behind him for his dagger, grasping nothing but the back loop of his jeans. Of course, it was gone. Everything that had held meaning in his life was gone.

As the vehicle drew closer, Brodie reluctantly decided to take action. Better to face the enemy than to let him surprise you. If it was something as harmless as a lost tourist, he'd give him directions and quickly send him on his way. If not, it didn't hurt to be prepared.

He slipped out the back so he could see the driver first, and approach him from the hidden vantage point of the woods. Brodie loped around the perimeter, moving silently through the trees. When he saw the truck's license plate, he skidded to a halt.

WIZ-KID.

Eight hundred years of survival training fell by the wayside. He ran into the clearing, his boots crackling in the dead leaves.

The driver, now on his porch, turned at the noise.

He should retreat. He should march back into the woods and lose himself in their protective shadows. But his feet didn't seem to hear the message from his head. They responded to the instinctive joy of seeing BJ again.

In a few strides, he reached her. He lifted her onto her toes and gathered her in his arms, covering her mouth with his. He drank deeply, needfully, a condemned prisoner clinging to his last taste of freedom.

Moments later he came to his senses and set her abruptly away from him. He stayed on the ground and left her on the porch, putting her beyond his reach.

"You shouldn't be here." His voice sounded thick and inhuman.

At eye level, he simply stared at her, unsure

if she were real or a vivid hallucination from his feverish dreams.

Fatigue lined her eyes, but flecks of blue light sparkled in the green depths. Her curves looked fuller, richer than he remembered. Maybe because he so desperately missed the feel of her in his arms. A mischievous pout curved her lips, tempting him to kiss her again into revealing whatever secret amused her so. A navy sweater of soft cotton cable draped over her high breasts, which were pushed forward because she hid something in her hands behind her back.

"What is it? What's wrong?"

"Nothing. That is, if you still love me."

Didn't she know? "I'll never stop."

She pulled her hands from behind her back and held up a little plastic stick tipped in blue. "Welcome to the land of mortals, big guy."

BJ tried to convey all the love and joy in her heart. But Brodie just stared at her, uncomprehending. After the fiery yearning of his welcome, she thought everything would be all right, that this would be easy. But Brodie didn't respond. He stayed too far away from her. He acted as if he didn't even hear her.

"I know they didn't have these in the thirteenth century. It's a pregnancy test. Blue means it's positive." His brows moved together, narrowing his eyes. She kept trying. "I've been to a doctor. We're going to have a baby."

Pain sheared across his features. He shook his head. "My God, it's only been two months. I expected you to find someone else, but . . ."

An eternity had passed as far as she was concerned. BJ closed the unnecessary distance between them, cupping her hand under his bearded jaw. "There is no one else. There never will be. This baby is yours."

Something cracked and melted in his icy gaze. "Darlin', maybe you want to believe it, and I'd love for the miracle to be true, but you're alive. It can't happen."

BJ pulled her hand away and paced the length of the wooden porch, willing patience to replace her exasperation. He just didn't understand. She had to make him believe.

"I died in that chamber, Brodie."

She stopped in front of him once more, looking him straight in the eye. "You accept that I was dead, right?"

"I don't know. Your sacrifice haunts me day and night."

"Damon accepted my death. He freed you from the curse."

"We don't know that. I won't risk endangering you again."

She realized that eight hundred years of doubt was a lot to overcome. This called for drastic measures. "Sit down, big guy."

He surprised her by complying to her request. How could she ever feel intimidated by her gentle giant when he always put his needs second to hers? Her hopes for convincing him of the truth went up a little. She felt his hungry gaze on her as she crossed to the cab of her truck. Good. She needed his undivided attention in order to make this work. BJ opened the door and released her secret weapon.

"Get him, boy."

Duke jumped down from the seat and bolted toward Brodie.

"Ah, Beej, no."

Once he realized her intention, he tried to get up, but Duke was too quick. The dog jumped into his lap, propped his front paws on Brodie's shoulders and licked at the skin exposed between Brodie's beard and his ear.

BJ crossed her arms and watched, letting Duke do his work. "Do you believe me now?"

"BJ." She worked her jaw muscles to contain her smile. Despite the disparity of sizes, Duke was getting the better of Brodie. Brodie put up one big hand to fend off Duke's marauding tongue, then stood, dropping the dog onto the porch and towering over BJ, trying to look put out.

"That doesn't prove anything except that your guard poodle is annoying."

"Two months ago he'd have tried to take your nose off. He recognized you and Damon were different. Damon made me try to kill him so Duke couldn't convince me of the truth."

"Your dog deciding he likes me isn't proof that anything has changed!"

His fists rode to his hips, straining his flannel shirt across a considerable expanse of chest. He might try to look tough, but BJ saw the chink in his armor, the slight possibility of belief that Duke had planted there.

She grabbed his hands and unfolded them palm upward. They were double the size of hers, calloused at the tips and palms, but they were undamaged. She lifted them closer to his face. "Where are the scars, Brodie?"

"The burns weren't severe enough to leave a permanent mark."

She tugged at his peppered, coffee-brown beard. "When was the last time you shaved this thing? It couldn't grow so thick and full if you still had the scars on your face."

He pulled her hand away. "There's only one mirror in the house, and I hide it in a drawer so I don't scare myself."

BJ nearly burst with frustration over his obstinance. "Don't you want to believe? The curse is broken. You're mortal now. We can be together."

"Don't you think I want that?"

"Maybe not badly enough."

A shadow passed over his face and BJ knew she had hurt him again. Instead of apologizing, she made one last attempt to get him to believe what she felt in her heart.

She grabbed a handful of his shirt and yanked the flannel up out of the waistband of his jeans. She batted his hands away when he tried to stop her. "No. You have to see."

He held his arms out to his sides in surrender, looking down on her as though he thought she had reverted to madness once more. BJ pulled his thermal shirt out next, loosening it enough to push it up his stomach and expose his chest for them both to see.

Tenderly, lovingly, knowing he watched her, BJ pressed her hand over his heart. "It's gone. Damon's mark. All the scars. They're gone."

His warm skin cooled at the brush of autumn air. But beneath her palm, she felt the beating of his heart thudding more rapidly with each breath he took. He pulled her hand away and looked down, seeing his true self for the first time.

BJ stretched upward, touching her lips to the healed skin, awestruck by the masculine beauty that encased the noble man.

She tipped her face up to his. "I died, and the curse was lifted. You made beautiful, glorious love to me three times that night. I'm due in late May. I hope that sometime before then you'll marry me and give our child the father that I never had. One who's there. One who loves with his whole heart and soul."

Her voice caught as she thought of Jake and the love fate had cheated her of as a child. "And if he's too smart or too strong or perfectly average, you'll be a father who lets him know he's special in your eyes."

"Darlin', I . . ." Brodie's rough thumb gently

brushed a tear from her cheek. "If I remember rightly, I'm an ugly mug even without all the scars."

BJ laughed, shutting off her tears with a grateful smile. She clutched at the soft collar of his shirt, wanting to be closer. "Yeah. But you're my ugly mug."

His hands encircled her waist and drew her up against him. "I'm old-fashioned, to say the least. I've got a lousy temper and I'm overprotective."

BJ tilted her head back. "I keep weird hours. I have childish hobbies. I'll always be a smart-mouthed brainiac."

"Yeah, but you'd be my smart-mouthed brainiac."

BJ's responding laugh faded in dumbstruck wonder. Before her eyes, a marvelous transformation was taking place. The centuries' old grooves beside Brodie's eyes softened, and for the first time in several lifetimes, Brodie smiled.

She gasped at the miracle of atrophied muscles coming to life once more. "Brodie."

He framed her face in his hands, beaming his love down to her. "I'm not always sure how things are done here in the modern world, but if you proposed marriage a few minutes ago, I accept."

"I did."

"I will."

Her heart soared as Brodie swung her up into his arms and pledged his love to her with a kiss.

Immortal Heart

She clung to him, answering the vow with her own eager mouth.

A while later, Brodie sat in a rocking chair on the porch, holding BJ in his lap. Duke dozed contentedly at Brodie's feet.

"Darlin'?"

"Hmm?" BJ tightened her hold around his shoulders and snuggled closer.

His voice rumbled with husky emotion. "Thank you for my life."

He placed his hand over her abdomen, surrounding her and their child in the secure haven of his love. "Thank you for my future."

BJ slipped her hand over his. "It's our future, big guy. And for us, the only thing immortal is our love."

DON'T MISS OTHER *LOVE SPELL* ROMANCES BY
AMANDA ASHLEY

Sunlight, Moonlight. He comes from across the universe—a tawny, powerful stranger more perfect than any mere mortal. Yet when Micah crash-lands on earth, not even his boundless strength can help him resist the temptations of one stunning beauty.

Long has Navarre dwelt in darkness, a vampire doomed to eternal night—searching through the ages for a woman brave enough to desire him, a lover bold enough to embrace him. And when Navarre at last finds her, he swears that they will savor the joys of undying ecstasy and surrender the dawn.
_52158-X $5.99 US/$6.99 CAN

Deeper than the Night. All the townsfolk of Moulton Bay say there is something otherworldly about Alexander Claybourne. But never one to be scared off by superstitious lore, Kara Crawford laughs at the local talk of creatures lurking in the dark. No matter what shadowy secrets Alexander hides, Kara feels compelled to join him beneath the silver light of the moon, where they will share a love deeper than the night.
_52113-X $5.99 US/$6.99 CAN

Dorchester Publishing Co., Inc.
65 Commerce Road
Stamford, CT 06902

Please add $1.75 for shipping and handling for the first book and $.50 for each book thereafter. NY, NYC, PA and CT residents, please add appropriate sales tax. No cash, stamps, or C.O.D.s. All orders shipped within 6 weeks via postal service book rate. Canadian orders require $2.00 extra postage and must be paid in U.S. dollars through a U.S. banking facility.

Name_____
Address_____
City _____ State _____ Zip _____
I have enclosed $_____in payment for the checked book(s).
Payment <u>must</u> accompany all orders.☐ Please send a free catalog.

DON'T MISS OTHER SPINE-TINGLING PARANORMAL ROMANCES!

Waitangi Nights by Alice Gaines. With her meager inheritance almost gone, young Isabel Gannon has little hope but to stake her future on a risky gamble. She accepts an offer to accompany a shipment of wild orchids to the lush New Zealand home of the darkly handsome Richard Julian. There she is determined to nurture the precious plants—and resist the lure of her employer's strong arms. But even as Isabel feels herself blossom beneath Richard's tender touch, she senses something else lurking on the exotic estate. A strange cry in the night, a mysterious light—something sinister that threatens to nip her newfound happiness in the bud. Now Isabel will have to unravel a web of secrets if she wants to preserve their halcyon days and savor the passion of their wild Waitangi nights.
_52153-9 $4.99 US/$5.99 CAN

Full Moon Dreams by Lori Handeland. Emmaline Monroe is not prepared for the deaths at the circus that occur on nights when the moon shines full and bright. Everyone has been warned to trust no one. But the lovely tiger trainer is finding her attraction to Johnny Bradfordini impossible to tame. Each time she looks into the handsome stranger's silvery-blue eyes, she feels pulled into an all-consuming passion—and an inexplicable danger.
_52110-5 $5.50 US/$6.50 CAN

Dorchester Publishing Co., Inc.
65 Commerce Road
Stamford, CT 06902

Please add $1.75 for shipping and handling for the first book and $.50 for each book thereafter. NY, NYC, PA and CT residents, please add appropriate sales tax. No cash, stamps, or C.O.D.s. All orders shipped within 6 weeks via postal service book rate. Canadian orders require $2.00 extra postage and must be paid in U.S. dollars through a U.S. banking facility.

Name_____
Address_____
City _____ State_____ Zip_____
I have enclosed $_____ in payment for the checked book(s).
Payment <u>must</u> accompany all orders.☐ Please send a free catalog.

Flames of Rapture

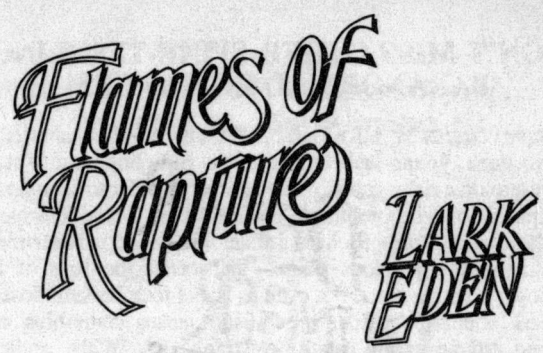

Lark Eden

"Great reading!"—*Romantic Times*

When Lyric Solei flees the bustling city for her summer retreat in Salem, Massachusetts, it is a chance for the lovely young psychic to escape the pain so often associated with her special sight. Investigating a mysterious seaside house whose ancient secrets have long beckoned to her, Lyric stumbles upon David Langston, the house's virile new owner, whose strong arms offer her an irresistible temptation. And it is there that Lyric discovers a dusty red coat, which from the time she first lays her gifted hands on it unravels to her its tragic history—and lets her relive the timeless passion that brought it into being.

_52078-8 $4.99 US/$6.99 CAN

Dorchester Publishing Co., Inc.
65 Commerce Road
Stamford, CT 06902

Please add $1.75 for shipping and handling for the first book and $.50 for each book thereafter. NY, NYC, PA and CT residents, please add appropriate sales tax. No cash, stamps, or C.O.D.s. All orders shipped within 6 weeks via postal service book rate. Canadian orders require $2.00 extra postage and must be paid in U.S. dollars through a U.S. banking facility.

Name_____
Address_____
City _____ State_____Zip_____
I have enclosed $_____in payment for the checked book(s).
Payment <u>must</u> accompany all orders.☐ Please send a free catalog.

A Vampire Romance In The Immortal Tradition Of *Interview with the Vampire*.

A DEEPER HUNGER
SABINE KELLS

For years, Cailie has been haunted by strange, recurring visions of fierce desire and an enigmatic lover who excites her like no other. Obsessed with the overpowering passion of her fantasies, she will do anything, go anywhere to make them real—before it is too late.

Mysterious, romantic, and sophisticated, Tresand is the man of Cailie's dreams. Yet behind the stranger's cultured facade lurk dark secrets that threaten Cailie even as he seduces her very soul.

_3593-6 $4.50 US/$5.50 CAN

Dorchester Publishing Co., Inc.
65 Commerce Road
Stamford, CT 06902

Please add $1.75 for shipping and handling for the first book and $.50 for each book thereafter. NY, NYC, PA and CT residents, please add appropriate sales tax. No cash, stamps, or C.O.D.s. All orders shipped within 6 weeks via postal service book rate. Canadian orders require $2.00 extra postage and must be paid in U.S. dollars through a U.S. banking facility.

Name_____
Address_____
City _____ State_____ Zip_____
I have enclosed $_____in payment for the checked book(s).
Payment <u>must</u> accompany all orders. ☐ Please send a free catalog.

ATTENTION PREFERRED CUSTOMERS!

SPECIAL TOLL-FREE NUMBER
1-800-481-9191

*Call Monday through Friday
12 noon to 10 p.m.
Eastern Time
Get a free catalogue;
Order books using your Visa,
MasterCard, or Discover;
Join the book club!*

Leisure Books

Love Spell